BONEYARD
11

BY
LINTON
ROBINSON

Boneyard 11 is the initial book in the BORDERLINES series, novels taken from scripts of the television series. All rights to any characters, properties, or teleplays from that series are reserved to Linton Robinson and Border Accomplices Productions.

Adoro Books is a Division of Escrit Lit LLC
South Carolina
info@adorobooks.com
See more titles at
AdoroBooks.com/bookstore

adoro books

Is a new, innovative independent press producing print and electronic books for the current century and posterity.

CONTENTS

Chapter One	1	Chapter Twenty-Eight	111
Chapter Two	3	Chapter Twenty-Nine	113
Chapter Three	9	Chapter Thirty	1116
Chapter Four	10	Chapter Thirty-One	121
Chapter Five	16	Chapter Thirty-Two	131
Chapter Six	18	Chapter Thirty-Three	137
Chapter Seven	22	Chapter Thirty-Four	145
Chapter Eight	27	Chapter Thirty-Five	149
Chapter Nine	30	Chapter Thirty-Six	151
Chapter Ten	34	Chapter Thirty-Seven	153
Chapter Eleven	40	Chapter Thirty-Eight	163
Chapter Twelve	44	Chapter Thirty-Nine	170
Chapter Thirteen	47	Chapter Forty	172
Chapter Fourteen	49	Chapter Forty-One	176
Chapter Fifteen	55	Chapter Forty-Two	179
Chapter Sixteen	57	Chapter Forty-Three	182
Chapter Seventeen	61	Chapter Forty-Four	190
Chapter Eighteen	63	Chapter Forty-Five	196
Chapter Nineteen	70	Chapter Forty-Six	201
Chapter Twenty	74	Chapter Forty-Seven	203
Chapter Twenty-One	75	Chapter Forty-Eight	208
Chapter Twenty-Two	77	Chapter Forty-Nine	212
Chapter Twenty-Three	81	Chapter Fifty	214
Chapter Twenty-Four	90	Chapter Fifty-One	218
Chapter Twenty-Five	98	Chapter Fifty-Two	223
Chapter Twenty-Six	105	Author	226
Chapter Twenty-Seven	108	Bonus Tracks	227

Dedicated To

Clarita

Chapter One

It wasn't going to stop unless she did something about it. She moaned and squirmed under the tousled turquoise sheets, but the nasty pulsations went on and on. A slim, pale forearm punched out from under the covers, slender fingers tipped with immaculate rose nails fumbled gracelessly on the nightstand. A Kawabata paperback fell to the floor, losing her bookmark. Two bottles of prescription sleeping pills rattled and tumbled. She knocked over a sleek digital travel alarm with violet digits indicating a ridiculous hour. She found the phone, lifted the receiver and let it drop back down. The shrill piping continued. The cell phone, then. Uh-oh.

She snaked the slim Nokia back under the sheets and mumbled sleepily, muffled by morning fogginess and 600 count pima cotton. "This is Nan. I think."

The phone chittered frantically as a long, shapely leg emerged tentatively from the bed clothes and manicured toes felt around the deep green pile. "Just because I'm a call girl doesn't mean I like calls at..." The sheet lifted enough for an accusing view of the clock. "Eight in the morning! Omigod, Maru, if I could handle morning I wouldn't have worked nights all my life."

Her foot found the sheepskin slipper and snuggled into it as the phone jittered louder in her ear. "Now?" She exclaimed. "There?"

"What?" Another foot slid to the floor and reconnoitered for the other slipper. "It sounds like a cattle call. Who's the client? The Godfather? Satan?"

The phone chirped twice and Nan sat up convulsively, the sheet falling away to reveal the clean, calm beauty of her classic Nordic features. She stared at the phone, as if demanding answers. After a full-body shudder and a violent shake of her nimbus of silvery hair, she spoke to it more seriously. "Oh. Okay, I'll be there in a half hour."

She shifted her hips and stood up, the sheets sliding off her lilac silk teddy. Her body was as fine-limned as her face, all slim curves and smooth muscle tone. She spoke into the phone once more before clicking it shut. "But don't forget who comes through for you. You old whore."

She tossed the phone on the bed and bumbled towards the bathroom, then reversed direction and pushed open the glass-paned doors to the front room. Flinching from the brutal morning sunlight, she moved through the sterile Danish post-modern order of her so-called living area. Her steps grew firmer as she padded into the efficient kitchen, shook off the pills and got with the program.

"First things first," she muttered, flipping on an elegant Swedish coffee maker pre-primed with bottled water and dark Yucatan grounds, then backtracking to the bathroom.

The teddy slipped silkily down chiseled calves as she waited a moment for the shower spray to warm up. She stepped inside and closed the glass doors, raising her face to the warm water. "Welcome back my friend," she grumbled into the needle spray, "To the show that just won't end."

Chapter Two

The whole place looked like a home office made over into a whorehouse by Martha Stewart. A perfect fit for Maru herself; a dated, cushily upholstered, over-decorated little cupcake on the shiny side of fifty. Everybody assumed her real name was Maria something, but nobody had known for sure for over thirty years, back when she was turning tricks herself instead of being the prime local broker for the very top crust in commercial grade love.

She dithered around the doilied red velvet furniture in her living room, not showing a bit of dealership pride in the unusual display of her whole line of goods, currently standing against one wall trying to look ravishing on short notice. The girls, ranging from highly fetching to drop-dead gorgeous, were either black or Hispanic, except for "Nikita", whose pale white skin and black hair threw her deep blue formerly-Soviet, eyes into startling contrast. They lounged against the wall like mugs in a lineup, unsure of the situation.

One sure thing: nobody wanted to offend the two men, big physical Latino types who looked dramatically out of place in the perfumed cushion of Maru's parlor. The older one that she called Alfredo was obviously a scarred street veteran who'd fought his way up to perks like his expensive Brooks Brothers suit. He leaned against the door to the kitchen at ease, offering the young hookers only an incurious gaze. The one that had them on their toes was Mongo.

He was a big block of muscle with a tight, dark face that looked as though a handsome mannequin for some roughtrade leather boutique had come off the line a little too angular and cock-eyed. His chopped-off hair was lacquered up into a stiff, vertical crest above his low forehead, the latest word in *cholo* chic. The presence of all this high-ticket pulchritude had put him on his volatile *macho* mettle, his consciousness hovering a few inches south of the sea crocodile belt that brought together his whole barrio mobster look. Tied the thousand dollar Armani in with the red acetate shirt printed with skeletons in sexual positions and the cowboy boots hand-stitched from endangered species skin. This

3

was a young man continually on the prod, and this particular cattle call was no exception.

He gave the girls another oily, cloying scan and spun around to Maru, who skittered away towards a bookcase crammed with collectible Barbies in 'ho rags.

"Listen, he's had it with the *raza* bitches," he sneered at her. "Who needs some *puritanca* little Chicana breaking your balls, then crossing themselves when you come?"

Maru eagerly nodded assent to that wisdom, glancing to Alfredo for assurance. She hoped he was in charge of this checkered-assed punk.

"And who wants any of those bushy-haired jungle monkeys?" he went on. "The only white *putona* you come up with isn't even a blonde."

The black escorts bristled at that assessment and Maru flopped placating hands at them. But Mongo was relentless, looming over Maru like a Doberman menacing a Pomeranian. "We said your best lookers, didn't we?"

He dripped scorn and malice, waved a dismissive hand at the girls against the wall. "The fine blonde white stuff."

"If I'd had entrance lines like that, I might have made a go of the acting thing." Everybody turned to the foyer, where Nan slouched against the doorway in a Bacall pose, her enticing body graced by a clinging sheath and shoulder-length strawberry blonde hair curving softly around the pale oval of her serene face. She moved into the room, raking Mongo with a dazzlingly fake smile.

"Hi, I'm Nan. But you can just call me Stuff." She walked past the staring Mongo towards Maru, tossing back, "Apparently."

Alfredo shifted on his feet, taking notice for the first time that morning. "Not blonde, exactly," he said appreciatively. "But definitely fine."

Nan shrugged and snatched off the wig, finger-fluffing silver-blonde hair in a short, athletic cut. "If you don't see what you like," she beamed, "Just ask."

Alfredo gave her a friendly grin and nod as she leaned over to kiss Maru on the cheek. The older woman was shooting her eyes around like marbles on a drumhead, trying to telegraph the whole setup and her apprehensions about it. Nan winked and wheeled elegantly to face Mongo, slipping the wig into place and smoothing it down.

The young hood had done nothing but stare artlessly at Nan since she entered, leaning forward on the balls of his feet like a birddog spotting a grouse. He liked what he saw, took it as a challenge, and was getting worked up over it. He moved towards Nan, encroaching her personal space, giving her the once-over twice removed. Nan nonchalantly stood her ground.

"Not bad, not bad," Mongo muttered, the petulance in his voice replaced by a toughfellah version of a coaxing purr. "This is more like it here, the real goods."

"Would you like to take a look at my teeth?" Nan opened her mouth to show off a white gleam. "Check for my VIN number?"

"These original equipment?" Mongo asked her with a leer, trying to stare down and intimidate her through sheer bulk. He raised a hand, fingers splayed as if to grasp a peach off a table.

"OEM," Nan replied, effortlessly meeting his imagined cobra gaze. "But listen. Free for looky-loos, but any contact starts up the old meter."

Mongo reached out anyway, slowly and sensually moving his cupped hand to make the contact she'd just denied.

"I said keep your hands to yourself, greaseboy," Nan snapped, blowing off all the patently fake charm. She slapped his hand away, glaring at him without temper, just a studied, dismissive contempt. Behind him Maru was stricken, frantically waving her hands and shaking her head. Against the wall, the chorus line of tarts drew a collective breath and waited wide-eyed for the results.

He reacted instantly, grabbing her by the nape of the neck and pulling her face up to his own, his other hand reaching to cup her ass.

Somehow Nan's hand was already in her purse. It came out flashing a small automatic pistol, which she dug into Mongo's groin hard enough to make him gasp. He went rigid, his eyes bulging.

"Well, well," Nan murmured with no trace of humor, "The incredible shrinking man."

She moved the pistol significantly and spoke with the incisive bite of a knife slapping into a chopping block. "Now back the hell off."

Mongo stepped back gingerly, removing his hands and instinctively holding them up at shoulder level, his palms toward her.

Maru shot a panicked glance at Alfredo, who was apparently not going to do anything about seeing his associate under the gun. He was watching the scenario like the wall girls. Front row seats for a little morning drama.

"Okay, Tiny Tim," she said, "Now close your eyes."

Mongo recovered enough of his shattered macho cool to give her a hateful glare instead of obeying. Nan slid the gun up his belly and chest and pushed it hard into the side of his throat. "You close those eyes or I'll close them for you, you needle-dicked sleazeball."

Fighting agonized resistance from his every instinct, Mongo fluttered his luxuriant lashes then squeezed his eyes shut.

Whereupon Nan measured him carefully and drove a full, powerful kick directly into his crotch. He jackknifed, fell to the floor and lay there retching.

Nan gave Alfredo a look and saw no trouble from that quarter. She stepped to an over-wrought recliner and plopped down. Filching a cigarette from Maru's pack on the coffee table, she brought the gun up to the tip, pulled the trigger to produce a flame from the barrel. She lit up, drew a deep drag, and blew smoke from her nostrils.

Maru leaned on a chair, her knees shaky with the quick release from panic. She shot a worried look at Mongo, struggling not to toss his enchiladas all over her new carpet. Alfredo moved towards Nan, smiling and miming a silent applause.

"Please excuse our in-house idiot," he told her. "Could I ask you to come down to the car with me, take a few Polaroid shots?"

Nan looked him over out of the corner of her eye, brought the pistol lighter to her lips, blew off imaginary smoke and dropped it back in her purse.

"We've already made arrangements with Maru," the big thug assured her.

Across the room, Treshanna, a black prostitute as tall, angled, and savage-looking as Grace Jones, mused, "Be takin' polaroys out in the *car*?"

6

Alfredo gave her a half-smile, but spoke to Nan. "We just represent the client, you understand?"

She replied with a cool nod and he turned to glare down at Mongo with his fists on his hips. Big, gnarled fists with some nicks out of them, Nan noticed. Much like his face.

"You can call me Alfredo."

"Hi, I'm Nan."

He nodded as he booted the groaning Mongo lightly in the ribs, "Hey Mongo, you gonna open the door for the lady? *Sí o no?*"

Mongo rolled away from him and pressed up to his knees. He looked at them both and Nan knew that there'd been a real possibility of him shooting them all. She'd sized up Alfredo as the authority of the two from the first, but what she saw burning in the kid's eyes just then offered no safeguards. He lurched to his feet, staggered to the door, fumbled it open and blundered out, leaving it open. They could hear him clumber painfully down the stairs.

Nan turned to Alfredo, a delicate eyebrow cocked, "Honestly, you can take the boy out of the barn, but..."

Alfredo laughed for the first time, a baritone rumble that told Nan a lot about the man. He held his arm towards her politely to usher her out. "Oh, yeah," he told her, "I think you'll do just fine."

As the door closed, Maru heard Nan say, "Do *what?*"

She practically collapsed in relief, and so did her whole stable. Four cigarettes snapped out like switchblades, straight to trembling, over-coated lips. Maru motioned them all to sit at the kitchen table and headed straight for the cabinet to grab glasses and a bottle.

"*Híjole,*" Mariposa, a leggy Veracruz girl with butterscotch complexion, breathed. "I was scared she was gonna get us all blowed down right here."

"I hear that, honey," Treshanna said, reaching for the shot Maru had just poured. "What a ball-bitin' bitch."

Maru jumped up and leaned towards her, clapping her hand over the drink. "Hey slut! Don't ever dis Nan around me, you hear?"

Treshanna placed a spread-fingered hand sporting two inch blue nails to her amazing breast and batted eyelashes like Venus flytraps. "Yeah? What you gone do 'bout it?"

Maru sat back down and handed her the glass. "Tell her what you said, see if she kicks that fat off your butt."

The girls all laughed a little too hard and simultaneously tipped back straight shots of Tequila.

Amarylis, the other black whore, licked a drop from the corner of her mouth and mused, "So who's the client, anyway? The Klueless Klan?"

"Don't ask," Maru said darkly, pouring again.

"Somebody don't mind discriminating race," Treshanna told her seriously, "That's for damned sure."

"That Alfredo's who I think he is, huh?" Mariposa asked without expecting an answer. "Not too bad looking. I mean, a guy his age."

Maru nodded fondly and winked. "You should have seen him twenty years ago. And damn well-hung."

Questioning eyebrows shot up around the table.

"You know," Maru said, giving it a beat. "For a *Mexicano*."

Treshanna shrugged and reached for her glass. "I was gone say."

Chapter Three

Magdalena Gaspar, ten year old Mexican-American Princess known as Magi to her many friends, adoring teachers, and shattered family, knelt prettily beside her plush pink bed to pray. It was a picture some Chicano Norman Rockwell might have done: a sweet kid in soft flannel Hello Kitty nightgown, hands folded piously, wide black eyes turned upwards in supplication.

From the doorway her mother Chela watched fondly, but hoped the prayers would get wrapped up so she could zip downstairs in time to see the cliffhanger at the end of her *telenovela*. It wouldn't be unkind to describe Graciela Gaspar, *nee* Floresta, as a fading Latina hotty and she could still show a good turn-out with the proper preparation. She leaned against the doorjamb barefoot in cutoff sweatpants and a Luis Miguel t-shirt, eavesdropping her daughter's chat with God.

"...and please bless Tia Rosalinda and her sick cat," Magi intoned. She paused and shot a glance at the doorway, where Chela still stood watching, then blurted out, "*Te lo pido estas cosas, Señor, en nombre de tu Santo Hijo. Amén.*" She scrambled up into the bed, snuggled in, and blew a kiss to her mother. Chela smiled and blew one in return before switching off the light and hurrying back to catch *Mirada de Mujer*.

Magi was out of the bed and back on her knees instantly, clasping her hands in the dark and speaking with a palpable fervor. "*Y Señor*, please watch out for my *Papá* and keep him safe. *Amén.*"

She quickly skinned back up into the bed and lay watching the light reflected off the pool dance and weave across the ceiling until she fell asleep.

Chapter Four

Hard to tell is which is weirder here in The Joint, he'd often thought; dealing with the other cons or the damned guards. But so far Gaspar had found the worst was trying to communicate with anyone from "the outs". It was like they lived on a different planet from the one he was getting used to so fast it sometimes scared him.

Not that he had many of these stupid conversations through the thick glass that made everything seem like a fish tank full of marine specimens talking on cheap, buzzy telephone handsets. He always met with his attorney Manny in a private room, his business associates and friends couldn't visit due to conviction records and his ex-family hated his guts. He was losing contact with what he didn't even think of as the Real World anymore. And after less than a year inside. He'd had to do something. And was about to get his first clue on how well that something might work out. He wasn't all that optimistic.

He looked at Nan when she came in, admired her looks in an abstract "under glass" kind of way, but in no way associated her with the polaroids he'd screened or why he was sitting in this embarrassing little booth toying with a greasy plastic handset. Then the guard pointed him out and she came over to sit in front of him. *¡Hijole!*

They stared at each other a moment, neither getting an easy grip on what they were looking at. The word that came to him was "innocent". She was a major looker, no doubt about it, but there was something vulnerable in her delicate features and bone structure. A fragile quality with a faint ache in the eyes. He felt a stirring he couldn't identify. This wasn't what he'd expected to drag in, but he was getting a much better feeling about the operation.

What Nan saw wasn't as advertised, either. She had known the name immediately, but had never seen a picture of the man himself. He was rough enough to fit the bill, no doubt about that. Even pushing fifty, showing signs of soft living and a little puffy from prison food, he was obviously one tough hombre; the stocky body softened but still brutal. His face was hard and brown, but

10

the inevitable mustache was too thin to complete the ruthless appearance. And the slightly slanted cast to his eyes gave him a sort of Fu Manchu thing. But the phrase that came to her mind was "commanding presence." Well, he'd commanded her presence, hadn't he?

What surprised her was his eyes. She'd expected an opaque, reptilian regard, but what she saw was intelligence and a very human interest. He wasn't looking at her like a John, but like a guy who wanted to know her better. Hope his first line isn't, What's A Nice Girl Like You, she thought. She smiled through the submarine glass and picked up her handset.

The first words he heard her say were, "I know we advertise outcalls anywhere in the county, but I'm betting they frown on it in here."

His voice was deep and somewhat chilly, distorted by the poor quality of the phone hookup. "Just a matter of arranging things properly."

She laughed, a silvery tinkle that nailed him, but good. A sound from some world alien to the stark, drab one he inhabited. "Wow," she said, "So you really *are* some sort of Godfather."

"Property of the State, these days." He showed her an unexpectedly open smile. "But no numbers, please. Just call me Gaspar."

"Ah, one of those single professional names like Madonna and Iman. Good branding strategy for finest domestic and imported contraband."

He didn't smile, just looked into her eyes through the thick window. He had an impulse and went with it. "Maybe their real first names are Humberto, too."

Nan didn't smile either. She had an instinctual tip-off that he'd just confided something to her. A man not given to easy confidence. She said, "Hi, Gaspar. I'm Nan."

He gave a half-nod that somehow managed to be courtly. There was a dignity behind this guy, but she'd seen men who had that air only because they could back themselves up with damage and death. And he was certainly in that category. He was making no move to control the conversation, just watching her. But in a removed way. Not the acquisitive edge she was used to. Maybe

11

I'm losing my touch, she joked with herself. Somebody had to say something, though.

"But I wouldn't be wrong in thinking of you as a dangerous criminal? And potential esteemed client, of course."

"Both, yeah." He held up a blunt finger and wagged it. "But my proposition is completely legal."

"Okay, a proposition," Nan nodded pertly. "That's familiar ground. Legal is somewhat less familiar."

"But you've got no jacket. No priors." Actually that was a matter that had made Gaspar curious. He circled the finger to take in the booth, the visiting area, the entire R.J. Donovan Correctional Facility. "Or you wouldn't be allowed to visit."

"So that's why Alfredo and that Manny guy gave me the third degree about my troubled past." She didn't know why she hadn't thought of that. "No, I've had a very careful career. Also why I wasn't worried about those tests at the clinic."

"Just means you're smarter than average." He looked at her with a wry smile teasing one corner of his tight lips. "Alfredo said he asked you about your record and you said, 'You're wondering if a whore is a criminal or not?' I love it."

"It's really funny now that I know who was really asking."

"Alfredo likes you. He thinks you're the one."

Nan's smooth white brow furrowed slightly. "Well, the Oracle said so, but I've had a few lingering doubts."

Gaspar didn't respond to the reference, but was getting more interested the longer he talked to her. Which, the clock over the guard's head indicated, would only be for five more minutes. Initial visit, non-relative, non-legal.

"I might make you an offer," he said, raising his hand like a cop signaling to stop, "Please, no movie gags. Think of this as an audition."

She looked around the stark room with the big, motionless guard and the hunched figures trying to communicate with loved ones in exile. "Audition for what? Prisoners Of Love?"

"You're in business, right? You advertise. Promote."

"Ironically, lawyers can take out ads now, but not whores. Where's the justice in *that*?"

Gaspar waved a hand like an emcee introducing a performer. "So make me want to give you money."

Nan studied him for a long moment. She's scanning me, Gaspar thought. Trying to read me for what I expect, what I'll pay for. Well, good luck honey.

She abruptly hung up, stood, posed prim as a prep school virgin for a beat, then pulled open her blouse to display the pale perfection of her breasts to Gaspar's view.

His eyes widened appreciatively. In a rare unconscious movement, he leaned forward and kissed the glass in front of her faintly pink nipples. Just as the guard grabbed her from behind and spun her away from the glass.

"What the hell you think you're doing?" the guard demanded. He shoved her away from the booth, motioning for her to cover up. Nearby visitors stared at her, not to mention the row of inmates goggling through the glass.

She buttoned up, looking at the guard contritely. "Sorry, phone sex always gets me so turned on."

Which put the guard decidedly off-guard. She winked at him and murmured, "So do badges."

Gaspar saw what she said, and the guard's nonplussed reaction. He laughed out loud. "When was the last time a woman made me laugh?" he asked himself out loud.

The guard recovered into a stiff, official posture and tone. "You're going to have to leave, Ma'am."

He turned and glowered, "Gaspar, you're on report."

Nan nodded understandingly. "Conduct unbecoming of a felon?"

This time Gaspar's laugh was an open, full body expression. "Oh, I think we've got a winner here."

The inmate beside him, a slight, shifty black burglar, said, "Shit yeah, you do." His wife glared at him, turned to stare daggers at the blonde hussy.

Gaspar yelled, loud enough to be heard through the glass, "You'll definitely do!"

As the guard firmly escorted her out of the visitor room, Nan called back over her shoulder, "Do *what*?"

The paint was fresh, and a few sad trappings attempted a look of sanctity and good tidings, but nothing could make the room out to be anything other than a cement box owned by The System, equipped on an overstrained budget, and only half-heartedly functional for mass spiritual needs. The clergyman looked pretty much the same. Prison Chaplain is not a highly sought-after calling. Inmates are an unreliable flock, their piety often misrepresented. And conjugal relations among them are seldom blessed by even the generic, official states of matrimony, much less Holy Wedlock.

The same guard from the visiting room stood stiffly by in a fresh uniform. He'd taken an interest, actually, but was there for reasons of ritual witness, not security. The chaplain looked like government issue: graying, hardened from use, and somehow shopworn. His black suit hung loose and his backwards collar was yellowed. He read from a black book, not being overly familiar with this particular rite of passage.

"By the authority vested in me by the State of California," he intoned, "I now pronounce you man...

He glanced perfunctorily at the groom. Gaspar had on new, starched denims, and wore an expression that was somehow proud and sheepish at the same time.

"...and wife."

The good reverend glanced at the bride with a great deal more interest. Nan was radiant in a very short, veiled wedding dress cut to cling, flatter and suggest that Fredericks of Hollywood had added a bridal line. Gleaming white, although both dress and veil were polka-dotted with tiny red appliqués of kissy lips. She held her bouquet of pink roses with a chaste expression.

"You may kiss the bride."

Gaspar raised his hands to lift her veil, somewhat restrained by his handcuffs.

"Awww," Nan cooed, "A double ring ceremony."

She turned her head to accept Gaspar's gentle kiss on her cheek, which brought her eyes to the guard, who couldn't seem to decide whether to roll his eyes in disgust or applaud and throw rice.

"And there's just something about a best man in uniform."

The guard smiled, shaking his head, and Gaspar chuckled. He patted her shoulder awkwardly with his manacled hands. He leaned close and Nan could smell bay rum. Did they have state-issue aftershave, she wondered. He said, "See you on the honeymoon."

Chapter Five

"He's powerful, all right. And rich. And a smart cookie, I guess," Maru said tentatively, like someone unqualified to judge. "Basically, he gets what he wants."

"Does he now?" Nan mused. She lifted the steaming cup to her lips and sipped tentatively, then blew across the frothy surface. "I think that depends a lot on what he wants."

"That's my motto, right there." Maru did one of her occasional self-aware smiles. "Give 'em what they want."

"I thought it was, The Customer Always Comes First."

"That's optional."

Nan laughed with the jolly little madam. She laughed a lot around Maru, which is why she liked to hang out with her sometimes. She didn't socialize with any of the other "girls" in her trade. Not with much of anybody, she sometimes realized. She worked, kept herself in shape, kept herself educated. Other than that, all she expected from the world was that it would let her sleep. Not that it always obliged such a simple desire.

Maru's social life was anybody's guess, but Nan figured it wasn't that much different from her own. Her apartment looked like the kind people have when they don't like to leave home if they could help it. Which is why Nan invited her to the Hotel Del Coronado for coffee. The classic look of the old wooden deck, the obsequious service and the air of deep-dish money were all heady delights for the pudgy procuress.

Maru was apparently on her wave length because she suddenly said, "Married. Wow. I don't run around with a lot of married women."

"Just their husbands." Nan gave her a soft smile. "I can't believe it myself, really. I mean, not that it's 'really', really. But still, hitched is hitched. Maybe we can rent some children or something. Lease an Airedale."

Maru laughed. She didn't always understand Nan's sense of humor, but she enjoyed what she did. She pointed an elaborately over-manicured finger between Nan's eyes and pronounced, "Cinder-fucking-Ella."

Nan laughed out loud. Perfect. Pretty Woman meets Goodfella. "Well, he's sending me a coach."

"*You* need coaching?"

"A limo, you wiseass. Maybe it's a stretch pumpkin."

"Limo?" Maru puzzled. "To go where?"

"Our honeymoon, silly." Nan touched her fingers to her heart and heaved her breast wistfully. "Don't you know he's going to take me somewhere just fabulous?"

Chapter Six

Nan lounged in the wide leather seat, her light touch on the fingertip control toggles leaning it soundlessly back. She wished she could just doze off to the gentle, expensively-suspended purr of the big car bowling along the empty desert roads on top of Otay Mesa. She'd slipped into the front seat as soon as Alfredo pulled the burnished black Mercedes to the curb in front of her sidewalk table at Croce's. It was probably silly meeting him there. Not wanting her own *husband*, for Pete's sake, to know where she lived. Like they hadn't known all about her from the jumpoff.

She didn't like being inside opaqued car windows. She wasn't that crazy about cars at all, for that matter. She'd wondered about it before. How many thirty-two year-old career women made six figures and had never owned an automobile? She wrote it off to her deep-seated distaste for all the registration, fingerprinting and data-giving. Which was better than thinking that maybe automobiles represented a work environment to her. Thoughts that might lead back to her early days, doing business out of backseats. Which was not a situation she much cared to revisit.

Besides, she wanted the chance to talk to this Alfredo some more. Size things up as much as she could. Barreling the car across the peculiar urban wilderness of the Mesa, he looked as impassive as you'd expect a bodyguard to look; face as stolid and impenetrable as one of those Mexican stone heads. But he'd seemed friendly towards her from the start. Somebody it would pay to cultivate, was her assessment.

She fiddled idly with the window controls, popping a slit of hot, buzzing air open and shut. The big driver glanced at the distraction. Nan took her hand off the buttons and said, "Are we there yet?"

He looked at her blankly. "Little nervous?"

"Well, a girl always has those first night jitters. Did I save myself for the right guy?"

He looked back at the road. "Cute. But I guess what it is, I just don't think of you..."

"As a whore? I don't either, I guess. But enough about me. What about him? What if we don't click? He doesn't like me after awhile? I'm betting the prison doesn't much go for Wife Of The Week."

"You're concerned about the Boss? That's funny." He looked at her again, his face more open. "Yeah, he's taking a chance on you, in a way. That you'll be worth the bother. No tryouts before marriage, you notice. You hook up and that's that."

"Kind of charmingly old-fashioned."

He laughed. She did have a fun way of looking at things. Time would tell, of course. "It's old-fashioned a lot of ways," he told her, getting serious.

"Let me guess." She pondered prettily, index finger under her chin. "High fidelity?"

"You got it," He slowed the car, gave her full attention. "You're a married woman. Exclusive."

"Know what, Alfredo?" She met his eyes squarely. "I'm all for it."

She leaned back, looked forward and speaking quietly. "That was a lot of what made me go for this setup. No more take-out."

He nodded his understanding noncommittally. Then she surprised them both by blurting harshly, "No more fucking *men*."

He nodded again. Made sense. But he had to make it completely clear. "Just so you know the score. And you probably figured out there's going to be people keeping an eye on you."

"Suits me fine. A girl can't have too much protection these days." She raised a finger, suddenly thinking of more immediate matters. "Speaking of protection, how does that work? Should I bring in my own? Do they have little machines in the restrooms? Can I put on my teddy? Can he ask his cellmate for a little privacy?"

"Cellmate. Funny," he grinned. "Don't worry, you get plenty of privacy. They got these nice trailers. You know, mobile homes. The whole boneyard is trailers.

She leaned forward to look over at him, which took him aback. He quickly amended, "Conjugal visitation area."

"The Boneyard. Now that's a charming bit of American folklore. What's it called at the women's prison?"

"Same thing, I guess," he replied brusquely. "That's what married inmates get: boneyard visits."

"Sure, they'd call it the same thing. The universal commodity that makes the world go around."

He kept his eyes carefully on the road and said in voice so soft it was almost menacing, "You shouldn't think of yourself like that. Commodity, goods. You know what I'm saying?"

"Oh, please. Do I look like Julia Roberts to you? All this is, a mobster figured out how to get his ashes hauled in the lockup."

Alfredo's jaw tightened. He jerked his hands roughly, and put an oversize foot on the brakes, spinning the car off the shoulder in a roostertail of dust. He turned and leaned toward Nan, who shrunk away from the anger in his suddenly fierce and threatening face, reaching behind her waist for the door handle. She'd located the lock overrides before she'd even fastened her seatbelt.

"Figure it out, *chica*," he scolded her. "You're not a whore anymore. Not even a girlfriend. You're the *wife* of a powerful, important man. You understand that?"

He must have seen the comprehension in her face because he leaned back, eased the tight clench of muscles in his face. "You had your past, now you have this future. Live up to it, is what I suggest."

Nan relaxed, her pose softening. She faced forward in her seat, hit the button to bring it to upright, and smoothed down her skirt. She tipped down the lighted vanity mirror on the visor, patted her hair.

Then she turned to him with a shy smile. "You're right. I'm in. Let's not be late to prison."

He studied her a moment, then nodded. He pulled on the handbrake and stepped out of the car. Nan sat motionless as he walked around the front end of the car, his dark bulk distorted by the heat waves writhing off the long black hood. He opened her door and offered his forearm. "*Señora* Gaspar?"

She placed her hand on his arm, gracefully pivoted her legs out of the car to stand, and stepped away so he could close the door. She looked around the surrealistic landscape of the Mesa as he walked to the rear door. Thinking, it could be a new colony on Mars. The dust and desert scrub stretching out from the blacktop for miles, the ghostly runway standards of Brown Field running beside the border fence, the loom of cubical, dirt-colored Mexican and Japanese assembly factories in the distance. And straight

20

ahead, the forbidding, expressionless hulk of Donovan. She walked back to where Alfredo was patiently awaiting her, holding open the door to the darkened interior.

He extended his arm again and she rested her hand on it as she seated herself elegantly and swung her legs inside. He leaned over to speak to her, framed by the fathomless blue of the border sky. He said, "You're going to do just fine, *Señora*. All I'm saying is, don't sell yourself short."

He closed the door without waiting for a reply. Nan waited while he returned to the driver's seat and pulled back into the lines of semi-trailers and delivery vans that filled the absurd connector road. She pondered a moment, then reached over to push the door lock button, which responded with a heavy, authoritative click.

Chapter Seven

Another click with much more authority: the gate of a chain link fence topped with barbed wire coils slamming shut, locking Nan into a drab, dusty enclosure with a dozen sun-faded tan single-wides. Nan looked up over the top of her sunglasses: yes, those men watching the yard from high towers were holding assault rifles. Oh, except for that one: he's got a shotgun. Probably a rebellious trend-setter.

To her left, past a double fence that partitioned off what was unquestionably The Boneyard, a few dozen inmates had left off loitering to lean into the fence watching her like a caged tiger might regard human babies in the zoo crowds. They were yelling the nastiest things they could imagine. Fortunately, she thought, they don't have much imagination.

The guard--"Corrections Officer", he'd corrected her--pocketed a cumbersome set of keys and started to walk back through three more gates to the reception area. He caught her confused pose; a small, tender-looking woman lost amid one of the most brutally masculine architectures imaginable and bayed at by a pack of animals. He turned back, rattled the chainlink to get her attention over the barrage of vile admiration and pointed. "Number eleven, ma'am. Right over there."

She looked towards the trailers and couldn't immediately summon the motivation to walk over to them. She'd spent most of her life wrapping an ugly business in the accoutrements of elegance and grace, but one glance at the fence full of inmates in slack denim and sweaty skin clambering on the wire and gibbering like a troop of monkeys crashed it all back to the ancient reality of jungle meat. She looked back at the guard, tempted to just ask for a pass. But a deal is a deal.

She must have looked as lost as before because the officer filled his lungs and bellowed, "GASPAR! Visit!"

The fact that the name instantly silenced the gallery on the fence wasn't lost on Nan. She smiled her thanks at the guard and turned back towards the trailers. The ribald heckling started up again, yardbird punks too chicken to show their fear.

Then her new husband stepped out of trailer number eleven and smiled at her. He turned to the pack of yahoos on the fence and made a gesture with his fingertips together like a pouch. They shut up. Nan looked at them, then him, raising an admiring eyebrow. He strode over to her, looking flustered.

Her first unshielded impression of the man was different from what she'd seen in the visiting area and chapel. He moved confidently here, his dominance apparent in his pose and bearing. But his face seemed less hard with the two of them alone, and his eyes were friendly.

The denim prison issue that had looked appropriate through the glass of the "fishtank" now seemed like a clumsy disguise. This was a guy for white tropical suits and a Panama hat, she thought. A big cigar. He could be some landowner kicked out of Cuba and running rackets in Miami.

"You're early. Sorry I wasn't here at the gate." He started to touch her elbow, but turned the gesture into a sweep of his arm towards the trailer. "Come on inside. Get away from this horndog trash."

Nan walked beside him towards the door, but glanced back at the staring cons. "Oh, they were talking about *me*? That's so flattering."

He smiled appreciatively. "This place could use a little humor."

He put his hand on the big black number "11" and pushed the door open. "Not to mention some beauty and class."

He motioned her through the door in front of him, but as she started to move past, he held up his hand. On impulse, he bent, cradled her knees and shoulders and effortlessly scooped her off her feet. She laughed delightedly as he carried her to the door. The gallery along the fence whooped and applauded at this chivalrous *geste*: Nan waved to them gaily as she was swept over the threshold.

Inside, he quickly set her down and stepped back. He closed the door, then started adjusting the blinds, tipping them up to cut the slash of California summer to a soft gold glow. Fiddling around because he's unsure of himself, Nan realized. Doesn't know quite what to do about being locked up in a bedroom with his Rent A Wife. Kind of cute.

She looked around the space, a ten-wide version of the standard hotsheet motel, but without the charm. Nothing shabby or dirty, but nothing indicating any human care involved. Built to state specs for convict carnality, she thought. The Boneyard Arms. "From now on," she told him, "Whenever I hear somebody say, 'Hey, get a room,' I'll always think of this one."

He looked around more critically, standing with his hands on his hips, frowning. Not his style either. "It's like the demo model for tidy trailer trash," he said.

The only furniture was a bed and, inexplicably, a dresser.

"I guess we sit on the bed," she ventured.

Gaspar swung around quickly, embarrassed. "Oh, yeah. Please have a seat."

She sat demurely on the end of the bed, patted the sheeny synthetic blanket invitingly. He sat an arm's length from her, looked around again. "Sorry about this place."

"Maybe next time the Presidential Suite will be vacant." She looked him straight in the eye, expressionless. "So, what have you been doing?"

"Time." He smiled, "Ask me how it's going."

"So how's it going?"

"It's going."

"You're really a standup kind of guy," Nan grinned. "Playing a tough room."

"It's like everybody speaks a different language in here. But listen, just ask me whatever you want to know. Everything's been through lawyers and paperwork up 'til now."

"Don't forget those phones in the aquarium."

"You got any questions about the deal?"

"Clear enough to me." Nan shrugged offhandedly. "We're married for the rest of your stretch. Or until death do us part. I got the 'signing bonus'. Thank you. Fee per visit is pretty standard. Generous, though. I appreciate the rent part. And the lump sum if I go the distance."

He grunted. "Only thing worse than getting divorced would be getting dumped in prison..."

24

He broke off but she knew the next thought had been, "...by a whore." And she had to admit that would be salt in any guy's wounds.

He also realized she knew what he'd almost said and paused before continuing. "Then when I'm released we split up. Or renegotiate, I guess."

"But no performance incentives."

Gaspar stared at her.

"No major medical," she went on, "Or free agency clause."

"You had me going," Gaspar grinned. "Hey, blame your agent. It's a pre-nup, is all. Wish to hell I'd had one the first time out."

A client whining about his divorce, Nan thought. There's a novelty. I think I can sing this one without a lead sheet. "Let me take a stab. Traditional Catholic Lupe Lu dumped your butt before the ink dried on your fingerprints?"

"Good guess. She made out like a *bandida,* too: house, car, kids, dog, works. Both lawn mowers, *fíjate.*"

"Incarceration constitutes abandonment, I understand." She held her hair away from her nape. It was getting warm in the trailer in spite of the grumbling little air conditioner under the window. "Hey, would that work if the guy was already in prison when you married him?"

Gaspar gave her a hooded glance. "Somehow I figured you'd know."

"Not that interesting." She made a dismissive gesture. "Why would I want to void a sweet deal like this? Of course, I could go for community property. If she left you anything worth picking over."

"Good luck finding any property. Not the divorce, so much. Manny was way ahead of her. It was more like for taxes and trying to deal with the beef in the first place. Anything I got, they can just come take off. So I don't own a damn thing."

Nan broke into a full, genuine laugh that he just loved hearing. "So I managed to marry a drug mob kingpin who's flat broke?"

He nodded "ruefully", enjoying the whole thing.

"Boy I sure can pick 'em."

Now he had the good, real laugh. This babe was shaping up to be a lot of fun.

"It's pretty complicated at the moment," he told her seriously, "But it works. Checks are good, right?"

"Oh, quite good." She looked around again, noticing that the fixtures visible through the open bathroom door were all stainless steel. Some twerp designer downtown could have yuppie posers drooling over that look. She glanced back at Gaspar, sitting on the bed and eyeing her with calm, open interest. "But there's one thing I don't understand about this situation."

"Shoot. If anybody's got time, it's me."

"Aren't we supposed to take our clothes off?"

Gaspar looked down as if to check that he still had his denims on. He didn't look back up at her, said, "Oh, yeah, well... I just thought we could talk a little. Get to know each other some, you know..."

She kept a straight face. "For a wiseguy, you don't seem to have much of a handle on how the call girl thing works."

He chuckled. "Yeah, but we're married. I got *no* clue how the wife thing works."

"Me neither," Nan nodded. "Let's stick to what I'm good at. Lie down. Relax. Then I'll do whatever it takes to give you your money's worth."

"Well," he cracked a wide, relaxed smile, "You want to put it like that..."

"That 'get to know each other' thing was truly sweet, though," she said as she pulled off her suit jacket. "It just happens I talk better afterwards."

He lay back on the bed and spread his arms. "Know what? So do I."

"Get comfortable, Boss." She still hadn't figured out what to call him. "Kick your shoes off. I'll take it from there."

Chapter Eight

It was a fairly austere office, though actually near the top end for what an SDPD Lieutenant would occupy. Everything straight issue except the basketball hoop some previous occupant had bolted to the wall and RayRay's framed Shaft poster behind the desk. Not the remake: Richard Roundtree in full blaxploitation splendor. The brass desk plate proclaiming "Lt. Raymond Mobley: Border Crime Division" was obviously brand new. RayRay had the job attitude of a man reluctantly promoted above his level of competence.

A sturdy black man in his forties, Mobley gave off the vibe that he could step in for Shaft any time he had to. But was currently pinned down by paper complexities he didn't care for, understand or even approve of. At the moment, for instance, he was talking to--no, "liaising with"--a Fed from some messed-up agency that couldn't get its own agenda or initials straight. He leaned back and stared over his scuffed BlackTops at the guy's slick wardrobe, wondering what was the point. Right enough guy so far, though.

"I'll say this much," he said, "I like the way you don't throw your weight around."

The guy in the tailored suit spread his hands in a self-deprecating gesture. "I'm new. Still learning how to be a Federal asshole."

"Hey, take your time." This might not be all that bad, Mobley thought. Maybe.

What Reach couldn't understand is why a division commander with international responsibility would come to work dressed like a street cop gone bad in a cheap ghetto flick. Maybe it was the Roundtree poster. He'd risen to his current job at a youngish age largely by looking the part. He was smart and professional and had a great record as a Federal Marshall before moving up, but so did lots of guys. But they didn't look as fabulous as Sean Reach, did they? The rangy, graceful athlete's moves and wide-shouldered slugger's body that draped so well in "*collezioni*" suits were impressive enough, but then he had to have curly blond hair, flecked hazel eyes, and the strong, clean features of a model or movie lead.

A former colleague had called him, "pinup puss porn", but it hadn't stuck because his features were strong enough to save him from prettiness. It was a jock face, the trusted quarterback in a forties film, the sort of look men didn't resent. All that much. Single at thirty four. Go figure.

RayRay swung his legs down and grabbed two cups and the Mr. Coffee pitcher. "I'm new on this block, myself," he said as he poured the cups. "Four months back I was in Homicide. Did so good they gave me this for punishment. Seems everything is focusing on the damn border now."

Reach nodded, letting the coffee cool in his hands. "That's where I come in, all right. But listen... you don't mind my being a little curious?"

"What, why they put a black guy doesn't speak Spanish on the beaner beat instead of a 'Hispanic'? Why we got a border operation being run by a nigger and an Aryan Honkyhood pinup boy?"

"Well, yeah, along those lines."

"God knows what you're doing here. But let me tell you, San Diego border policing makes some fucked-up politics. If they'd put a white guy on it--an "Anglo", you know--everybody would have bitched, you can see that right off."

Reach nodded, tentatively sipping his coffee. Not too bad, surprisingly.

"But if they brought some Julio on, then it starts looking token, and frankly--just between we two--San Diego ain't exactly Boston. Not even L.A. It's Omaha By The Sea. I don't think the brass trust Mexican cops to stay clean, not side with their 'border bros', push come to shove."

"But nobody can bitch about you, right?"

"Bingo, amigo. I'm the perfect political solution. Functionally useless."

"Well, I hope not. This Gaspar guy was the Big Enchilada in this area..."

Mobley nodded, "With extra salsa."

"And we've got his ass. He's got the answer for the whole schmear. If we can wring him out."

"Easy to say. But I dunno. I've been working it a little. You gotta meet my counterparts over in TJ."

"Tijuana cops are interested in him?"

"Yeah, but from like, homicide angles. The whole racket thing, too. Mostly they're seeing him as one finger of a local honcho named Altamira. Ring any bells?"

Reach thought it over. "No big brass ones."

"Major mover over there. Very low profile until last year. Then suddenly he comes out of nowhere to get elected mayor. Gaspar's his dog in the California fight, they're telling me."

"What's the connection?"

"Nothing I could put my weight on yet. But it's why I've been picking at his outfit. Keeping a monitor since he became our respected guest. Any new shit."

"Like he got married?"

"Yes, he certainly did that, all right. Miss America Emeritus. Former Miss Nowhere In Particular. She visits him once in March, next thing you know it's all matrimonial. Comes in regular."

"The trophy wife? Maybe why his old lady divorced him?"

"Could be, but he never transferred anything to her name. Not in the picture previously. Cherry as they come: No record. Make that, no *records*. No job, no background, no car, *nada. Nada* fuckin' hint."

"Hmm. That doesn't intrigue you any?"

"Shit, you got intrigued first look at her picture, huh? But I guess she'd be worth leaning on. Maybe she's a gold-digger, could be tempted. Maybe we could squeeze out some assets, some dirt. Get some associated names, shit like that."

Reach nodded. "She might be some sort of loose cannon. Who knows whose side she might come down on?"

"Be easy enough to ask her about it. You been out to Donovan yet?"

"Haven't had that pleasure."

"It's a real garden spot. Southern California penal lifestyle at its finest."

Chapter Nine

Gaspar and Nan were sitting on the bed, leaning back against the headboard in their underwear, beaded with sweat in the stuffy room. They'd placed a cheap box fan, stenciled with the Donovan label and supply numbers, to blow towards their bodies from the rickety dresser. Her dress and his dungarees hung on the bathroom door. Both sipped from cans of lukewarm soda from the vending machine out in the yard.

Nan stared at the blank wall across from the bed while half-listening to an anecdote about the oddly static weirdness that apparently went on in the dormitories. It really bugged her that there was no crappy painting hanging there, like there would be in your average "no-tell motel". A cheap K-mart print of some smudged European scene with the impasto and canvas texture faithfully reproduced. She idly wondered what style would best suit this prison playpen.

Gaspar had shown her examples of inmate art, mostly done on envelopes. Major motifs seemed to be walls, wire, chains, clocks, and calendar pages. People in the artwork tended to be fierce, noble outlaws with bulging muscles or doe-eyed, buxom women wearing nothing but perhaps an occasional gang sign. She'd have to think of what art "ism" would work here. It could be a "School", she thought. Temporalism? Maximalism? She already knew what sort of literature would find favor: Escapism.

A twist in the story caught her attention and she laughed. "He didn't really say that," she said.

"Swear to God," Gaspar held up his hand and placed the other on an invisible bible hovering in midair. "Then this Rivera guy from H Block sticks his head in and says "That'll feel better when it stops hurting".

Nan laughed again, holding her soda can against the side of her face, where strands from her short brunette wig were starting to stick to her cheek. "You've got a pretty wacky clubhouse here, all right."

"We're very carefully selected." He sipped his soda, seemed to consider pouring it over his head. "By invitation only."

"A real elite." She pushed her hair back with both hands and turned to face him. "Look, we're running short of face time here. Maybe we better get down and get dirty before checkout time."

"Yeah," he replied tonelessly. "Boy, it's hot for that stuff, though. We're already sweating like pigs."

"Excuse me?" She gave the words the full Queen Latifah treatment. "Women don't sweat. We glow. Pigs do not glow."

He nodded a mock apology and she gave his shoulder a light punch. "I would have thought you jailbirds would kill for a shot a real-life hot, wet woman."

"Well, sure," Gaspar hastened to say. "I mean, just look at you."

"Yeah, look at us. An old married couple, sitting here chewing the fat on an unmade bed."

"Hey, we got our needs, right? I mean, you're a lot younger..."

"I can take it or leave it," Nan cut in. She patted his thigh. "You're not that old, either. And not a bad lover. But there's nothing wrong with a man your age not being a horny kid."

Gaspar sat for a moment, careful not to look at her. Not a bad lover, huh? Somehow that sounded more personal than stock whore talk. She picked up on his thought and leaned close to his ear. "And no, I don't say that to everybody."

"You know what I was thinking the other day?" There was something pensive and tentative in his voice. Nan sat still, careful not to derail his mood.

"I think I look forward to talking to you more than I do the sex." He paused to take a sip of Diet Coke, surreptitiously glancing at her for any sign of derisiveness or scorn or whatever it is men fear from confiding in women.

"It feels good." He seemed encouraged to explore this a little more. "Just, you know. Talking to the wife about the life."

She waited, but he put the can down by the bed and turned to her. "But yeah, we probably ought to do something here."

"*Ought to*?" She couldn't decide whether to be amused or insulted. "Gasman, what is it with you?"

He seemed to realize what he'd said and drew back a little. He leaned against the presswood headboard and looked at the blank wall as he spoke. Maybe he's seeing a painting there, too, Nan thought. He spoke suddenly, not looking at her.

"Look, I'm gonna tell you a few things, okay?" He went on without waiting for her okay, "Like why I went to all the trouble to do this whole marriage thing."

"I can't wait to hear this," Nan said with a soft laugh in her voice. But she gently touched his leg as she said it.

"Well, it's kind of embarrassing." He paused, seemed to miss having the soda as a prop. "I got worried about my prostate."

Nan went to some trouble not to laugh, just levelly say, "I'm seldom at a loss for words..."

"No, serious. I heard a guy my age, he has a regular sex life then all of a sudden isn't getting any... well, it can cause prostate cancer."

"So you were afraid of that. That's very touching, really."

"Afraid?" Bad choice of words. But he went back on the track. "No, more like, I was concerned."

"About having cancer up your butt and around your sex plumbing? You'd be nuts not to be afraid of something like that."

"I don't normally tell people that kind of stuff." He turned towards her, his head leaning against the wall. She could see an unaccustomed uncertainty in his eyes. Not a guy much given to coming clean.

"See, I can't sound weak," he went on in a rush. "I didn't even talk to my wife like this. There's something about you." He looked around the tacky room. "Something about this."

"I've pretty much heard it all." Nan's tone was calm, the voice she used to reassure and gain confidence. "Well, actually the prostate thing is a new one on me. But I wouldn't worry about that."

"I thought I'd be nuts not too."

"Did you hear that from a doctor?"

"No, one of the guys in here."

"Think about that a little." She patted his cheek and turned to face him, their heads lolling against the fake wood paneling. "Meanwhile, let me tell you what I think we ought to do."

She leaned close, whispered, and zipped the tip of her tongue into his ear.

"Sounds kind of nasty," he said, miming shock.

"Nothing of the kind," Nan coolly rejoined, swinging her leg over him and pushing him back, sitting against the headboard. "It's for medicinal purposes."

She straddled him with her hands on his shoulders, stroking the sides of his throat. Then she leaned back, shook her hair free, and reached up to unfasten her bra.

Chapter Ten

Nan turned a few heads as she strode past the benches of visitors waiting to see inmates. But even in her stylish mint-green suit and coppery hair she didn't rate top ten in sheer flamboyance among some of the women dolled up in their Saturday Nite Special to visit their men. Maru should run a recruitment drive in here, she thought as she moved around the seating area to sign in with the guard who admitted the pre-screened to the various visiting venues. Then her Inner Schoolmarm chided her for tacky thoughts: Be nice, Nan. These are the gals who are sticking it out.

The guard gave her a friendly nod and clicked at his keyboard, then his head come up with a sharper look. Uh, oh, she thought. Nan was not a great fan of being in databases, much less having them consulted about her. The guard, keeping his eyes on her, pulled a telephone handset from a strongbox-looking desk drawer and said, "There's a Fed flag on Gaspar."

I'm as patriotic as the next girl, she thought, but Federal flags just can't a good thing.

The telephone muttered incomprehensibly and he replied, "Well, she's here."

Yeah, here she is, Nan thought. Right here inside the bars. Just ducky.

The guard spoke to her with that official courtesy so ostensible it comes off as a snub. "Ms. Gaspar, it's been requested that you speak with enforcement officials."

Nan rolled her eyes up theatrically. "How many times am I going to have to fix that darn ticket, anyway?"

"If you could please step over to that door," he pointed, "An agent will speak with you."

"An agent?" She asked, wide-eyed. "Sheesh. Is this X-Files or a Geico pitch?"

The guard smiled, friendly again, and watched her walk to the blank beige door.

The door was locked--what else do I expect in the lockup, she thought--and her gentle tap brought no response. She turned back to the guard with a questioning look just as it opened behind her.

She turned to take in the impressive visual display that was Agent Sean Reach. And he was confronted with the sight of Nan Gaspar.

Neither spoke for a long moment as they drank each other in. Finally he produced a leather wallet that displayed a badge and identification card, showed it to her perfunctorily and pocketed it again without taking his eyes off her.

Nan was having trouble not staring at Reach. It felt like some sort of setup: somebody had bugged her brain, figured out what she envisioned as the Ideal Man and rigged it up for her. Blond, beautiful, fit and athletic, dressed in perfect pearl gray, and obviously a man who was all about Responsibility, Authority, and Reliability. Keep breathing, dear, she reproved herself. After all, you saw Brad Pitt in the lobby that time in Palm Springs and didn't swoon.

Reach stepped aside and held the door open for her, his pleasure in looking at her quite obvious.

"Better manners than Mongo, at least," Nan said as she stepped into the doorway. "Could I trouble you for a closer look at that badge?"

Standing in transition, one hand holding the door open, Reach didn't seem the least off-balance. He pulled the wallet out and flipped it open in front of her eyes, held it steady. She examined it closely. She would have been just as judicious about it if it had been written in Hebrew. This was one step you took with people who showed you official badges and laminated material. Then she turned just as thorough examination on Reach himself. He stood calmly, waiting.

She stepped into the corridor and he fell in step with her, the door closing itself behind them. He motioned casually to the first doorway on the right.

"Sean Reach," Nan mused. "Federal Investigator. My, my. Are you good at it?"

Reach gave her a boyish, sidelong smile that knocked her flat. It was like meeting an ex-lover or older brother she'd been away from so long she'd forgotten. He said, "Don't make me show you my last performance evaluation."

As they continued down the featureless hall, she eyed him some more. "Seems like such a waste of a perfect 44 long. Are you their token Chippendale model?"

"It's a waste of a guy who hit .427 career at Brigham Young, too. But this career lasts longer and has better medical."

Just letting me know he's not all show and no go, Nan thought. Interesting he would bother doing that. She took another glance. Whew.

"You remind me of somebody," she said. "I'd best watch myself with you."

"I'm just a rookie, really," Reach said as he opened the plain steel door. "Who you'd better watch out for is him."

He nodded his head at the room inside, where Nan could see empty walls, slot windows, a gray steel desk and RayRay Mobley.

She stepped into the small interrogation room, nodding a greeting to Mobley and waiting to be invited to sit. And hassled.

Mobley had been examining a manila file folder, but didn't play any cheap officer games with her. He stood and nodded to her, his nubby black face totally empty. I like his eyes, Nan decided. He's a man working as a cop, not a cop trying to be a man. He motioned to a state issue steel chair in front of him and she sat demurely down. He's got nice hands, too, Nan thought. Then, like a chessmaster after the handshake, she looked at him blankly and he became The Adversary.

Mobley sat and picked up the folder again. "So it's Ananda Gaspar?" he asked her politely.

"One more nuisance from my hippie mom. People call me Nan." She looked around the forbiddingly generic office then back at Mobley. "What did I do this time?"

But it was Reach who answered, from his perch on the corner of the desk. "For one thing, you recently married a major international drug dealer and known Mexican Mafia figure."

Nan looked shocked and clutched her bosom dramatically. "Do you mean..." she quavered, "That I'm... Married To The Mob?"

She was playing to Mobley, having sensed he was in charge, even if he didn't flash Federal paperwork around. Mobley inclined his head slightly, acknowledging that he knew she was having some fun, and pushed the file across the desk to her, turning it so she could see. A collection of photographs, faces of people she didn't want to have to meet, for the most part. Oh, except that one really mean-looking guy. And she was married to him.

"See anybody you know?" Mobley asked.

Nan pushed the pictures around with her fingertip, examining them with brow-wrinkling diligence.

"Well, see, we haven't been married that long," she told Mobley earnestly. "And he isn't the type to bring his work home with him."

She held up a photo of one particularly wanted-looking Latino and examined it. "If you'd let him come home, that is."

Reach spoke up again, "Are you familiar with RICO laws?"

Nan looked at him then back at Mobley, shrugged. "I heard it was Kangaroo for 'guilt by association'."

Mobley had to hide a smile over that one. He leaned back and spread his hands. "You're associated."

"How?" Nan demanded in a firmer voice. "By injection?"

She looked from Mobley to Reach, the ingénue demeanor gone. "Look, I have to apologize," she said flatly. "I thought this little song and dance would be entertaining, but I'm having to lead and you aren't keeping up."

What did she mean by that, Reach wondered. Is she trying to send us a message? Feel us out for an offer? He said, "I'm afraid I don't follow you."

"That's what I just said," Nan snapped. "Let's cut to the finale here so I can go do my visit and you two can get back to intimidating jaywalkers or something. If you're fishing for any information or co-operation against my husband I'd recommend you take up beach activities."

Reach wasn't going to bite twice, so RayRay smiled slightly and said it. "Beach activities?"

"Pounding sand, for example." Her tone was as flat and neutral as the desktop.

"I don't understand your hostility here." Reach came on official, concerned and yes, just a little hurt in his warm eyes at her attitude. "Or why you wouldn't want to co-operate with..."

"Save it, cutie," Nan said, not too unkindly. "Here's the bottom line we'll get down to no matter how long this takes: He's my husband."

"And as a spokesperson for family values..." Reach began but Mobley cut in with, "Are you telling us you had no involvement with Gaspar before you married him?"

Nan laughed out loud. "Some great files you have there." She closed the folder and pushed it back across the desk. "The first time I met him he was right here in Donovan, doing his time."

"So you decided it would be fun to marry a strange felon twenty years older?" Mobley was as curious as Reach.

"Not as strange as a lot of them, from what I'm hearing."

Reach was too genuinely puzzled to hold back. "But why?"

Nan turned slightly in her chair, offering Reach a long, cool look. "In your line of work you never run into powerful gangsters who hook up with almost-beautiful and still-fairly-tight younger women?"

Reach didn't react, but Mobley nodded as if that much was pretty obvious.

"Well, you put it that way," Reach said. Then delighted Mobley by blurting, "You just don't seem like the kind of woman who'd be for sale."

Nan clutched her bag and stood. Gotta hand it to her, Mobley thought, she's got the timing of an actress. Or politician. She moved a half step closer to Reach and looked him straight in the face. "You don't look like the kind of cop who's for sale, either. And unless somebody comes up with an offer that matches your needs, we'll never know, will we?"

She stood expectantly as Reach looked to Mobley, who shrugged cynically. Broad has a point, he seemed to be signaling. Reach kept his voice carefully neutral as he told her, "Well, thanks for all your help and co-operation, Mrs. Gaspar. Have a nice visit to Donovan. We may want to speak with you again."

She nodded at Mobley and took a step towards the door, then turned and gave Reach a much friendlier look. Game over, Mobley thought. Visitor slamdunks the homeboys, now she can talk like folks.

"I like this trend towards gorgeous young cops," she said. "And don't take me wrong. You don't look like you could go bad if you wanted to. That noble chin and brow. Those eyes. Wow. You're the true blue type, aren't you?"

Reach made an affirmative gesture with his right hand. "I take my oath of office seriously. And the trust that comes with the badge."

Thank you, Dudley DoRight, Mobley thought.

"So maybe you can understand that I took vows, too, Agent Hotty," She told him earnestly. "Which I also take seriously."

She did a statuesque pivot, walked to the door and half-turned. "A pleasure meeting you. You, too, Lieutenant."

She tried the knob and it opened, so she walked out without a backward glance.

Both men looked at the door for a moment without speaking. Then Reach asked plaintively, "How come the scumbags get to have women like that?"

Mobley stood and scooped up the file. "I just heard her tell you."

Chapter Eleven

One thing Nan liked about the space she thought of as "Boneyard 11" was that it was calm, an island of muffled quiet locked away from the whirl of the world. Two people doing simple, basic things with minimal props and no need for the games that complicated those things in relationships out there in the buzz.

It took only the few seconds required for her to mention the conversation she'd just had with Reach and Mobley to blast that cocoon of calm into a hot wind of stress. The world resents a vacuum; needs to push people around and mess with their heads.

She was sitting on the bed cross-legged in her panties and bra, watching Gaspar pace in agitation. Shoes off, shirt open, his whole body a heaving mass of pissoff.

"But they never came out with anything they wanted from you? Like, specifics?"

"Why would they?" she answered dully. "I wasn't very encouraging."

"Just, 'co-operation', you're saying?"

"A few hints at pressuring me. Accessory. Associated. A bad joke, really. Look, why don't you come over here and sit down?"

He snorted. She could see the mobster in him now, a bull taunted by the flirt of the red cape of authority. "Co-operation! Sounds better than 'snitching', huh? Better than, 'just lie still and enjoy it.' So you told them..."

"To go screw themselves." Nan almost barked the words, stopping Gaspar in mid-pace. He looked at her and she shrugged her shoulders slightly. "Saves a lot of time and awkwardness."

He took a breath and looked down at his fists, unclenched them. He came to the foot of the bed and looked at her with a fond smile. "I'm starting to really appreciate your style, *nena*."

Nan patted the pillow beside her, motioned him to it with a toss of her head. "Well, we hear so much about how you mafia types treat stool pigeons and various tattletales."

Gaspar had moved to sit by her, but stopped and shot her a look. "And you think...?"

She raised an eyebrow and he relaxed, smiled, sank down beside her. "I should know by now that everything you say is a joke on all the rest of us."

He turned to her and very gently brushed back damp hairs from her throat. "But in case you don't know, this thing... you and me? It's not about fear. It's about loyalty."

"That's exactly how I see it," she told him matter-of-factly. "You're the client: I stick by the fine print all the way."

"Looks that way. But you can't just buy up loyalty, you know. Not really."

"Not even with fear?" She asked him guilelessly.

"Lots of guys do things that way, but it's really worthless in the long run. People who're afraid of you hate you and are just waiting for their shot. That's the movies. Always look at the dark side of things."

"And what's the sunny side of mob discipline?" she asked brightly.

He smiled, but turned serious again. "Long as we're talking about this stuff, you know what really holds things together? Respect. In a way it's a thing like everybody pitching in to survive."

"Surviving is a good perk."

"You always got one of those comebacks, don't you? Look, it's like living on a *rancho* in the desert or something. Everybody's in it together to get by. Like family."

"So you went out and bought yourself a family."

Gaspar started to speak, then gave her a pained look and heaved a sigh. He scratched his stomach and leaned over to kiss her bare shoulder. "I bought myself a whore with a smart mouth."

Nan bent forward to kiss the spot he was scratching. "Educated mouth."

"You can say that again. Ph.D. At least."

While Nan and Gaspar enjoyed a new level of intimacy brought about by the application of outside threat, Reach and Mobley were walking across the shimmering blacktop of the parking lot. Neither felt a warm sense of accomplishment about their expedition to Donovan.

Reach finally said something. "She's tougher than she looks."

41

"Tough?" Mobley touched his car to gauge how much the sun had heated it up. "That what we're seeing there? Tough? Tell you how it looks from here. Committed."

Reach opened the door that Mobley had unlocked from inside. Jesus, wouldn't have to worry about a soufflé falling in there. He wished male protocol allowed him to stand outside and wait ten minutes for the air conditioner to deal with it. He slid inside, careful on the baked seat cover. "I have to admire that, in a way."

They sat with the doors open, motor running and air conditioner on full blast. "Among many other ways," Mobley said with friendly sarcasm. "She kicked your butt and took your name. You'd best check yourself, young blood. Entrapment can cut both ways and I'll tell you right now which one of you got the best bait."

Gaspar lay on his side watching her as she stepped out of the cool shower. She wrapped a sheet around her instead of a towel, saw him looking and gave him a flash and grin. He motioned her over to the bed and she shuffled across the tacky carpeting trailing a train of damp percale. She sat and shook her damp hair on him, then said, "You're a kind of a crash course in irony, GasMan."

"What'd I do now?"

"All those years I was hooking without one single bust. Then I get married and immediately have cops all over me like static cling."

He nodded ruefully, "Trying to twist you up. I hadn't really thought of that."

"Great. Anything else that might have slipped your mind? Aside from big cops and slick Federal agents? Anybody out there with car bombs or hijacked 747's?"

Gaspar rolled on his back and stared at the ceiling for a long moment. She dried her hair with a corner of the sheet, watching him and waiting. She'd been half-joking, but the longer he took to answer the more serious it got.

Finally he said, "Maybe the Maras. They're the main reason I'm even in here."

"Another gang?"

"It's more like they're *the* gang. Swarming up out of like Nicaragua, Salvador, the barrios. They probably really are a threat because they're too crazy to control."

42

"Oh, you shouldn't have," Nan crooned. "My very own dayglo bull's-eye right on my very own ass."

He spoke with decisiveness and drive, making it clear that it bothered him to have overlooked a threat to her. "I'm moving you someplace safer. And putting more people on watching you."

"Oh, goody. A whole squad of Mongos around."

He gave her a disgusted look. "You got a problem with people trying to keep you safe?"

"Did they keep you safe? Take a look where you are."

Unexpectedly, he lay back and stretched luxuriantly then looked up her with obvious relish and affection. "I am looking. And know what? It's not so bad. Some ways, this might be one of the best times in my life."

That blew even Nan's deep-seated unflappability. She just stared at him.

He shrugged widely, turning it into a caress of her closest flank. "Serious."

Nan laughed delightedly. "So we've moved on to Irony 102?"

Chapter Twelve

Gaspar's first impression of the attorney conference rooms had been that they were designed for some complex, high-level competition. International backgammon with the players sealed in until it was over, something like that. There was like *nothing* in the room except a table and two chairs, not even a trashcan or clock. Just the green-topped table waiting for two guys in sterile coveralls to come and start playing a game. Which, he supposed was what he did there. He and Manolo Basto, his attorney.

Who was looking as slick and burnished as usual. His long, bald head sleek as a marine mammal, his nails glossy on smooth hands. The aquiline nose always raised as if to sniff out problems, or pushing ahead to cut through a sea of red tape like the prow of an icebreaker. He was fiddling around with the latches on his slim briefcase of buttery Argentine leather, the way he always did when he was saying things Gaspar didn't want to hear, his supple fingers fluttering like minnows around the titanium fittings. "Don't get me wrong," he was saying, "She's probably okay. But she is a weak link."

Gaspar was giving him the stoneface over the whole issue. "She's either okay or she's not, *wey*."

Manny nodded, but kept on track. "She's a woman. She's where they can pressure her. Lots of ways. She's not really... you know..."

"Know what? Ask Alfredo what he thinks would happen if somebody tried to put some fear on her." He leaned forward and thumped the briefcase with a hard finger. "Like Mongo muscling her or something?"

"I think he'd say, God help the poor son of a bitch."

Gaspar laughed along with him, the discussion now resolved. "She's one in a jillion, that's for sure. But you're right, Manny. Put that thing in her purse, wherever. If nothing else, we get tapes of cops talking shit."

Manny nodded, stood and flicked the latches with final, businesslike clicks.

"Oh, yeah," Gaspar said without standing up, "Speaking of her. Could you put a rush on getting the place ready? She's getting tired of playing musical hotels."

Manny hefted the case. "And wire the new place."

Gaspar nodded. "For everybody's piece of mind."

The following week was even warmer and the trailer was not quite oppressive, but definitely a sweatbox. Nan wore only panties as she straddled her husband's broad, rough back and massaged his shoulders. Perspiration droplets worked down her breasts, fell off her nipples. "One thing about no air-conditioning," she said as she dug into the softening slabs of sweaty shoulder, "We're saving a fortune on massage oil."

Gaspar chuckled, mellow and content under her kneading hands. "It's always hard to tell with you," he said softly over his shoulder, "But it sounds like you're okay with the house."

Nan gave him a double-handed squeeze and leaned sideways to catch his eye. "It's wonderful, Gasp. It's like Architectural Digest meets spy movie. I keep expecting Pierce Brosnan to walk into the bedroom with a dry martini."

"He'd have to be James Bond to get into that place, way they went over it."

"Yeah, the security's a little obsessive. But I guess security has to be that way."

"That's what it's all about. But I'm glad you're happy there. I figured you'd get tired of shuffling around suites."

"Think about that one a minute," Nan said, shifting her attentions to his heavy upper arms. "Who's a Different Hotel Every Night kind of girl? I didn't exactly spend my youth looking for a cozy nest with long-term security."

"So how about you give security a chance, see how you like it?"

"It's working for me so far. I love the sun deck and hot tub. You're pretty plush for a guy who doesn't own anything."

"Somebody owns it. But nobody connected with me. I mean, they can try to connect if they want to."

"And you're sure they'll give it back when you want them to?"

"No doubt in my mind. I never see my asshole, but I'm sure it's there when I need it."

"Well, it's nice to have assholes you can count on."

Gentled and somnolent under her deep rubbing, Gaspar spoke as if about to fall asleep, his thoughts drifting lazily. "Some day I'll be out of here, have a lot of stuff, you know what I mean?"

"No I don't. And I don't think it's such a great idea if I do."

"Right," he breathed. "But after this settles down, I'll have it again. You'll see."

"I will?" Her hands stopped moving. "You know, I think that's the first time you ever mentioned, Is There Life After Prison?"

Gaspar craned his neck to look at her, gave up. "I'm just saying."

"Yeah. I know." She jostled his head affectionately and returned to her rubdown.

Chapter Thirteen

It was an emphatic contrast to her old place. There was nothing impersonal or unisex about this bedroom. In fact, forget "bedroom", Nan thought: this is a "boudoir" if ever there was one. The russet carpet pile was so deep she could lose visual contact with her toes. The walls were a rich cream color but it was hard to tell because you could hardly see them behind all the hardwood shelves, book cases, sandy paintings of deserts and beaches, giant television, and rich, sexy drapes. A tent of peach gauze surrounded the bed, the same color fabric wafted around the door to the balcony, filtering the light warmly. Dimmers controlled indirect lighting, but at the moment twenty candles in glowing earth colors took care of that and gave the room its faint odor of almond. Comfy little nest, she thought as she shuffled around in her slubby Turkish robe and frothy periwinkle nightie, rubbing her face with a cream that promised women everywhere skin as perfect as Nan's.

She set the jar on the apparently antique walnut nightstand beside a half-read Bulgakov from the Chula Vista library, picked up a plastic vial of pills and moved over to the softly swaying drapes. Slipping through the flimsy material, she stood quietly on the balcony. The pool was the main light source for the tiled, landscaped courtyard inside the high walls, a soothing blue lozenge nestling close to the bright white eye of the Jacuzzi. Small courtesy lights glowed like fairy lamps in the bougainvillea and lantana. Motionless, silent and utterly reposed.

She couldn't see a living soul. The neighbors' houses were lower and set back, she couldn't spot any of Gaspar's men in the courtyard or garden. But she knew they were there. She drew a deep breath of the dry, cool air and slipped back inside. They were there: hard, functional men with guns, radios and prior convictions.

So this is how security feels, she thought, gliding around barefoot to blow out candles. Like nobody is going to walk in on you unwanted. Nobody is going to wake you up, confront you, disturb whatever fragile peace we all try to knit out of the world's twisted skeins. What's outside stays outside.

She laid the robe across the back of the plush cherry chair at her enormous vanity and sat on the turned-down bed, contemplating. No rent was due. There was plenty of food in the restaurant-class kitchen. There was nothing that had to be done, nobody who had to be pleased, no schedule to keep. She had a man she could go to when she wanted, but couldn't come to her when she wasn't conscious or prepared. She had more than she could read, could sleep around the clock if she felt like it, either in this cool, shadowed bower or in a chaise under the soporific touch of the sun outside.

She had, it suddenly came to her, somebody taking care of her. The idea hit her right between the eyes. Could she remember a time in her entire life when somebody had taken care of her?

Gaspar might have something about this security thing, she thought. She looked at the pill bottle in her hand a moment, then opened a drawer in the nightstand and dropped it inside. She picked up two more bottles from the stand and dumped them in as well. Then lay down in the silent dark. She watched the sinuous undulations of the drapes for four minutes before she was asleep.

Chapter Fourteen

She'd come to think of it as the "Chamber of Doomed Questions". She sat comfortably, trim and contained in a floaty dress the color of orange sherbet. Her dramatically white wig was swept up in a fifties Audrey Hepburn do that went well with the unbleached macramé espadrille that dangled off one foot. She felt no tension waiting for Agent Reach to come up with something to say: she was soaking up the view.

Much more than just a pretty face, she was thinking. Well, the face and the classy, virile body. He was more than smart and dedicated. He actually cared about what he was doing, you could tell that. And also cared about her. As a human being. Not to mention certain signs she hadn't missed, indicating that she wasn't the only one whose thoughts occasionally strayed towards what two great bodies like hers and his might look like in a closer proximity. And feel like. His concern for her must create a certain amount of conflict, she thought. Well join the club, copper.

He didn't seem so much irritated at the polite stonewall she'd been handing him; more like sad and resigned. Disappointed, maybe. Finally he blew out his breath and leaned his chair back. "I'm not the only player in this thing," he told her and she definitely saw his dissatisfaction with the interview. "There's more pressure coming on me all the time. And on Ray. And therefore on you. And I hate to tell you but we're the Good Cops in this scenario."

"I've got no complaints so far," she nodded affably. "Well, the coffee could maybe be improved."

"I've been hoping we could work something out. You and I."

Oh, I'll just bet you have, she thought. "Well, it's hard to bargain with somebody whose only position is No Way, Jose."

"I'm not kidding around with you here. I'm the best it's going to get for you."

"Oh, I know. You'd love to give me a killer deal on the used convertible, but there's your demonic sales manager in the back office."

"It's not like that. My superiors are pushing me, the local people are moving. Even the prison staff."

"The prison? Why would *they* be after his ass? They've already got it."

"They're getting concerned about his activities here inside. His continued direction of narcotics business outside. What channels he's using." He gave her a hard, meaningful look.

"So of course he'd use me to run a sensitive business, not somebody with attorney privilege. Or just buy up some guards. Who from what I'm seeing would probably work for the price of decent haircut."

"I told you, this isn't about busting him. And certainly not you. It's about protecting people."

"And I told you. You've got nothing coming. Not one word."

He regarded her without speaking for a moment. Her beauty was so refined, so delicate. He figured he could span her waist with his hands. That she'd break if not handled with care. So when she showed the steel beneath the chiffon like that, it excited the hell out him. What a sick waste, he thought, of all this woman.

What he said was, "So I took my cuts and fanned out. Meet the next guy in the lineup."

He flipped open a sleek metal cell phone that had apparently been on all the time and spoke into it, "Okay, see how you do."

The sad shrug he showed Nan said, I tried my best to help you. And she believed it. Almost immediately the door opened and a tall, chesty man in a western cut suit walked in and stood looking at her with his hands on his hips. Not a friendly look.

Reach stood and moved to the wall, where he leaned with his hands in his pockets. Whoa, I could sell that shot to GQ in a hot second, Nan thought. If he loosened his tie and tousled his hair a little he'd be eye candy of the month for the ladies and queens alike.

The newcomer gave Reach a very pointed look, but he stayed right where he was, a fly on the wall. The big guy took the vacated chair and sat statically, both hands on the table, checking Nan out. She didn't get the feeling her sex appeal had anything to do with what was going on in his head. She imagined the robot in *Terminator*, browsing down a list of human-sounding response variables.

He had huge hands, well-maintained but carrying their record of use. His face was narrow for his bulk, but strong-jawed with high, hard cheekbones and brow ridges. His skin was light olive with a matte look, as though buffed with fine sandpaper but never finished. She doubted he had sweat glands, or used them if he did. His eyes were very carefully blank. Her take on his gaze was of a guy who'd banked all his emotions into an inner cage where they chewed their own paws while waiting to get out to hunt and hurt. She'd known the kind of guy who, after they'd knocked somebody down, didn't just kick them but stomped them flat. Let me guess, she thought, the Bad Cop?

"Ronald Gaithers, *Miz* Gaspar," he said with a straightforward cop-to-street-scum delivery, "D.E.A."

He showed her his identification, but she didn't bother examining it. Finesse was beside the point with this guy. He had a sledgehammer awareness, was her guess. He started asking her questions.

It was like a powerful drill rotating against an armored bank vault door. Sound, motion, heat: but nothing getting through. Nan handled him the way she would idly stroke tennis balls back over the net to her neighbor's ten year old. It's so easy when you don't want anything and have nothing to hide. Finally she broke the monotonous rhythm of question and menace. "Do you have a card, *Mizter* Gaithers?"

He almost blinked at having his script interrupted. She leaned forward with a soft smile. "Why don't you leave me your number and if I ever find out anything about these mobsters I never see, or my husband commits some crime during the six hours a month I see him, I'll call you up. Do you have voice mail?"

Reach, lolling against the wall, didn't even try to hide his grin. It was fun watching somebody else bang their head on the wall, try to pick the pretty flowers that burned your fingers. The skin tightened across Gaithers' cheekbones and he seemed to draw inward, consolidating inside the boundaries of his body. He spoke in a very measured monotone.

"We'd hoped you'd be more willing to help us, Ms. Gaspar. Since you aren't I can only tell you that this makes you, in my assessment, an accessory. Withholding evidence. You're becoming a person of interest to us, and I'm not talking about just when you're in here visiting that vicious piece of sewage you're married to."

That outburst surprised Reach but Nan took it in her lazy stride, tipping it back over the net. "Can you really have a 'piece' of sewage? Isn't that a collective noun or something, like drainage?"

Gaithers ignored her, trudging on in his quest for intimidation. "I think you'll find that your life is going to become a lot more public, and much more closely scrutinized."

"More closely than the alleged hoodlums allegedly associated with my alleged husband?"

"Your credit records..."

"I don't have any credit."

That stopped even the juggernaut of Gaither's bullying scorn. He looked at her blankly like an actor who had given the right cue and gotten a bird call in response.

Reach was enjoying this immensely. "You shop for the kind of clothes you wear without having credit cards? Is that allowed?"

Nan shrugged prettily, "I guess they just give credit where credit is due."

"Your banking, investments, in your workplace..."

"I'm retired."

Reach cut in again, courting Gaither's annoyance. Mobley had called the guy a "four door, hardtop, V-Eight, donkey dick" and he'd been right. "I wondered about that actually. What was it that you did?"

"High ticket, outcall prostitution."

That wiped the smirk off his face. And almost made Gaither show something on his.

Reach chuckled uncertainly, "No, I mean seriously..."

"You think I'd kid around about doing sex for money?" She turned a very direct look on Reach. "So much for your keen eye for who's on for sale, huh?"

She wouldn't have thought it possible for Gaithers to look more superior and disgusted, but he pulled it off. He practically sneered as he said, "I think you can count on being stopped and searched anywhere you go. And long delays for your visits here."

Nan gave him a look that clearly stated: Let's cut the kidstuff and play hardball, tough guy. "So I'd only be making five hundred an hour when I come up here, instead of a thousand? Well, with the economy like it is, we all have to cinch up our garter belts a little."

"Embarrassing searches, I would say," Gaithers ground on. "Including explorations of body cavities."

Her look peeled all the cashmere back off the tool steel. "You cops always get for free what criminals have to pay for, don't you?"

The look in Gaither's eye was murderous. She was glad Reach was there. Even in this bastion of law and order, she'd just seen the look of a man who would lash out and maim.

"If it will save you some time," she said in a voice with all the soft compassion of commercial oven cleaner, "I'll tell you exactly what you'll find in my 'cavities' on the way out."

Gaither stood up without a word and walked out with no backward look, no slammed door, no variation in his stride. She'd have been more comfortable with some show of temper.

Reach stayed where he was, looking at her with an injured wonder.

"Nice friends you have, Sean." She stood and picked up her purse, turned towards him. "Aw, poor Agent Hunk. You've had it haven't you? Look, why don't we just call this one a draw and let me go visit my husband? We can do tag team again in two weeks."

Reach nodded numbly, but as she reached for the doorknob he snapped out of it. "Can I ask you one more thing?"

"Or course. My life is an open book. Which is at least partly your fault."

"Forget all this. Off the record, okay?" He didn't wait for her nod, plunged on. "I just want to figure things out."

Nan waited demurely, dangling her purse in front of her.

"Why you..." He stopped and regrouped. "Your getting into... you know, the life..."

"Whoring, you mean?"

"Okay, sure. But somebody like you? There must have been some reason."

"Why a nice girl like me would charge for it? Something noble and tragic? Like a daughter in an iron lung?"

Reach brushed off the way she was playing with him. "I just want to know."

"Actually," she told him with eyes downcast in "shame", "We could only afford a cardboard lung."

He didn't brush that off. She regretted his disgusted look and smiled at him. "I'm sorry, Sean. Look, as a matter of fact, I did start making it with men who didn't appeal to me in order to support a poor little girl. She was shocked and hurt. Abandoned by her mother, abused by her father, tossed out hungry and cold and defenseless on the streets. That help any?"

Reach felt a combination of relief and commiseration. "I knew it had to be something like that. How old?"

"The homeless girl?"

"Yeah, how old is she now?"

She spoke flatly, a bucket of cold water in his face. "Thirty two."

When she opened the door and left, he didn't say anything to stop her.

Chapter Fifteen

Manny Basto wasn't exactly comfortable on the stiff steel chair in the sterile, overlit attorney contact cubicle, but at least he was relaxed. Doing the job. Not like his *patrón,* who was either trying to pace in the cramped quarters or leaning back in his chair, away from the matters at hand. Finally Manny leaned forward in his chair and stuck the sheaf of typed paper almost in Gaspar's face. "Look," he said with a hint of exasperation, "You said wire her up, we wired her. Why? So you could pass on reading the transcripts?"

Gaspar made no move to take the transcripts. Hard evidence of a lack of basic faith in probably the only one in his environment that didn't invite suspicion. "You say she stood up, I believe you."

"Oh, she stood up like a trooper. What she did, she handed them their ass. So we aren't spying on her, really. We're spying on them."

"Yeah," Gaspar reflected. "She wore our wire in there. She's right, this shit is ironic. Well, they started it."

He took the transcript of the broadcast of Nan's interrogation as broadcast from the state-of-the-art, high-end, European-made gizmo concealed in Nan's purse, and started to read while Manny carefully re-ordered his power-ops briefcase and stood to leave. He was moving around the table towards the door when he was startled by an outburst from Gaspar.

"*Hijo de su madre!*" he exclaimed. "I *knew* there was something like that."

He came to his feet and paced the little room again, reading from a page of the transcript.

"I knew it. Thanks, *compa.*"

Manny stared at him, clueless, then peered at the papers still on the table. He spotted what was happening immediately.

"*Oye,* Boss. I think you should read the next page here."

Gaspar waved him off, intent on the sheet he was reading. "*Sobres, mano!* This thing paid off a lot of different ways. You were all the way right. See you next week."

He was obviously too wrapped up in his reading to talk to, so Manny spread his hands and pushed the button to request the door be buzzed open. "Read on, man," he called back as he left.

Gaspar paid attention only to the page in front of him. "Oh, man. '...shocked and hurt. Abandoned by her mother, abused by her father, tossed out hungry and cold and defenseless on the streets.' That's some heartbreaking shit, right there."

"Yo, Gaspar," the slim black guard from the control room hailed through the speaker in the ceiling. "You gonna move in there or something?"

He moved out the door thumping the rolled-up paper against his hand. He had a lot to think about.

Chapter Sixteen

Even as stark a space as Boneyard 11 could be lent a domestic air by its inhabitants. Gaspar lay on his back in his shorts, hands clasped behind his head as he smiled at the ceiling. Nan sat cross-legged beside him, biting off the thread she was mending a torn-off pocket of his jeans with. Practically a scene out of Bruegel.

"I qualify for it," he was saying with the provisional air of somebody open to feedback. "But I don't see any reason I should take it."

"Are you out of your mind?" Nan asked rhetorically. "Look at you."

He did look, pulling his head forward with his clasped hands to stare down his body. "What? I look like a farmer to you?"

"No, that's my point." She looked up from her repair job, serious. "You're pale and getting soft. You aren't going to inspire faith and dread like that. Wouldn't you really rather be outdoors, on the soil, than sitting around that dusty yard playing dominos with the usual pack of losers?"

"Losers?" He put on a little faux indignation. "Those are my colleagues."

"Four of whom," Nan pointed out, punctuating with the needle, "You have described to me as--and I think I'm quoting exactly here--'three time losers'."

Gaspar held up his palms, conceding her point. "So I'd be less bored shoveling cowshit?"

"Gasp, you're in prison for crissakes. I'd think *any* change would be worth it. Besides, didn't you have to go to some trouble to qualify for the farm gig?"

"It's all just classification points." He motioned dismissively, but could see she wanted more details. "See what it is, your status down here--where you do your time, your living conditions, all that--it's based on like, numbers."

"Wasn't numbers one of the charges that got you in here?"

"Oh, cute." He shook his head in amusement as he went on. "See, you get points for being educated, being married, having a job offer, having a family. No points, you live behind walls. More points, you're here behind fences. More points, maybe honor camp, work release, early parole."

Nan thought it over a moment. "I get it. The more good citizen brownie points you get, the more slack they cut you. Because you've got more to lose."

"You got it. Go to school inside, get your GED, and boom, a few more points."

"They're smarter than I thought. Of course the real sociopaths will just manipulate that system, too."

"Definitely. Get a job offer, get married, get a diploma: they all carry points."

"Well, now I feel all cheap and used," Nan pouted. "So you only married me to con your way closer to a pile of cowshit?"

Gaspar laughed and sat up. "You finish that sewing and breaking my balls, we might have a little fun around here."

"Careful, there, sport. I'm holding a needle and presumed dangerous."

Nan had just toweled off after a cool shower, but could already feel the sweat beading on her stomach and nape. She took another swipe with a sheet then stepped into her panties. Gaspar wasn't watching her dress as usual: he seemed pensive, lying there naked, staring into middle air.

As she slipped her dress on and snugged it down, she saw him come to a decision and roll up to a sitting position. She smiled as he laid a pillow over his lap. He spoke with a quiet significance that told her to take him extra seriously.

"Hey, listen up a minute."

Nan put one bent leg on the bed and sat facing him, her other foot on the floor. "Don't I always?"

"Yeah you do listen, don't you? You sure you're really a woman?"

Nan looked down, then smirked at him, but he didn't react.

"Look, I want to get something settled here."

Nan folded her hands in her lap, gave him the undivided benefit of her clear blue gaze.

"There's a thing or two Manny could set up. Like in case something happens to you."

Nan did an incredulous take, saw he was serious. "You've got cops, Feds and gangs after you, live in this kibbutz crammed full of violent criminals. And something might happen to *me*?

"Just hear me out, okay?" He held out his hand like an orator asking for a following. "I want to fix it up so your little girl is taken care of, no matter what. A trust thing, maybe. I could even adopt her."

Nan's face stayed completely blank as she stared at him for a long beat. Finally she said, "Did we just move past irony to surrealism? My little girl?"

"Yeah. That little girl out on the street. Why you got into this escort thing."

The light dawned behind her sky blue pupils and her smile broke open. She couldn't decide whether to laugh out loud or lean over and kiss this guy to pieces. "This is just too funny," she told him, smiling wider at his shock at her response. "But truly, deeply moving. You're always at your most endearing when you're completely full of crap."

She moved quickly to reward his feelings. No matter why he got his wires crossed, he deserved a medal for stepping up. "Hey, hon, I don't have a little girl. I was one, once. And yeah, out on the street. You weren't listening."

"Oh." He sat frozen, grinding inner gears. "Ah, wait. I get it now. Well, hell, never mind."

"Never mind? You wish." She sparkled merrily as she wagged a finger at him. "I don't even know where to start torturing you over this one. For openers, how many points would you have gotten for my poor little spastic wheelchair kid?"

Chagrined, he grumbled, "Not enough to make a difference."

"So you wanted to use me *and* my non-existent child. Well, that does it, you brute. You're cut off. Let your old cowshit cop your joint for you."

He stared at her curiously. "You serious with this BS?"

Nan grinned slyly, "caught out", "Of course not, tough guy. It's just that we've been married two months now and I thought we should have a spat. You know, just for normality's sake. But you wouldn't play along and ruined the whole game,. You insensitive pig."

He scowled, leaning forward with his forearm raised for a backhand. "Watch yourself, bitch. Or I'm gonna..."

He broke off, laughing. "Know what? For a macho Chicano, I've never been too good at the wife abuse thing. I guess I always got that stuff out of my system on the job."

Nan laughed with him. "No wonder Chiquita Banana dumped you. Well here's a lesson on spatting with women. What it starts over is never the real issue."

"Now you tell me."

"Well, I shouldn't. It's supposed to be a secret of the sisterhood." She swung her other leg up on the bed and scooted up to within a foot of him. "Now, in this particular case, the real issue is this. Ready?"

"Can I get a notebook?"

"Oh, I think you'll remember it. The quiz question is: How'd you hear about my autistic dolphin daughter?"

He stared at her with his mouth half open, totally busted.

"Cat got your tongue there, hubby mine? There aren't many multiple choices on that one, are there? You're bugging my ass."

Gaspar admitted it with a shrug and hangdog duck of his head.

"So I've got a free pass to bug yours."

"Couldn't we just screw, instead?"

"Well, if you're going to get all worked up about it, like that," she said dryly, slipping from the bed to her knees and reaching up to tweak away the pillow. "How can I refuse?"

Chapter Seventeen

RayRay had the phone handset cradled on one shoulder as he worked. He'd had a big corkboard set up and was pinning photographs to it. Extremely important to have a corkboard for an investigation, he'd been assured by a retired bunco detective he still shot some leisurely hoops with now and then. Easiest way to make it look like you're doing something.

The pictures pinned to the board made a multi-apexed pyramid, like a mountain range. At the center peak was a telephoto shot of Gaspar in a broad-brimmed white hat and dark aviator glasses.

"I don't think you're understanding me," he said into the phone. "He's fine. Good cop, smart, easy to work with. I'm just saying it might be a good idea to move him away from this end of the operation. The whole Gaspar thing."

He listened, and rolled his eyes upward in a why-do-I-get-the-morons take that he'd always done rather well. "No," he said firmly. "I'm not saying anything like that. What I'm saying he's young, he's single, he's kind of exposed here, might lose some perspective."

He placed a picture of Nan beside Gaspar on the theoretical organization chart. Somebody had marked it with a large question mark. He looked at her face in the professional headshot somebody had dug up at a modeling agency in L.A. "Totally understandable," he said.

"Yeah, she's hot. But not that way. More like, she needs protection and guidance to keep her safe from the baddies of the world, know what I'm saying? Sort of thing appeals to a cop's better nature. Hell, *I* like her."

He picked up a shot of a low-level *cholo* with tattoos on his neck, then paused, smelling a rat. "Yeah, she seems to dig him, too," he told the phone in a slow, measured tone. "He's pretty cute, you might have noticed. So what?"

They told him what and his face clouded over, seeming to grow darker as the furrows and hard spots appeared. "Play that card?" He demanded, all inter-agency protocol gone. "That what you said? Let me make sure I got it straight, we being less sophisticated than you federal types. You're talking about maybe seducing a married woman in order to infiltrate the family?"

He had the phone off his shoulder, gripping it angrily while leaning over it as if to browbeat it. "No, actually, that *was* what you were saying. That Gaspar babe might be right after all."

He listened again in obvious disgust. "Yeah, she's got this theory that being an asshole is completely relative to your viewpoint."

He started to hang up, but paused. "You figure out what she meant. You've got experts. And listen, you don't want my opinion on your people, don't call me up, okay? And see if you can pull that Gaithers shithead off this. Before somebody punches his ass out. And I'm talking friendly fire, here." He banged down the phone and stood fuming. He looked up at Nan's modeling photo and picked up a magic maker. He reached up and drew an exclamation point beside the question mark.

Chapter Eighteen

Location, location, location, Sean Reach thought as he cruised slowly up the canyon street, lowering his head to look for house numbers on the elaborate gates of these walled enclave homes. Lobo Mesa had to be the southernmost cluster of nouveau riche in the West. Isolated up here on a mesa with only one access road and a drop-off view to the south, they could look over at Tijuana or down at the shacks of Barrio Lobo scrabbling up the foot of the mesa and feel twice as good about their pools and air-conditioning and clever porte-cocheres with grass growing up through the fluted paver blocks.

And there it was, number 1347, perched out on the rim with a sheer drop behind it and fortress walls around it. He parked across the street from what he thought of as Nan's "safe house" and checked it out. A fine piece of faux Spanish architecture, fortified like a citadel. He liked the slot windows in the curved front tower and would bet that the graceful wrought iron gates and window grills were actually hardened steel. Value? He couldn't even guess. San Diego realty was a streaking comet anyway, and he figured that an offer of three million might get laughed at.

He sat looking at the house, fidgeting and sipping 7-11 coffee, feeling increasingly like a teenaged moron. How about I just put on a tape of "The Street Where You Live", he thought mockingly. Maybe I could sing a few bars under her window. He noticed a charming balcony on the second floor of the main structure, sheer curtains blowing in an open sliding door. I should go buy a ukulele, he thought, reaching for the ignition key. But he couldn't do it. He leaned back and watched some more, nothing on his mind. He had no idea why he was there, that it was a stakeout of the heart.

He'd run out of coffee and rationalizations and was about to fire up the Nissan 350 Z he was thinking of trading because it was too flashy for field work. But as he reached for the key again, he caught movement in his rearview mirror, a van coming up the canyon from behind him. There was something just plain sinister looking about the van: flat black, lowered front end, windows the purplish black of the "*blindado*" film the *cholos* and *narco-*

63

wannabes all loved. He slouched low in his seat to watch the van pass. And saw it coast to a careful stop six inches from the wall of Nan's house.

If he'd been suspicious from the look of the van, he went into full alert at the appearance of the driver who stepped out the back doors. A big guy sporting a gangbanger brushcut and the weird combination of Sonora cowboy and disco duck that might as well have had a pop-up caption reading, "Mexi-mobster, junior grade". He reached under his seat and found the Hogue combat grips on his Python .357, eased it out and snugged it into the Bianchi holster clipped on his belt.

The van driver walked over and peered through the bars of the gate, then returned to the van. Reach sat motionless, completely intent. He tightened up more when the driver emerged from the rear doors with a rigid black case, longer and slimmer than a suitcase. About the size of a rifle case, actually. He slid the case up on the roof of the van, looked around the street for about the fifth time and climbed up a chromed ladder attached to the rear van door. He picked up the case and boosted it onto the top of the wall, then grabbed two of the decorative iron spikes on top and hoisted himself up. Reach was now on full alert status.

There was apparently a roof immediately on the other side of the fence, because the van goon was a yard past the spikes, squatting to open the case. He pulled out a nylon rifle stock and reached inside the case again, obviously assembling components on the stock as he peered down into the compound below him. Reach was out of the car in one smooth, quiet flow, sprinting across the street with the Python out in his hand. He ran silently in his rubber-soled oxfords, and went up the ladder without a sound.

He jumped to grab the spikes and curled himself up and down for a quick peek. What he'd seen was the hood from the van lying prone on a red tile roof, the stock at his shoulder, aiming down into the courtyard. He kipped up from the waist, his feet against the wall, then punched hard with his legs, swinging himself upwards. He got a foot on the wall between the spikes and powered on up through sheer leg strength. He crossed the sloping roof in two quick strides.

The sniper sensed him coming and turned his head towards him, but Reach was on him, his gun pointed with both hands. The guy started to roll over, but Reach continued his motion, kicking him in the chest, flipping him over on his back. The stock disappeared over the edge of the roof, falling soundlessly into a potted palm. The goon continued to roll, then popped to his feet, shouting in Spanish. Reach closed with him, but the guy was big, strong, rough, and dirty. Punching and kicking viciously, he screamed, "*Ayudenme! Las placas, cabrones!*"

Even with his size and gutter skills he was out of his league against the trained, athletic Reach, who blocked pretty much everything he threw and landed two good solid shots before the roof gave way beneath them and they both fell three yards to the deck below in a shower of dust, broken timber and clay tiles.

Nan was lying prone on a lounger beside the Jacuzzi, topless in the sunshine and intent on the Zen mp3 player pumping Jessica Williams' virtual Miles into her earphones. Blissed and oblivious until the skies opened and dropped two men in front of her, trailing clouds of terra cotta. She bolted upright off the lounge and stood with a towel clutched to her bosom, agog at the sight of Sean Reach and Mongo, covered with ocher dust and slugging it out like a John Woo movie.

Mongo had a luckier landing and got in two vicious kicks to the midriff of Reach, who was on his knees blinded by dust. The agent absorbed some brutal punishment as he fought to his feet. One punch to his chest knocked him against a roof support, which brought more tile down on them both.

But he fell into his drilled-in defensive posture, standing sidelong and bobbing away, his open hands blocking half-seen punches at his face. He caught a punch and twisted, bringing Mongo halfway around and allowing Reach to sweep a kick to his knees, taking him down. In the second that bought him, he wiped his eyes and blasted the heel of his hand into Mongo's nose as he bounded up off the floor towards him.

Mongo lost balance as the blood burst from his crushed nose and bent forward at the waist, allowing Reach the luxury of a full-frame uppercut from out of the cellar. Bouncing off the roof pillar in a new rain of tile, Mongo was helpless as the agent pounded him to his knees then kicked him unconscious. Reach caught his breath then, none too aware of his surroundings, stepped over to pick up his gun.

He was dissuaded from that by the lock-and-load sounds of a dozen Hispanic heavies brandishing military-grade heat. He stopped, raised his hands, and stepped away from the gun. And saw Nan standing in her bikini bottom, a gold-brown towel held to her breast like Venus on the halfshell. He stared at her, at the gunsels, back at Nan. She was smiling and shaking her head in amazed humor.

"Relax, boys," she said, laughter bubbling up through her words, "It's Officer Friendly, come to call."

She pointed with her bare foot. "Oh, and could somebody please scoop up Mongo and toss him in the dumpster?"

Two of Gaspar's retainers slung their AK's and picked Mongo up unceremoniously. The others stood down, regarding Reach with mocking superiority. One of them stepped over to the planter, grabbed the rifle stock and pulled it out of the bulrushes. He turned to Nan, saying, "I think it's some kind of camera."

Reach, deeply chagrined, affirmed that. "It's a digital surveillance rig." He stooped slowly to pick up the Python and carefully replaced it in its holster. The bodyguard squad, openly derisive, slouched off dragging Mongo toes-down behind them.

"So it seems Mongo is a bit of a collector," Nan said lightly. "If I'd known, I could have given him more of a show."

Reach looked engagingly sheepish. And well he should, she thought. But he said, "I thought he was going to shoot you," which made sense under the circumstances, so she nodded understandingly.

He looked back at the roof and piles of broken tile. "Your bodyguards don't seem to be very good at it."

"He *is* one of my bodyguards." That put him back to that boyish awkwardness she rather enjoyed. It had been pretty exciting watching him take Mongo apart and she didn't think being excited was a good thing under the circumstances. "The others must have assumed he was acting under orders. Not that he's very well-trained."

"I'm a little surprised he keeps his job."

"Oh, you know Mexicans. He's somebody's sister's shirttail cousin." Standing there idly shooting the breeze in a thong, holding a towel over her chest. He couldn't believe it. He was trying to come up with something to say that wouldn't be idiotic when she zinged another one in.

"But this nice chat is sort of evading the larger question, wouldn't you say?"

"You mean, like, what the hell am I doing here?"

"This isn't 'Jeopardy'," she admonished. "You're supposed to come up with the answers."

"I came by for a look," he said, determined to plow through this thing. So then he had to say why he came by. "Frankly, I'm worried about you."

She just kept looking at him, head slightly to the side.

"And okay, intrigued. I just drove by on an impulse, have a look."

"And leaped to my rescue. Wow. Highly impressive. I'd swoon if was wearing anything."

He took a step towards her, voice low and earnest. "Does any of this maybe tell you that you're in something over your head? This isn't a normal afternoon by the pool."

"How do you know?" she teased. "Maybe last week I was mowing down Columbians with a grenade launcher."

He kept his eyes on hers, took a deep breath. "Okay, I'm going to stick my neck out here, look like a jerk. What the hell? I don't think you belong here, mixed up in this."

She shook her head, smiling gently. "That is just *so* sweet. You could really turn a girl's head with that manly but vulnerable stuff. Yow."

He showed just a touch of color in his cheeks, but soldiered on. "It's wrong. Criminal. Maybe we can't prove it in court, but this house, everything here, comes out of vice money. From exploiting peoples' weakness."

She laughed, but with a note of sadness in it. "And I'm one to get judgmental about *that*?"

"Get serious," Reach snapped at her in frustration. "This is for real. Your hubby and his goons kill people."

Nan stepped close to him and reached to tease open his dirty, battered suit coat. She nodded her head at his waist. "So is that a real gun?"

"Not the same thing, dammit."

"Listen to me," she said in a low, dry voice. "When I was fourteen I killed a man for trying to do what I let people do to me for money now. I've killed people before they even got a chance to be people. And for more selfish reasons. If you want to try laying guilt on me, the line forms too far back to get to."

He threw his arms wide in an embracing, I-give-up shrug and sagged. He was outplayed, outscored, off-base.

"Why don't you wait a minute while I get decent?" she asked in kindlier tone. "We can have some iced tea before you go. Brush you off a little."

He looked at her mulishly and it tumbled out of him. "You're kicking me in the guts. I never met anybody like you. I think about you all the time."

It was as though his words fell through a glassy silence, parting the air between them. She smiled at him, then shook her head sadly. "Uh, oh. We'd better skip that tea, I guess. Go straight to the brush-off."

"Yeah, square one." He was completely abashed now, to have spilled his lame declaration and have it taken like some buddy's mom dealing with an amorous boy. But he hadn't hit bottom yet. "Well, I'll tell you something. Not bragging or trolling or anything else. But I bet you think about me a lot, too."

"No bet," she said briskly. "Lucky for you I'm an old married lady or I'd turn you inside-out and gobble you right up."

He looked at his feet, crushed, then slapped dust off his ruined suit and turned away. But took one more look at her and snapped into motion so fast he didn't even expect it himself. He grabbed her behind the neck, pressing her face to his, finding her lips and kissing them greedily. With his free hand he snatched away the towel and tossed into the burbling hot tub. He clutched her to him tightly, trying to bury himself in her.

He turned his head and kissed her throat. He spoke in a rush, like a man expelling wind after a punch in the chest. "I can't keep my hands off you. You're all over me, all through me. I've never felt this way about anybody before."

His hands slid down her back as he tried to engulf her totally. His lips were urgent on hers, his hands strong and sure.

While up under the eaves of the house, barely visible, a small digital security camera hung motionless and silent, making a lasting record of their every move.

Chapter Nineteen

Gaspar didn't fidget or pace as Manny opened his pretentious damned briefcase and took his own sweet time fooling around with the gadgets inside. He was too anxious and upset to bother laying it off. He sat motionless with his hands clenched in his lap, staring straight ahead.

Manny pulled the portable DVD player out and opened it, turned it to face him like some accusing little eye. He looked at Gaspar and gave him an eloquent shrug. Gaspar waited a beat before nodding for him to proceed. As he reached over to hit the "Play" button Gaspar blurted, "All this spying *chingadera* sucks. Who are we, 'America's Sneakiest Videos'?"

Manny stopped and gave his boss a bemused look. He couldn't remember seeing him this uptight. He thought it was kind of cute, actually. Another side to the man he'd known for thirty years. He set those years aside for a minute by recalling a name from the past. "Listen to me a minute, Humo."

It got Gaspar's attention. Old times. He looked at his lawyer alertly, waiting.

"One thing I gotta say, here. You know the business we're in. You know I've been through three wives already. But here it is: you get married you got to have some faith. Even if things look bad, even if they don't pay out, it has to be there somewhere. If you can't believe in what you got going, where are you?"

You know where I am, Gaspar thought. But you get to go home when you're done. He said, "Already I don't like it. Just play the damned thing."

Manny started the machine, then started jumping ahead, the onscreen scene jitterbugging as it jerked forward in time. Shattered stills of Nan, of a fight of some kind. Manny was saying, "Let's just jump forward to the scene of maximum interest."

On the tiny screen, degraded by the poor sound and picture quality of miniature remote cameras, Gaspar watched Nan and some fag model type standing in the courtyard. She was holding a towel in front of her, otherwise seemed naked. He could almost feel his blood pressure jump up a couple of notches. Then the guy reached out, grabbed Nan and pulled her close to him, embraced her, tossed her towel in the tub.

The tiny, pixelly Reach was very clearly saying, "I can't keep my hands off you. You're all over me, all through me. I've never felt this way about anybody before."

Gaspar flicked a glance at Manny, who sat expressionless, but felt like reaching out and patting his boss's shoulder or something. Hang tough, big guy, he thought.

On screen, Nan relaxed, sagged up against the handsome agent. And said, "Will you handcuff me first?"

Manny was studying Gaspar's face and read it as much more shocked than angry.

Reach buried his face at the side of her throat. She said, "Will you take me downtown? Lock me up? Read me my rights, if any?"

Reach pulled away from her, staring at her face.

"Do I just have to do you?" Nan went on in the same drifty voice. "Or the whole squad room?"

Reach released her and slumped, embarrassed anger radiating from his pose.

Gaspar's reaction was almost spasmodic. He had been leaning closer and closer to the screen, now he recoiled back in his chair. His face was exultant, the dimensions of his relief blazing off him like he was some kid dodging his first bullet in life. Manny gave him a wry I-told-you-so expression. The DVD continued to play, again capturing Gaspar's interest.

"I just don't understand you," the Fed was saying. "You're this refined, solid woman. Then you're a whore with this messed-up loyalty to a drug dealing monster."

Gaspar looked at Manny with a broad "hurt" expression. Who, *moi*?

"I got married," Nan said crisply. "End of story."

Reach snorted contemptuously. "Get serious, will you? I'm as sincere as I've ever been and you're talking like this was a real marriage."

"It's a legal union under the laws of California. That's not real?"

"You know what I mean." Reach sounded thwarted, almost pleading. "That's just a piece of paperwork."

"A legal contract doesn't get respect?" Gaspar knew the light needling in her voice was going right through the guy. "Interesting attitude from Agent Squeaky Clean."

"But you only married him for money!" Reach almost yelled.

"Have you ever been married, Sean?" Nan had covered up with the wet towel.

"No." He was more subdued, sounded miserable. "I don't think I've even been really in love until now."

Gaspar watched closely how she took that. He could see it hit her hard. What she said was, "Oh, Sean, that's really humbling. And believe me; I'm not worth it."

Hell you're not, baby, Gaspar thought. He was actually kind of starting to feel a little sorry for the guy at this point. He knew the presence the guy was up against. Getting nowhere and it was killing him. Or he was a really great actor. What he looked like, actually.

"But my point here, Mr. Investigator," Nan went on in a kindly tone, talking down to him really. "Is not to investigate too closely why people get married. You'll run into all kinds of motives they didn't mention in Police Academy. Or the Lifetime Channel."

Gaspar cracked up, his relief and pride showing in his overly loud laughter. Manny smiled and gave him a thumbs-up. "Is she too much?" he asked the world in general. "I think I'm in love for the first time, too."

He caught Manny's glance and brushed with his hand. "You know what I mean."

"Oh, absolutely," Manny enthusiastically seconded. "I'm lovin' it, too."

Gaspar continued to chuckle happily as he reached to turn off the DVD player. "I still don't like this spy treatment, though."

Manny waited.

"But keep it on."

Manny nodded: understood. "Sure *Jefe*. Know what, that disk right there could probably get Agent Hollywood fired."

"No need. Think he'd ever show his face again if that thing was on the street?"

Both rotten drug monsters laughed and swapped a hand slap.

Manny stood and stowed the player in his case from space, looked at the Boss leaning back with his hands behind his head, smiling. "Know what?" he said as it occurred to him, "You seem really different lately. You're getting more and more... I don't know what the word is exactly."

Gaspar grinned. "Relaxed? Mellow? Human?"

"I was thinking more like, 'pussy', actually."

Gaspar laughed. "Eat your heart out, ya friggin' citizen."

Chapter Twenty

Nan woke and stretched like a cat in the big bed. She lolled languorously on the soft, scented sheets, gazed around the luxury of her room, shrouded in tawny haze by the softly billowing drapes around the canopy. Impulsively, she rolled over and pulled open the drawer of her nightstand. She fumbled inside and pulled out a bottle of sleeping medication. Teasing open the flimsy curtains with her toe, she lobbed the pills across the room into a wastebasket. She made a two-fisted gesture of success when the shot dropped in, then flopped back on the pillows and burrowed her face into them, smiling.

Chapter Twenty-One

There were two cars in front of them at the drive-up coffee kiosk. If there'd been three, Mobley would have blown it off, gone to Jack In The Crack or something. He wasn't an impatient man, just had priorities on what he'd sit around waiting for.

He tapped his fingers on the steering wheel of his black Dodge Magnum while he waited, keeping time to a CD his wife had made him, a jumble of Isaac Hayes, Ohio Players, Tower of Power. Cold Blood playing at the moment. Hard to believe Lydia Pense was a white girl.

He looked over at his Trusty Fed Sidekick, as he referred to him when speaking with other local cops. He'd been kind of withdrawn this morning, not the usual sparkling commentary on cases, the incisive analysis of Padres games. "So. Got a little action yesterday? Leaping over rooftops at a single bound. But nothing for your scrapbook."

Reach looked at him, kind of spooked. "How'd you hear about that?"

"Documented fact, my man." Mobley enjoyed the look that one got. "What was on your head, anyway? Jumped one of Gaspar's goons, then fell off the roof, I heard."

Reach could barely answer. Documented? "I wanted to get a look at the place. The actual site, not just pictures. Some dickhead drives up, gets on the roof and pulls something that looks like a weapon. How'd you hear about it?"

"Place is surveiled. Low key, but we've had an eye on it since they turned it into Fort Knox and moved her in." He pulled the rumbling car ahead and signaled for his usual with two fingers.

"He's had that place awhile? Stashed girlfriends there or something?"

"Could be. She pays a dollar a month rent to a realty service in La Jolla, who remit to some octopus-ass holding company in Guadalajara."

"One more of his non-assets."

"Little chunka his non-empire." Mobley turned from watching the cute little barrista pounding his grounds. "But when you say, 'looked like a weapon'? What weapon? Sure he wasn't just stroking off, sneaking a peek at the lady of the house?"

Tattooed arms handed two coffee cups into the car, and waved. Mobley smiled back but no money changed hands.

"Something like that. It wasn't a gun, turned out. Some safari camera rig."

He accepted a cup of coffee, opened the little drinking spout in the plastic lid.

"These clowns are all about overkill, aren't they?" Mobley set his cup down in a molded holder and put it in gear. "First they come in and fortify it into a nuclear bunker. Then they wire it up like a Hollywood sound stage. How many more cameras they need?"

Reach spoke like there was a hand squeezing his Adam's apple. "Wire it up?"

Mobley nodded as he pulled around the drive-up and waited for a pause in the traffic on El Cajon. "Like a motherfucker. Scratch their ass anywhere in that house or grounds they've probably got three-camera feed on it."

Alarmed, he looked towards Reach and yelled indignantly, "Yo, what's wrong with you, man? Gotta spit coffee, do it out the window, not on my carpet. Damn!"

Chapter Twenty-Two

Nan reclined on the bed nude, the heat continuing into the fall, but not as bothersome these days. Gaspar stood at her feet, peeling off his shirt for a deliberate reveal of tighter musculature and a "farmer tan."

"Working on those forties down toward the border is interesting," he told her with a genuine interest that she found amusing. "You can almost look at the water level quotes and predict how many gallons of milk you're gonna get."

Nan cruising his bod with lowered lids, laughed. "Omigod. Farmer Gaspar."

He looked at her and grinned. "E I E I O."

"Well I guess you can afford to buy all the vowels you want. Say, you're looking pretty butch, there, Country."

He looked down at his body with pride. "It's not just the farm. I've been working out a little. Couple of the younger guys have been sparring with me, checking me on the weight pile."

"They could probably charge yuppies to come here and get in shape."

Gaspar lifted one leg to pull off his jeans. "Not with this clothing line."

He draped his pants on the dresser and flopped on the bed beside her. "I owe it to you, some ways. Come in here, my sagging old guts lying next to physical perfection. I just felt like I should shape up a little."

She gave his bicep an admiring squeeze. "Nothing like a younger bimbo to make an older guy dash out to get jogging shoes and a coronary."

"Coronaries are for suits. I'm a cowpoke, now, ma'am."

He rolled over to kiss her, then lolled back, trying to lounge like John Wayne.

"I hate to say it," she said seriously. "But prison life seems to suit you."

Gaspar gave a short laugh. "When I think how much effort and money I put out trying to keep outta here."

"Careful," she warned playfully, "Sounds like lifer talk."

Gaspar stared upwards for a minute, not smiling, idly caressing her thigh. Finally he said, "Look, I wouldn't say this to anybody else, but you know what? I really am having a good time. Working with the cows, horsing around with the boys, simple food, exercise, very little stress. No decisions."

"I guess they figure if cons made their own decisions they might decide to leave."

"I'd have to think it over," he grinned. "Seriously, though. I might be about as happy right now, feel about as good, as I ever remember."

"Permanent summer camp? Every boy's dream?"

"You got it. Camp Snoopy for Badfellas."

She turned towards him and ruffled his hair. He was growing it a little longer. The inmate barbers weren't in a league with the expensive ones he used outside, but it didn't look bad at all. Shagging a little, curly around the ears with a dash of gray. "You might have a different attitude if you weren't in the Boneyard Key Club."

He took her hand and put in to his lips, held it there a moment. "You're a big part of it, yeah."

"A weekend wife," she teased. "Sort of a hobby, like a bowling league. Perfect."

"Hey, I wish I'd thought of it fifteen years ago." He dropped the bantering tone, though, to look at her and say, "No, it's something about you. I mean you in particular."

"Now quit," she demurred, lowering her eyes missishly. "You know pink doesn't become me."

Then it was her turn to get serious. "Know something? This is probably the best time in my whole life, too."

He saw her eyes turn inward. And sad. As she said, "Not like that's saying much."

He didn't know how to respond, but then the usual sparkle came back into the baby blues. "Which is pretty depressing when you consider I'm a beautiful blonde with nice tits."

Gaspar nodded at the humor, but kept looking at her with a deeper interest. "You don't have to tell me stuff like that."

"Oh. You know," she breathed airily. "We working girls get so used to faking it."

She'd caught him on the change-up again. He was trying to sort out where she was coming from when she knuckled his head and growled. "I'm serious, hoss. I like it here. I like you. I'm just not too sold on your decorator."

Gaspar lay there sorting out what he knew of her motivations and inner landscape. And not for the first time. Finally he said, "Sounds like you don't mind the security after all."

"I'm sleeping much better."

That seemed like a big issue for her. Maybe he'd find out why. They had time. Suddenly time didn't seem like such a bad rap.

"I have to say," she went on, "you were quite a surprise for me. I guess I expected some greasy mob pig rooting around."

"I could introduce you to a few of those."

"But what I got was this middle-aged guy who just wants a wife, maybe a pal. You're mostly looking for a little affection and understanding and it's not that hard to give it to you. I might burn in hell for saying this, but I think you have it coming."

"Jesus." Gaspar felt as if some carnival psychic had suddenly laid bare his inner life for him. "Know how often you say things that I never would have come up with, but as soon as you say them they're like really obvious. Scary."

"Think I should have one of those Sally Jesse shows?"

He turned on his side and pushed up on his forearm, leaning over to look down into her face. "So, how about you?"

"I'm kind of enjoying having a man who pays my bills and treats me right and doesn't jerk me around. And doesn't wake me up or steal all the covers."

Gaspar laughed. "Too bad they won't let you sleep over."

"Maybe if I promise to commit some crimes later." Then she was more serious. "I never spend the night with men. If I have to, I don't sleep."

He was thinking about what that might mean about her life when she flipped back to flippant. "Plus, I always know where to find you and don't have to worry about you cheating on me. Where else do you get armed guards keeping your husband faithful?"

Gaspar dropped the serious stuff, smiled into eyes as wide and blue as tomorrow morning, reached to touch skin as warm and soft as redemption. "I don't know, there's this cute new kid in the laundry with a fantastic ass."

"So it's true what they say about prison?" She reached out to touch some skin, as well. "The way they separate the men from the boys is with a crowbar?"

Chapter Twenty-Three

His new family had decided to call him JoJo, so that was his name now. When he found them he was ten and had already killed people, had led other boys through the jungles, living on whatever they could find or steal or take from the bodies of people they shot. The other boys, even older ones, had thought of him as a skilled, cagey commander with a frightening intensity of will. But that whole life had turned out to be child's play, an apprenticeship for the Mara.

He was fourteen now, prime age for fighters, and had attained respect among his new family, as well. For instance, they'd picked him to bring Syco across the border. And not just because he'd lived there awhile. He was a right hand, a boy to be reckoned with.

He didn't like the stupid clothes he was wearing, jeans and long sweatshirt, Padres cap. Or the lame car he drove so carefully. But that was what those La Neta clowns had given him, and he knew they were right: he had to blend in, not get pulled over by the *placas*. So he slouched in the rumpled Corolla, one more scrawny teenager with big black eyes, and drove slowly with extreme care. He wasn't that good a driver, anyway, and didn't want Syco to notice. He'd been traveling with Syco three days now--crossing the border through the river swamps at night along routes he remembered from seven years before, hiding in culverts and shacks, scoping out the San Diego environment, and conferring with the Barrio Lobo gangbangers--and begun to almost worship the man. This guy was what the Mara Salvatrucha was all about. Stone cold.

Syco hadn't paid that much attention to "JoJo". Just one more guide to move him into position to direct and put pressure. So far it had barely been worth the effort to jump the border. Those La Neta gangbangers were the only thing he could scrape up to help them combat the Altamira machine on the U.S. side and he hadn't been impressed. They really didn't have any choice about opposing the Gaspar group because he had practically choked them out of any distribution at all. They postured with their big weightpile muscles and cool cars, but they were weak and disorganized, street trash. What the Mara had been before adversity and balls had made them into the most powerful gang in the world. They needed Mara power more than he needed them, but they might do. When it came to dealing with Gaspar, though, he'd handle it himself.

JoJo found the address easily enough, a rarified strip mall at the edge of the Lobo Mesa enclave, snuggled close to the wealth in order to offer boutique experiences. Syco pointed and he pulled into a parking slot he immediately recognized as perfect. Close to the front door, too far to one side to be seen from inside, easy to cut off anybody heading for Starbucks.

As he examined all the sleek, expensive cars on the lot Syco thought, this country is just a big, sweet, fat, dripping pussy, and all we have to do is grab it. Of course their humble ride didn't blend in with this environment. Stuck out like a priest's dick at a whore's confession, in fact.

But they shouldn't have to wait long. He had to admit, La Neta did a good job casing things. And this JoJo kid was good to wait with. Patient and didn't talk too much. Plus, look, he'd gotten them some Pepsi and *churros*. Solid kid. Meanwhile JoJo, who spoke almost no English and couldn't really read, was studying the storefront, trying to decipher meaning from the words "Pilates Salon". He didn't think it was the Pilate from the Bible, but who could tell?

She came out the door just after three, right on time. Slipping on dark glasses as she stepped into the full sun. A looker, all right. He took in the supple body, purposeful stride, waves of caramel hair, smart cream suit with hemline a few inches above killer calves. Gaspar's woman. If you wanted to press on soft spots, she looked like the perfect place to start.

Nan felt as great as she always did after a session at Monica's; long, loose, limber. Hungry. Just enough to nosh a brownie with her mocha latte at Starbucks, scan what passed for the local newspaper until Alfredo showed up with the car. She didn't really register the two young men getting out of the crummy gray Toyota until they headed to cut her off. Something in their gait focused her in. They were just two Latino kids wearing typical clothes and mirrorshades but something about them rang up Totally Wrong. She pulled a remote from her coat pocket, pointed it towards a nearby car and pushed the button. She pushed it three times.

Which puzzled Syco and JoJo. She wasn't supposed to have a car. They heard no answering beep, but she looked at the remote, shook it, tried again and scowled as she dropped it into her pocket. She looked at them and smiled radiantly. Syco moved within a few paces of her and took off his shades. She stopped smiling.

JoJo automatically faded to his left as Syco moved to accost the Gaspar *morra*. He pulled his glasses off, too, hung them in his belt like Syco. He looked at her and could feel the cold pressure of the pistol at the small of his back, the warm pressure of his cock in the jeans. She was the ultimate feast, no doubt about it.

She took a careful scan of Syco's face. Normal features of a Central American Indian under the waxy, brown-streaked flattop. A couple of minor scars, also normal around the barrio. Typical wetback in his early twenties. Except for the eyes. They weren't just flat black, they looked dry. As expressionless as any shark or predatory bird: windows to nothing much. Not exuding menace, which Nan found threatening in itself. These guys weren't here about a job mowing lawns.

She glanced at JoJo. A thin kid barely in his teens: short, skinny and shaved almost bald. A long, tapered face. His expression wasn't empty of humanity like the other one, it just had the stillness of somebody waiting to be told what to do. She looked back at Syco, who would be the one to say what would be done. She stood still and calm. She could wait, too.

Alfredo hadn't gone home after dropping her off. He'd driven down to the Barrio Lobo middle school and parked by the fence, watching the girls' gym classes romping around in tight little shorts. He found the sight pleasurable and relaxing, but it embarrassed him a little, too. Girls his own granddaughters' age. They were just so pert and bouncy and alive. Pretty, coltish innocence and the constant chime of girly laughter: he could watch this all afternoon. Then he heard the three shrill beeps that meant, ALARM!

He fired up the Lincoln with one hand and flipped on the GeoLocator with the other as the big car leapt backwards, spun around, and surged towards the exit of the school's dirt lot. She was still at that Pilots place. Good. He'd be there in a couple of minutes. He had his phone out and was punching some alarm buttons of his own. The fat, soft tires screamed when he hit the pavement and cut a hard left.

Syco didn't like the way the conversation was going. But he had to admire the Gaspar bitch. Even if he wanted to just slap her off her feet right here and now. Not the greatest idea here in front of all these people, but it might come to that. She was a major pain in the *culo*. "Let me say like this," he said haltingly in his painfully acquired English. "You go to him, tell him. Then we don't having to do."

"Well, if you can get in to see him, let me know how," Nan said, shaking her head in frustration. "They're just so impossible to deal with up there at that prison."

"You don't get it, do you bitch?" The first time he'd used any language on her, but it didn't faze her at all. She just sat waiting, with her head cocked like somebody listening to a parrot. "We own that prison. Half of they inside are us."

"You must be so proud."

"Where we *come from*, understand what I say? Our country."

"Who'd you say you were with again?"

JoJo, keeping an eye peeled for trouble while watching Syco talk with the Gaspar woman, could see that he was losing a little of his cool. She must really be full of crap.

"The Mara," Syco said gratingly. "Mara Salvatrucha. *Eme ese trece.*"

Nan knew enough Spanish to understand MS-13, which rang a faint bell, but she stuck to projecting a wide-eyed desire to be informed. "Well, that's what you say. But everybody else who hassles me these days shows some kind of ID."

Syco stared at her for a moment, no flicker of movement in his face. Then on a *macho* impulse he reached up to tear open the front of his shirt. Nan took in a torso completely covered with a maze of blurry tattoos. She saw the 13, the words Mara and Salva, devil horns, barbed wire, hand grenades, obscure meat graffiti that mostly said, We Be Bad in capital letters.

JoJo, who had lived four years with guys who competed for number and ugliness of tattoos, couldn't fight his reaction to the underlying significance of Syco's tat job. It was like a boy feeling inadequacy at the sight of his father's big member. He had tats of his own, but nothing like the battle record and rankings Syco displayed. This wasn't the mindless scrawl local gangs pricked into themselves: each of those grenades meant a fatal bombing. It was a skintight rapsheet of killings and scores. Syco wasn't just the new *comandante* of the Mara in Tijuana, the man was a big shot down in Salvador as well. Lots of guys had tats all over their hands, feet, throats, even faces and shaved heads. But Syco had a new-school, hipper thought on that.

He was looking to a future where they'd need to pass in society, was even recruiting college kids who would stay clean and help them with business and political infiltration. If he or JoJo buttoned their necks and cuffs you couldn't see any ink at all. JoJo didn't realize that another main factor with Syco was that he liked to approach unaffiliated women in nice bars, saving the tats for when they undressed him. He loved dragging civilian women down into his driving indoctrination to the world of the bangingest gang.

Nan surveyed the squalid glory of his chest and said, "Very impressive. Looks like a comic book for hoodlums. If the comic artists were religious sadists who never heard of perspective."

Syco was a hair away from going off on this *jaina*. In his coldest, most insinuating tone he said, "I could show you more of them. Even more interesting."

Nan thought a moment before speaking. "Wait, let me guess. The popular barber pole motif?"

Barbaro? Motive? She was fucking with him, moving in loops. He started to say something, but she went on, "Or just the standard government disease warnings?"

He was weighing whether to sort that out and come up with a response, or just grab her neck and shake her limp, when JoJo hissed, "*Trucha!*" Alerted, he swung around to see the Gaspar Lincoln cut across three lanes and charge into the parking lot.

JoJo was already running for the car, where they had their real guns, and he was right behind him. As he swung into the little Jap piece of crap he looked back at Nan, standing on the sidewalk with one hand on her hip, shaking her head at him like a teacher watching a slow student screw up. He felt something white-hot blast from his outraged brain straight down to his crotch. Teeth clenched, he watched her wave goodbye as JoJo floored the little car into flight.

She could see that the Maras were trapped in the mall lot. There was only one exit and Alfredo, punching the big Lincoln towards the Toyota, had them cut off. Other than that, there were only storefronts and a forty foot drop-off to the arterial below. Worse yet for the little gangsters, she could see two familiar charcoal Suburbans making the turn up from the access road. She'd be interested in seeing what this pair had to say for themselves. If they lived through the next ten minutes.

JoJo spun the Toyota around the lot, looking for an exit while trying to avoid a trap by the Lincoln. He ricocheted off stylish sedans and clipped off small palm trees as he flitted around the lot. He had his pistol in his lap and Syco held both of their assault rifles ready for action. He saw a shot when Alfredo veered towards the Pilates place, and smoked his clutch heading for the exit. Then cut hard to his left to avoid a head-on collision with two Suburbans that came up the ramp side by side.

Alfredo released the door latch, so when he braked in front of Nan the door swung open by sheer inertia. Nan plopped unceremoniously onto the passenger seat and quickly swung her legs inside. Alfredo touched the gas and the door slammed shut as he punched forward, away from the three other cars in the chase. A quick glance at Nan showed that she was perfectly okay, so he circled, glowering at Lico and Chuy in the Suburbans, getting to have all the fun.

Syco jammed one of the Chinese AK-47's into the crack between his seat and the transmission hump, where either he or JoJo could get to it quick. He cleared the other one and thrust it out the window. He found the position he would hook his foot on when he leaned his upper body out the window and opened fire. They weren't going to be able to run out of this one, so they'd have to do the other. He wondered how many men were in the Suburbans. How many guns.

The lot was in a panic, people dropping bags and snatching up children, running like ants across the hot pavement. JoJo paid no attention to them, just kept tearing around looking for a way out of this. They'd trusted him to take Syco to California and guard him. He wasn't going to stop trying to do that as long as he was alive.

He screamed up to the south end of the lot: nothing there but a waist-high barrier and sheer drop off down the canyon. Maybe as a last resort.

He saw the pursuing cars split, forking around him. He jerked the wheel and leaned on the rickety gas pedal, forcing between them but heading straight towards the Lincoln. He saw the window come down. A big guy inside grabbed the woman and pushed her down, then aimed a pistol at him. He saw a gap between parked cars and took it, careening between two bulbous SUV's and badly scraping them both. He didn't hear a shot. He looked straight ahead and saw what he needed. He felt Syco move and glanced to that side. He was moving to lean out the window. "*No, no!*" he yelled. *Espera!*"

He grabbed his belt and tugged him back into the car. Shocked, Syco glared at him, then looked through the windshield and braced his hands on the dashboard. A second later they plowed into the glass front of a Coldstone ice cream parlor.

JoJo had seen straight through the vacuous white tile interior of Coldstone, nothing but glass walls on three sides, to the street beyond. The Toyota took a sickening jump when it hit the curb, then plunged into the glass. The customers had been standing, staring at the live car chase, but scattered as it landed in their laps. Two weren't fast enough.

As the Toyota entered in a resounding shower of glass, its left front bumper struck a man in the uniform of a Little League umpire, knocking him under the car where a rear wheel crushed his head. The right mirror slammed an eight year-old girl in the ribs as she tried to run, hurling her into the counter hard enough to break her neck. A table flew across the store, snapping two ribs of a woman who'd come in promising herself she wouldn't break her diet. Six other patrons were severely injured by big shards of falling glass. As the car hit the glass on the far side, the teenaged boy behind the counter threw a scoop at it, bouncing it off the rear deck.

The Toyota powered through the empty chairs outside, crunched across a six inch high barrier, further damaging its suspension, and crashed down four feet of landscaped slope to the street. Where JoJo cranked the wheel hard right and the shell-shocked Toyota gamely tried to comply, but came to a skidding, sparking stop when the left front wheel simply bent under and snapped off, turning the car into a sort of sled for twenty feet.

It impressed Syco that while he, not accustomed to being in automobiles, much less under Dirty Harry type maneuvers, was still getting his head together after their plummeting spin of fortune, JoJo was already out of the stricken Corolla and seeking further solutions. He grabbed the rifles and kicked open his crimped door. Looking for JoJo, he saw him running towards a Ford mini-van with his pistol thrust out in front of him. He vaulted the hood and followed, an AK in each hand.

JoJo ran up to the car, which contained a mother and four children, brandishing the gun. The soccer mom, panicked, pushed the door lock button instead of accelerating through the red light. JoJo screamed at her inarticulately and smashed his gun into the window, scattering it all over the kids in the interior, who were howling in terror. Syco veered to approach the passenger door. JoJo wrenched the door open and tried to pull the screaming woman out of the vehicle. He could see Gaspar's men turning down the ramp toward the street. A battered switchblade emblazoned with a gold scorpion came out of nowhere to slash the restraining straps away. He hauled the woman from the car and gave her a push that sent her reeling to the pavement three yards away.

He jumped into the seat just as Syco got the other door open and didn't bother evicting the sobbing little girl in the passenger seat, just flopped into her lap and yelled for JoJo to go. Which he was already doing. The minivan actually burned rubber for the first time in its life as he pounded the pedal to the floor. Gaspar's men had run into a mass of halted traffic at the street, piling up behind the cars that panic-stopped when the gunmen started running around. One Suburban humped up onto the sidewalk and gave chase, but was stopped by a crying woman with the knees torn from her designer jeans and blood dripping across her face. She stood in front of them and wouldn't move.

In the Suburban, Chuy looked at Martín, hunched forward over his submachine gun, and suddenly slumped behind the wheel. "*Chale*," he said, "she's just not ugly enough to run over."

Martín burst out laughing and the tension release swept through the other three men in the car. When Chuy lowered the window, the sudden sound of five men laughing socked the mother out of her tears. She gaped at Chuy's broad, dark face. "They took my children."

Martín stopped laughing, leaned out and spoke to her softly. "We won't chase them, lady. They have no reason to shoot or drive too fast. Or to hurt your kids."

The mother stared at him, desperately wanting to believe, hands clasped to her bleeding forehead. "Come on," Chuy said. "We'll drive you back up to the store, let you sit down while the ambulance comes."

The woman looked at him, then at the other men holding intimidating firearms. She turned and ran. Chuy looked at Martín, shrugged, and they all started laughing again.

The soccer mom burst into the gutted Coldstone, blanched at the carnage there, and started screaming. Nan stood up from where she'd been calming a young boy with a bruised leg and moved to her swiftly, pulling out her phone. "Come on, sit over here."

She led her to a chair and handed her the phone. "Here, call whoever you need to. It'll be all right, trust me. Hey, son, can I get a big cone of cherry vanilla for this lady?" Nan was a firm believer in the power of sugar to combat shock.

In the plummeting minivan, Syco had gotten the squealing girl out from under him and into the back seat, then terrorized the kids into shutting up. He turned to JoJo but didn't even have to speak. The kid said, "We're eight kilometers from the border at Otay. We can ditch the van at the McDonalds there, dump the guns, and walk across."

Syco nodded. This *chavo* would do, by God. He turned to the children and gave them a friendly smile that utterly convinced them he was going to murder them all and suck their bones. "*Pues,* my childs. Do you like go to McDonalds?"

They sat silently as he pondered Nan Gaspar. He realized that he admired her intensely. But he had to live this thing down. He'd had a lot of options in his mind on how to deal with her, even after he saw what she looked like. But at this point nothing would do short of making her his, breaking her down completely. That went without saying... and was largely due to his admiration of her.

Chapter Twenty-Four

The disorder and death at the Pilates mall drew the inevitable attention of every paper and station in the region and even national media. Hard to imagine anything more un-American than swarthy thugs with machine-guns killing Little Leaguers in an ice cream parlor. But it also rang the bells of watchers very distant from the border terrain itself. New forces in play, new parameters, new questions and loose ends. Big red Federal flags popped up on a lot of dossiers, not least Nan's files at Donovan.

Mobley had gone over to Tijuana to confer with his proprietary Mexican colleagues concerning the killers who'd dumped a carload of pink-faced blonde children at the drive-up window of the border McDonalds with ten bucks to buy cokes and fries, then fled on foot to Mexico. Reach wanted to go with him, meet his contacts there, but Nan had a visit scheduled and he was slated to debrief her on the incident. He expected to get zip in the way of information but was far from reluctant to stick around and sit across the desk from Gaspar's breath-taking, exasperating young wife.

He didn't feel any different about what he'd so embarrassingly declared to her at her home, but he was a professional and could restrain himself when talking to her. After all, being with her half-naked by a pool was a far cry from an interview in the sterile office of a state prison. He'd decided to use the small interrogation room that opened off the little office for visiting officials.

He handled himself very well when she showed up, highly professional. Her cool greeting carried no shadow of reproach from the episode on her patio. She followed him into the office, quiet and docile. Reach motioned her to the door of the interrogation room and she nodded politely, set her purse on the desk in the ante-room, and took a seat inside. As soon as he closed the door and turned to face her he blew his game plan.

"Look, I'm really sorry about the other day," he blurted suddenly. "I don't know what came over me. Well, I do know. But it shouldn't have. Please accept my apologies."

And thanks, she thought, for not reporting a sexual advance? But his contrition was so real and so abject she could only smile. Okay, no spanking this time.

Then he got off on entirely the wrong foot all over again. "We're interested in you having been present at an armed confrontation between known criminals..." he gave her a significant eyebrow, "...and some extremely dangerous armed illegals."

"I found it a rather interesting afternoon myself. They aren't just rotten drivers who kill little girls and kidnap soccer teams, they were downright rude."

"Has it occurred to you that the whole event was about you? That your presence there might have caused those deaths?"

"I wasn't even driving. I was the attempted victim. Things got out of hand when my husband's friends tried to save me. I can't have you around leaping from rooftops every time somebody wants to treat me to a fate worse than death."

"What did those guys want?"

"Not ice cream, apparently. Actually, I don't speak Spanish."

"My information is that you do."

"In fact, I don't even speak English except within the parameters I've already laid out for you."

"So you have nothing to say about this? The danger to you, the damage, the deaths of innocent kids?"

"Oh, I have comments on those, but it's all been said. I just don't have anything to tell you about the armed crazies that can apparently operate in this country without you and your super-troops doing anything about it."

He shook his head, but couldn't help a disgusted smile. The same as always: he didn't know whether to applaud her cool or get pissed off at her obstructionism and obvious lack of awe. Something leaped inside his chest as he looked at her, a wild hope and determination that was just plain crazy. He put his head down and riffed papers in her file until it passed. He had probably over-estimated his ability to handle himself with her.

When he looked up, she was gazing into his face, fighting against unbidden feelings of her own. He suddenly thought of her dead in that parking lot, or dragged off by those drug crazies. He spoke in a low, choked tone. "Don't you see the danger you're in? Didn't this convince you of that? Let me get you out of there before it's too late."

He could see it clearly. Reach to the rescue. Pull her out, protect her, save her from this insane and destructive involvement.

Nan's thoughts weren't that coherent. She was sailing uncharted waters and completely awash. She saw his desire to save her and the idea curled up in her belly like a warm kitten. Held safe in those arms. She hadn't felt the entire impact of his embrace at the house, had been too concerned with extricating herself before anybody saw them. Now it swept over her like a rogue wave, the memory of her bare nipples against the hard slabs of his chest, staring into the dazzling gold flecks in his eyes, feeling the firmness of his strength and the golden shine of his goodness. She had a feeling she'd better leave.

She stood up without comment and looked for her bag. Oh, yeah it was out on the desk. Covering her fluster, she nodded crisply and turned towards the door.

"Wait!" it came out of him with no warning, a completely unguarded plea. He was moving around the desk, making soothing motions with his hands. "Wait, wait. Look, I'm only trying to help you."

She turned, a shutdown remark right behind her teeth, but she was face to face with him now and all she could see was his eyes, the spray of freckles across the bridge of his nose, the shock of hair trailing his broad brow. The strong hands that came up to cup her cheeks. All he said was, "Please. Don't be upset. Let me help you with this."

She couldn't speak, couldn't move. It wasn't fair. This was all new to her. Her heart was the only virgin part of her, shocked into silence even before her sexuality had been nipped in its bud. Her capacity for love was like a damsel locked off in a tower, the untried response of a pre-teen feeling her first flutter at boys. Unfair.

Reach wasn't thinking about fairness. He wasn't thinking about his position. He wasn't thinking at all. The touch of her face had disconnected him from all that bother. His hands ran down her throat, down her shoulders, down her waist. He buried his face in the hollow of her throat and breathed in the hot musk of the scent she'd worn for her husband and the warm bouquet of her awakening desire. He felt her reach trembling hands to touch him and lost what little control he'd had at that point. This was the woman, this was the time!

She threw her arms behind his head, hanging from him as he bent her back over the table. Her breathing caught, then raced. She didn't have a name for what was going on, had never before felt this impulse to give herself up entirely, to take everything in, to glut herself to death on a man. The arch of her foot touched his calf and slid around behind him. She pulled him towards her as he smothered her with a kiss. He was trying to crawl into her mouth; she felt like she was drowning.

Her foot came up behind his thighs, pulsed with the motion of bringing him in, shoving him into her. She felt hot, felt soaked, felt like bursting into laughter and tears at the same time. She felt her dress pulled up over her buttocks, the cool surface of the table on her bare skin. Now she could lift both legs and put them behind him, could encircle him and stuff him into her. Her arms lost their grip and she fell back on the table, stretching and mewing like a cat.

He leaned on her breasts, fingers rubbing over her hard nipples. She didn't want that, so much. Just wanted him to swallow him up, to absorb him... to become him. She was head over heels with his shining gold star, with his straight, firm stance. She was besotted with the Good Guy and just wanted to be all over him, get it all over her. Fall into a dreamless sleep in his arms.

She heard him murmuring into her cleavage. He loved her, there was nobody like her. He wanted her, wanted to keep her alive, wanted to save her. She knew all that. Or at least she was finding out about it, lying there pulsing with her first tastes of it. Then he moved a hand between them, pushing past the fold of her skirt, past the flimsy, sopping fabric of her thong. His finger drew a line of sparking red light along a slick, pulsing fold of sensation. Then slipped inside. And just like that, she woke up.

Her reaction to coming to her senses was visceral and dramatic. She snapped forward from the waist, banging her forehead into his nose. Her hands snapped up like a martial arts master, slammed into his chest, pushing him off her. His eyes watering from her head butt, his mouth dropping open in shock, he reached out to her but she punched hard again, driving him off. Twice more, hard shots to his pectorals. She jumped off the tab, pulled her skirt down and headed for the door. Holding his bruised nose, he stepped in front of her, hands held up to stop her.

He looked at her face and saw only a fierce drive to escape, like a trapped animal lunging out in desperation. She was hunched like a boxer, breathing in ragged gasps. He had no doubt that if he tried to touch her she'd attack in a flurry of kicks, punches and screams. He stepped aside and she circled him warily, reaching behind her for the doorknob.

She looked at his face and read shock, disbelief and heartbreak; a violated angel tossed out into darkness for nothing more than loving too much. Choking, she pushed through the door, grabbed her purse and ran out into the hall. She ducked around a trustee who was mopping the floor, not seeing Reach pop out the door behind her with an arm raised to entreat her, then slowly sag in defeat, retreat into the office, and shut the door behind him.

Flustered and humiliated, Nan slumped in the back of the car without speaking to Alfredo, who was probably picking up all sorts of bad signals, and certainly wondering why she'd blown off her visit. What was wrong with her, anyway? Or had there been something wrong with her all her life and now there was a chance it could go right?

By being deceitful, she thought? Cheating on a husband and client? She reached for her purse and suddenly remembered setting it down outside the office door. Premeditation. Her cheeks burned for the first time she could remember. Subconscious, maybe, but there it was: prior intent. She felt like grabbing the purse and screaming into its microphone, "But I'm not like that! I just want one shot at the real thing!"

As the car swooped down off the mesa, she leaned back on the seat, replaying what she could stand of the scene in the office. It was creeping her out, but at the same time detonating new centers of sensation in her. What would it be like to feel that way about somebody when it *could* work out? When you could actually do something about it? Would she even want to find out?

She went back over the moment she'd snapped out of the lush new vertigo she'd discovered inside her, shoved away the only man she'd ever gotten that close to being in love with. What had popped? What little psychic vial did her subconscious break under her nose?

She hoped desperately it wasn't what she was thinking, that when it came down to genital contact everything had reverted to "workplace" reflex, that her dreamboy had suddenly turned into an unpaid john and her accommodation fallen back into that rut. She replayed and peered into it in the glum back seat, probing at what had flashed into her mind. And finally came up with it. It had been a shrill little ringtone, going off like a bucket of ice over her head: This is just *Wrong*! So she'd given Mr. Right a sore nose and blue balls.

At the house she slipped from the car without speaking to or looking at Alfredo and fled to her room. Lying in bed staring at the peak of gauze curtains above her pavilion bed, she kept trying to figure it out, trying to apply the rules and ethics of the normal world she didn't really understand. What was so wrong about it? And kept coming up with: just about everything. Except that Sean was The Man and for a minute there she'd almost been The Woman.

About three in the morning, without having slept at all, she suddenly hit on what it would have felt like afterwards. Lying on a steel table in a cop's third degree room in a penitentiary with a man crawling off her wishing he hadn't done it. Apologizing. Sorry, Ma'am, I don't usually fuck married women on duty. At that point there was no longer any question in her mind. There was obviously more going on between men and women than she'd ever dreamed, but for whatever reasons she was who she was and it would have been the wrong thing to do. And she knew exactly what she had to do to make it right. There was a soft, sad frown on her face as she drifted into sleep.

Reach avoided Ray Mobley's eyes as the big cop sauntered into the room and stopped in front of the desk, arms folded over his massive chest, waiting. Finally he looked up into a glare of dark, deep disapproval. "You just must be out your mother-lovin' mind."

Reach sagged in his seat, but met Mobley's gaze. "I'd say that about covers it."

95

RayRay appreciated a man who 'fessed up, but was far from done. "Let alone screwing around on official duty, okay. Let alone she's visiting an inmate and hauled in here by your authority. You realize the flavors of shit *that* leaves you open for?"

He let that one sink in for a beat, then bored on in. "But noooooo, better than that: you pick the wife and possible material witness to the focus of your entire federal witchhunt which my department is unwillingly being dragged into and not nuts about being left holding a bag for."

Reach didn't respond so RayRay leaned over the desk and droned in a flat voice, "You trippin', you dumbass fuggin' honky hard-on?"

"I know, I know. I didn't..." Reach wasn't used to being shaky, but the past hour had really dragged his emotional structure through the mud. He was madder at himself than Mobley was, but... "*Look* at her! *Talk* to her! God, I just..."

"I am looking at her. I warned you. I got a johnson, too, you know. Only reason I'm not on the phone to your boss right this minute, selling your stupid butt down the river."

"But that doesn't set any of this right."

"Damn right it don't." Mobley caught his eye again, and dropped some of the hard disdain from his tone. "You gotta cut this shit out. If I were you, which I'm damn glad I'm not, I don't rightly know how I'd manage putting something like her down, but you gotta get it done."

"I know, I know. I know what I should be saying right now, but I can't promise. She's like a fever all over me. I'm a goner."

"Gonna be lollapa-goner on this job, too. Maybe even gone from this mortal realm, you hear what I'm saying? Remember anything about who her husband is? The one with all the gunslingers and asskickers and throatcutters on retainer, just dying to go all medieval on some gringoboy can't seem to keep his damn pants up?"

Reach shook his head, then shook all over like a wet dog. He stared around the room, kind of wild-eyed, Mobley thought. Then looked back at him, more under control. "Look, you want to pick up the phone, drop the dime, I don't blame you. No hard feelings."

Hell, no, Mobley thought. What's a career? You shoulda been one them Catholic priests, get a little more slack for this kinda crap. "Let me ask you one question."

"Shoot," Reach shrugged. "I might as well get used to ugly officials asking me humiliating questions."

"You didn't do this because of that thing, did you?" Mobley gave him his most intense lie-detector stare. "Thing Sayers was saying about using your overactive dingus and boyish grin to infiltrate the fam?"

That jarred Reach out of his self-recrimination. What? "Are you kidding me?"

"Kidding!" Mobley exploded. "Why the *fuck* would I be jiving you? Somebody told me I'd walk in here and smell illicit perfume and your jizz all in the air, I'da told them they were kidding."

"If I'd been doing some scam like that for Sayers, I wouldn't have to worry, would I?"

"Depends. He the type you can trust when a some sex abuse scandal hits the fan?"

"I doubt it. But why does that make any difference? You going to roll me over, or not?"

"Nah, man. We're cool." Mobley glared again. "Some of us cooler than certain others among us."

"Thanks, Ray. Sorry."

"Oh, now suddenly you're thinking how this might reflect on *me* a little? Better late than never." Mobley walked over to the coffee maker, his back to the desk. "You're not so bad for a Fed, Reach. You can't help it if you're pretty. And stupid. And strung out on your own hormones."

Reach thought it over as he watched the black cop pour two cups. "It sounded like you were saying my motivations made some sort of difference to you."

"Just my personal respect. That Gigolo General shit is just too shabby." He came back, set both cups on the desk and sat down facing Reach. "But I'm a sucker for an insanity plea."

Reach nodded gratefully and picked up his coffee.

"Course I got to weed a little envy out of there, too." Mobley blew across the surface of his coffee, took a cautious taste and shook his head. "Man, oh, man."

Chapter Twenty-Five

It had been an antsy week for Gaspar. Nobody likes having their wife unexpectedly no-show for conjugals. Sitting in the day room, gradually realizing they're not going to call your name. Wondering what the hell, and almost any answer you come up with sucks.

Worse yet because he'd asked around and found out she'd been down. Had come inside the gates, had gone into an interrogation room with the cops. Then suddenly, she didn't show up to visit. Make a good scenario out of that one.

Then Manny had come up and looked grim in the attorney room. Yeah, the Feds had grabbed her, taken her in for almost an hour. She'd come out practically in tears, didn't talk to Alfredo in the car, just sat there chewing her nails and looking bummed.

Gaspar grunted at that news. "Hmmp. And she's not an easy babe to rattle."

Manny had nodded emphatically. He'd heard the story of the mini-mall mashup from Alfredo, then from Chuy, from Lico, from every man who was there. "No, I'd say it would take a lot to get on her nerves."

"They've found a place to stick something in and wiggle it around, huh?"

Poor choice of words, Manny thought. "Something like that. See, this trustee, janitor in the visit area said that prettyboy Fed tried to follow her in the hall, and he was like unbuttoned, messed up, face all red."

Gaspar grunted again, with more feeling. That was serious. "That fashion plate asshole ought to learn to hit on women someplace private."

Manny spoke very carefully, without any inflection or expression. "Maybe it's a good thing he doesn't."

Gaspar tensed and scowled, then relaxed, studying his lawyer. "I know what you're saying. You think I should worry?"

Manny had thought it out in advance. "I gotta say, if there is such a thing as a stand-up broad, she's it. But still..."

Gaspar nodded absently, thinking it out himself. He'd learned to trust Nan, no doubt. But women were one thing, business was another. Not just himself involved, is the thing. "Yeah, still. But I'm not in a position to worry about it. She's coming up next week, right?"

Manny nodded. "But first she's coming in to talk to me Tuesday afternoon. Says she wants some paper fixed up."

Gaspar pondered that and got nowhere. "Sure. Think you should ask her what went on up here?"

"I plan on seeing what she has to say. You can ask her whatever you want next week. If we've really got the cats in the henhouse here I'll come see you right away."

Gaspar nodded somewhat absently. No point worrying without knowing what was up. But it was definitely a rough week.

Nan was precisely on time, like always. Manny had asked a secretary to bring one of the mocha lattés she liked from the coffee emporium in his office complex, knowing she'd walk in before it got cold. He heard her speak to the girl outside his office door, thanking her for the latté. He sat watching the door, anticipating his usual pleasure at seeing her walk in, looking like a million bucks and smiling like desert sunrise.

And here she was in knee-length boots of supple yellow leather, a swingy orange corduroy skirt, embroidered Andean peasant blouse with an alpaca shawl, and a tight glossy black hair swept back with bone combs shaped like doves. But the smile wasn't really all there.

He motioned her to a seat with unfeigned pleasure, then waited to see if things would get less pleasant.

She sat, sipped, gave him a look so long and pointed that he felt a little uncomfortable. You called this meeting, *güera*, he thought. It's on you.

Finally she said, "You already know. How much?"

Well, that gets right to it, Manny thought. He parried, "About?"

"Come on, Manny. Up at the prison. I don't think there are any secrets in that place."

"All I know is whatever you tell me. Is there something you want to say?"

She laughed but not with a lot of heart. "Sure, Manny. Look, here it is. Are you afraid I might be cheating on your boss?"

Not "my husband" Manny noted. He gave her a smile that admitted all. "Hey, he's so cute I'd be tempted myself. You know, the right cellblock and all."

She smiled, not at the lame joke, but that they were out in open terrain. "And then there's that whole thing about women being treacherous and not to be trusted."

"Well, they write all those *ranchero* songs about if for a reason."

"Well in my considerable professional experience," she said dryly, "a lot more cheating gets done by men."

"Yeah, well, you know, that's..."

"Different?"

"Yeah. Different." He hoped this wasn't leading where he was afraid it was.

"Well, let me tell you, Manolo." She moved forward in her chair, capturing his eye. "I'm different, too. Okay?"

He nodded. She could say that again. But it didn't answer anything.

"I don't screw people over," She said, not softening the words a bit. Then she leaned back and got less intense. She seemed to be talking to herself, but he was all ears. "It's funny. The one thing I wished, all those years making my living in the sack. Know what? Just to be married. Be a one-man woman. And now I am. Do you understand what I'm telling you?"

"I think I do." He watched her drink her coffee, not looking at him. "Know what, that's really sort of..."

Nan looked up and smiled, "Not 'ironic' again?"

He shook his head. "I was thinking more like... you know? Touching. *Triste.*"

"That, too. So what I want you to do, I want to amend my contract with Gaspar."

Any positive view on the situation blew right out of Manny's head. He stared at her with definite alarm. "Amend? Listen, lady, I gotta tell you..."

She waited, but he was casting around for the right words.

"You know this goes beyond just a marriage contract, right? This is business. And I mean *Business*, am I clear?"

She nodded calmly. "Completely clear."

"I have to tell him about this before I even look at any proposed amendment."

"I wouldn't have it any other way. I'm going to be up there Saturday. I'll tell him myself."

"Why are you here, then?" For the first time he felt a little annoyance. Why did he have to be more a part of this soap opera than necessary? It wasn't like she was some ingénue seeking guidance.

"I thought it out and wrote it down. Here."

She pulled two folded sheets of typewriter paper from her purse and laid them on the desk. Manny grimaced and spread his hands in a "no touch" gesture.

"This is what I want done. As soon as you can. I'm sure Gaspar will okay it after I talk to him."

Manny looked at the sheets of paper unhappily. "This is about that damned agent, isn't it?"

"Absolutely."

"And I don't mean in some official capacity."

"No. Purely personal."

"Well hell, Nan."

"Thanks, Manny. Talk to you later."

She stood and walked to the door, Manny for once failing to enjoy the grace of her movement. She turned in the doorway and gave him the warmest smile since she came in. "Thanks for the latté, Manolo. That was sweet."

Then she was gone and he sat looking at the papers on his desk. Finally he picked them up, unfolded them and read.

Gaspar's welcoming kiss seemed pretty perfunctory for a prisoner who'd missed his last shot in the sack, Nan thought. Well, she probably came off a little ambivalent, herself. She didn't check him out too blatantly as he ushered her into Boneyard 11, but her vibes radar was turned all the way up. All he said was, "Missed you last week."

"Me, too. I felt bad about not coming." Really bad, actually.

"Well, here we are." But he didn't sound a hundred percent sure.

She sat demurely on one corner of the bed and motioned him to the other corner. When he sat, watching her blankly, she said,

"Look, I've got something so say, so let's get through it first, then see if you still want me around, okay?"

"Oh, shit."

"Look, you know my contract?"

Gaspar stared, caught off guard. "You're talking about a *contract* thing?"

She stopped and sized him up for a moment. "What you were expecting me to be talking about?"

"I don't know. You know, you start off like that..."

He'd heard something. I'm really lucky, she realized. Lots of mob bosses might have just snuffed a woman for the very whisper of something like getting physical with a cop. She changed her tack immediately. "Look, I'm really sorry. It's just that I a met a man who pushes all my buttons. I can't understand it: I never feel this way about men. I just go all weak over him. He's all I ever wanted, in one package. And he seems to be pretty taken with me, too."

Gaspar didn't show anything, but he was strobing through feelings about this. Suspicions confirmed, jealousy, a sense of loss that stabbed him deeper than he would have thought possible. And a slice of admiration. "You don't go in for a lot of pussyfooting and bullshit, do you?"

"I made a career of it, actually. But this is no place for fooling around. Would you say?"

"No. This is pretty serious. I heard a little about this."

"You want to hear any more, just ask me."

"What I want to hear is what you want out of me."

Nan relaxed a little, and surprised her husband with a very tender look. She held his eyes as she said, "I want to renegotiate our prenuptial papers. I already talked to Manny about it."

Renegotiation wasn't a concept Gaspar had grown to love over his career in illicit import and wholesale. But he kept cool. "Renegotiate? I sweat this thing out for a week, now you're not talking shape up or ship out, you're talking rewrite? That's pretty disappointing."

Let me tell you about disappointment, she thought. But I'm going to fix this. Right here and now. "There's nothing in the contract about exclusive services. None of that 'forsaking all others' stuff."

"That was kind of understood, I thought." He was confused. She comes in standing tough and now she's going to plead on the fine print?

"I want it signed and delivered. Black and white. Okay?"

"Wait a minute, hold on here." His confusion had collapsed into total mystification. "You want *what* in writing? That it's okay for you to get some on the side?"

She gave him a smile so sad he wanted to reach out to her, no matter what he was feeling about this whole development. "I'm afraid I deserve you thinking that way. I'm sorry. But, no. I want just the opposite."

By now Gaspar's head was reeling completely out of control. *Carajo!* What the *fuck* did women want, anyway? She seemed to be saying... "You want to rewrite the pre-nup so it says you can't cheat on me?"

She gave a shy smile. "If it's not in the contract, it's not cheating, is it? Can we just do it? Make an honest woman out of me?"

That took awhile to digest, and she was sitting there waiting for him to get around it. Finally he said, "Let me get this straight. You've got this really bad temptation to go behind my back here?"

She nodded and dropped her eyes.

"This really strong itch, and you might do it even though we're married?"

She nodded again, barely.

"And even though you've got to worry about what might happen to you if you did?"

No nod, this time. She just sat like a Catholic school girl awaiting punishment from the head nun.

"But if it's written into your contract, you'll honor it?"

She looked up and he saw stone-cold certainty behind her embarrassment. "That's what I'm asking for. And yeah, that's why. Hey, if I was perfect, I wouldn't have still been single."

Another cocktail of emotions swarmed up inside of him. Look at her. Just look at this woman, here. And he was married to her. He said, "You're just too much, woman."

"Too much?" She seemed genuinely shocked that he'd say so. "Huh! Apparently I'm the kind of girl who a financial contract means more to than love or passion or morality. No wonder I'm a whore."

He came off the bed and swooped to her, dropped to his knees and grabbed her by her upper arms, his emotional overload making him too rough, too abrupt. She didn't react or resist. "You were a whore before I met you. That's over. What you are now is my wife. Can we get that straight for once and always?"

She smiled into his face with an unfeigned joy and affection that moved and excited him. He didn't know whether he most wanted to wrap his arms around her or his legs. She said, "I'd rather get it in writing."

"You got it. You just really, really, got it."

"Okay then," she piped in a girlish tone, her eyes sparkling. "Wifely duties, coming right up."

He leaned forward, pushing her back down on her back. She wriggled backwards, drawing him into the center of the bed. He lowered himself on her, worming his arms underneath her to pull her tight. "You're one weird wife. I'm one lucky sucker."

She thrust her mouth upwards to nibble his ear and quickly whispered, "You'd better believe it. And I think maybe I am, too."

Chapter Twenty-Six

Nan emerged from the steaming bathroom still damp enough to adhere to her thin cornflower cotton robe, wrapping her wet hair in a towel, moving with the groove of the Blondie songs she'd been singing in the shower. She stopped in her tracks at the sight of Mongo lolling in one of the lowslung teak chairs on her balcony, a drink in his hand and the wolf in his eyes.

She regarded him like she might look upon some messy dead bird dragged in by a proud cat. "I just hate asking obvious questions."

He smiled proprietarily and gave a languid, wised-up, shrug that said as much about him as his clothes and hair. "I figured I could keep an eye on you better here."

"But it turns out just an eye isn't enough, is that the size of it?"

He nodded with a slow, ponderous emphasis. "You got that right. I got something to show you."

"What a coincidence," she chirped brightly. "So do I. Excuse me just a second."

She darted into the walk-in closet so huge she'd once referred to as "The Outback". Mongo, moving with anticipatory leisure, set his drink beside the phone and binoculars on the deck table and started to rise. But she was back, wearing a honey-blonde wig, pulling a taupe raincoat over her robe and clutching a cell phone in her free hand along with a small automatic pistol.

Snugging the coat tight with the clever integrated belt, she pointed the pistol at Mongo, who smiled and sat back down.

"Attaboy, sit. Just pant there for a minute while I make a phone call."

"You already did that number on me. Remember, *puta*?" He started to rise, his smile tighter and uglier. "Only one to a customer."

The pistol gave a small, polite slam and Mongo's drink exploded all over him. He froze, half up and half down, gaping at her and dripping expensive Scotch.

"Did you ever get the feeling the world is one step ahead of you, Mongo?" she asked with a touch of genuine sympathy at the guy's hopelessness. "And always will be?"

She popped the phone to her ear, the pistol pointing rock steady. Mongo sank slowly back into the chair, trying to regroup. He was in charge here, right?

"Alfredo? Hi, it's Nan." She spoke to the phone with her usual bright friendliness. "Listen, could you send somebody over to break Mongo's knees so I don't have to shoot his balls off?"

Mongo saw her expression take a dive. Somebody had said something that shocked that smirk off her face, all right. Wonder what?

She listened, the shock spreading on her face. "My God!" she exclaimed, all her attention on the phone. "What happened?"

Gaspar walked into the cool shade of the storage shed, slapping dust off a pair of rough cloth work gloves. The wheelbarrow wasn't where he'd left it, but he could see it in back by the sacks of Teramiacin crumbles. He took four steps into the doorway before a shovel swung in from the darkness beside the door, slamming the back of his head and knocking him on his face as his head flashed into bright white spirals and a din like a big iron drum.

"When?" Nan asked in a small voice, looking at the interloper on the balcony but not seeing him.

A hoe swished down from the other side of the doorway, chopping brutally into his back. He heard it hit him, smelled manure in his mouth and nose, felt nothing.

"Who?" Nan demanded, her tone strengthening. "Why?"

The hoe slashed down again.

"No, never mind," Nan said sharply, getting back into stride. "I'm on my way."

And again and again.

"Yeah, okay. I'm there," she spoke tersely, running a jumble of different thoughts at once. "Oh, wait. Mongo..."

She stopped, seeing Mongo again, but with a cold new light. Her face froze over and even as dull a *machista* as he was, he felt a chill.

"Hold on a second, Alfredo." She let her phone hand drop, pressed it against her thigh to muffle it. She looked at Mongo with a shining chrome fury. "This isn't a co-incidence is it, you weaselly moron? You knew. You'd never have had the balls..."

She clapped the phone back to her ear. "Alfredo? Any idea who did this? Or why?"

She listened, nodding. "Well, I think Mongo might have something to contribute to the topic. Send somebody over. He's in my bedroom."

She listened and gave a smile that made the big thug's neck hair crawl. "Oh, he'll be here."

She snapped the phone shut and dropped it in her pocket. Mongo took a shot, trying to explode out of his weak position in the low chair. Her first little .25 slug, carefully cut to dum-dum quarters with a nail file, hit him about an inch above the right kneecap, tumbling and disintegrating through the delicate structures that permit humans to stand erect. He cried out wordlessly and fell forward, grabbing the door jamb for support. The second shot blew shreds of the frame into his face and drove his hand full of lead and aluminum shrapnel. He fell heavily.

Her third shot was intended to hit his left femur, hopefully breaking it, but instead grazed the bone on its way through the muscles and tendons, emerging in a spray of bright blood. He jerked as if electrocuted, sobbed, and passed out.

Nan scooped up her big purse, stepped into a pair of soft leather *huaraches*, and headed out the door. She dropped the gun in her purse, but at the top of the stairs fished it back out and held it in her pocket as she hurried down. Who knew what mood the rest of her palace guard was in?

Chapter Twenty-Seven

She still wore the wig and raincoat, but they didn't come off as very chic. She looked like somebody with a carload of care who'd been up all night and slept in their clothes. Because she had. She slumped in the awful, gummy, orange plastic chairs, talking on a cell phone that was about at the end of its charge after so many frantic calls. "I know you're working on it," she said wearily. "Look, I know. It's no picnic barging into trauma units in the real world. This one, forget it. They've got guards and cops in here like roaches on a dumpster."

She listened, lipping the last cigarette from a crumpled pack and flicking a lighter. "That's good. Yeah, work on that." She almost hung up, but remembered, "And look, did you get those numbers for me?"

She lit up and sucked in the smoke. Nerve food, she thought. She went days between cigarettes when the world wasn't hitting her fan. "I know that, Manny," she said a little testily. "I'm not calling them right now: there's no point. But I want them, do you understand?"

Listening, idly waving a pattern of smoke, her face hardened. "So get them for me. I'll call you about it this afternoon."

She softened, looked tired. "Thanks a lot, Manolo. I know you mean it. No, I'll be all right. Find me those numbers. *Ciao*."

She looked at the little battery graphic on the phone, wondering if it had another call in it or not, then snapped it shut. She closed her eyes, feeling exhaustion and frustration. She calmed herself, drawing from what she envisioned as a spring of clear blue water flowing from a seamless stone well deep inside her. She sniffed, opened her eyes to see a cup of hot coffee a foot in front of them.

She reached to take the cup from the large, hard hand of RayRay Mobley, her gratitude evident in her glance and smile. He offered her packets of sugar and creamer, pocketed them when she shook her head. He pulled a chair in front of her, straddled it, facing her with his arms crossed on the grubby back of it. He sipped from his own cup and made a face.

"For an attractive woman," he said conversationally, "I gotta say you look like home-made shit."

Nan smiled and reached out to tap cups in a mock toast. "For a cop," she said, mimicking his broad street diction, "I gotta say you've got pretty useful timing."

"Can't say I'm bleeding for your old man, but I sympathize for what you're going through," he said remotely, eyeing her. "You're taking this pretty hard. You might not be quite who I've been thinking you are."

"Pretty simple, really. I'm a wife worried about my husband."

"Yeah, I think maybe so." He sipped, looked around the waiting room. "Said you've been here all night trying to get in, see him."

She waved an airy hand at the grimly anonymous waiting room. "I only come here for the atmosphere. And the coffee, of course."

He liked her resilience as much as the care he'd seen pressing down on her. "Well, good luck getting in."

"Thanks. Why is it easier to get into prison than a hospital?"

"I meant 'good luck' in the sense of, you know, 'fat chance'." He looked at her steadily for a beat. "But I might be able to change your luck."

"Now I thought it was just black girls who could do that one."

He smiled slightly and leaned a little forward, opening a hand towards her. "I can get you in to see him. Right now. But you have to do what I say."

They have a funny idea of what "private room" means, she thought. Gaspar, the only patient, looked small and eroded in the tilted bed, a mass of bruise and bandage plugged into a spaghetti of tubes, hoses, and wires leading to a bank of instruments, screens, and gismos that looked like they could launch a Mars probe if they felt like it. But one wall was almost all window, allowing the scrutiny of nurses and the two guards detailed to keep Gaspar prisoner while the Sharp Memorial staff tried to keep him alive.

Nan sat by the bed, leaning her head on the sheets. She felt a spasmodic jerk in the bed and popped erect, looking at what could be seen of her husband's face. His eyes opened, fluttered, swam into focus. He seemed about to yell, but oriented himself and looked at Nan incredulously. Before he even tried to speak, she had her hand over his lips. She stood and leaned over him, kissed his forehead. "I'm going to speak those three magic words you never expected to hear from me," she said.

Between her hand and his thick head bandages, Gaspar's eyebrows rose in curiosity.

She summoned up a brilliant smile and said, "I'm. Wearing. Wires."

Which totally blew the demolished crime boss's mind, but there wasn't much he could say or do about it.

"It was the only way I could get in to see if you're all right." She patted his cheek with her silencing hand. "That nice Lieutenant Mobley set it up. Like you might blurt something out to me."

Gaspar scowled wanly but she shook her head. "Don't. I think it was an honest favor. Go figure."

She took her hand from his mouth and slipped it into his, which lay weak and pale on the covers. "No, don't go figure. Go back to sleep. I can't stay very long. Unless you want to rat out a bunch of Latino wiseguys for the tape recorder?"

He liked that one, but was fading fast. She was probably just another one of the bizarre dreams he'd been living in, anyway. One of the nicer ones.

"I'll be back," she was saying. "Manny's on it. Alfredo's on it. I'm doing what I can. Just get well, okay?"

Gaspar nodded feebly. His eyes fluttered shut but she felt a light squeeze on her fingers.

"I got your back, hon," she said softly. "Sleep."

Chapter Twenty-Eight

The office windows offered a panoramic view of the border from its glassy sweep across the entire facade of the top floor of the tower above the Tijuana Country Club. A severe, minimalist space with an almost Japanese tendency towards unfinished wood paneling and stark black functionality, it had a quiet, static feel, like a modern art museum where the display itself is the work of art. Everything in the room led the eye toward the wide desk at one end, pale wood plaques supporting a flat black top that looked like polished metal but showed no fingerprints.

And all routes to favor and fortune in the northern border region led to the man who sat behind the desk in a black leather chair as rigid and futuristic as a starship command post. *Don* Aquiles Altamira de las Ronches was more powerful and connected than the average multi-millionaire due to the accident of his birth into one of the controlling families of Mexico. He'd moved his operations to the border, but was in no way removed from the central pathways of influence, be they politically financial or violently criminal. He was the distant superior to anyone living in Tijuana who had a desire to continue to live there. Among his many minions was a minor narcotics functionary on the California side who liked to be referred to simply as "Gaspar".

The stark simplicity of *Don* Altamira's dark clothing would have made it hard to realize that he was superior to the distinguished, urbane attorney who stood in front of his desk dangling a briefcase that put even Manny's futuristic prop to shame. Except that the posture and attitude of the urbane lawyer spelled out deference much more obviously than any superficial signs. He spoke to his boss with a bantering, cavalier air, but to any experienced observer the lines of power were clearly drawn.

The lawyer much preferred briefings here in the actual power center of the Baja region to hanging around the pretentious public prefab of the mayor's office in the *Palacio Municipál*. This was the environment he was born to occupy, and he was working on getting bigger and bigger slices of it. These things came to men who served *Don* Altamira well, and he more than earned his lavish pay and perks. The only thing that limited his effectiveness in representing those interests was the fact that he often just didn't understand what the man was thinking, the mercurial directions his machine slipped off into.

"The basic problem with the Gaspar situation," he told his boss with an all-to-common feeling that he was going off in the wrong direction, "Is not him. It's that it weakens his organization for him to be in bed instead of prison."

"Not an altogether bad thing."

Okay, the attorney thought, we spend a lot of money setting up and protecting this guy, and make him our largest funnel for drugs into California, but weakening might have a happy face to show us? "But if these cowboys move against the organization now, maybe cut into the territory..."

"Then they might come up with the strength to resist," Altamira interrupted, "Perhaps even produce a leader better than Gaspar."

Great, thought the sleek lawyer, one of those "what doesn't kill us makes us stronger things". But he said nothing.

"Or they'll be weakened enough to welcome whatever assistance and leadership we can provide them."

Ah, the light dawned. "Perhaps accept a local boss that didn't come from their own roots? Maybe somebody you've already got in mind?"

Altamira nodded very slightly. The lawyer grinned at him. You had to hand it to the *Jefe*, he was always three steps ahead of the world. He switched mental tracks, running down the ways and means of implementing the new contingencies just mapped out for him.

Chapter Twenty-Nine

Manny Basto's luxurious legal office in Bonita, its decor inspired in equal parts by interiors from the Godfather films and the upscale *rancho* chic in Vicente Fernadez videos, served as an *ad hoc* nerve center for the complex machinations of his only client. He hunched behind an imposing *colonial*-style darkwood desk, fiddling with the latches of his briefcase as Nan, withdrawn and moody, sat on a leather love seat in front of a wall full of bullfighter bravado. Alfredo, hunkered on the front few inches of a modernistic wrap chair upholstered in black leather, also hung on her answer.

"How do you think he looks?" she answered in a tired voice. "He looks like he got the stuffing beat out of him with garden implements."

"But he seemed okay?" Manny pressed. "He knew you, talked all right?"

"He knew me, understood me. I didn't let him say anything. I told you, I was wearing a federal wire at the time."

Alfredo shook his head, disturbed by all the implications of that. "Man, that's messed up."

"Look, it got me in. And didn't get the cops diddly. Now..."

She stopped and swept the men with a very hard gaze. They didn't know how to take her at this point and she wasn't quite ready to help them out with it. "What happened up there? Who did it? And what were they trying to accomplish?"

"We're thinking the Maras paid some guys inside to do the hit. They didn't want to kill him, I think. Just weaken us. Send a message."

"We have Instant Messenger for that," she was unrelentingly tough and grim with her speech and outlook. "Not weed whackers or whatever. But here's the main point. Who besides Mongo knew about it?"

"Three guys," Alfredo said. "They were gonna make a move."

"Higher-up guys," Manny explained. "*Cabos*. Guys who could take it over and run with it. Cut a deal with the Maras."

"Where are these guys now?" Nan said in a voice even these two men heard as menacing and merciless. "I want to talk to them."

She saw the expected glances between them. Who does she think she is?

Alfredo looked away. "We sort of had to let them go."

Nan laughed, but there wasn't much fun in it. "I'll bet you did."

She moved forward in her seat and gave Alfredo a very stern look. "Listen, guys, don't spare me any details. I want the works. We have to deal with this thing."

"*We*?" Manny said, amazed at her attitude. "This is a business thing. Our business, you know. You don't..."

"Yes, I do," she said rigidly. "You bet your ass I do. Let me level with you here. I don't really give a damn if the whole drug biz goes broke and we all end up burning burgers at a drive-up. But when they try to kill your husband, you have to care about it. You have to make them stop."

There was a very long pause in the room, the subliminal hum of the air conditioner growing louder as she faced them down. They eyed her, each other, objects in the vicinity. They didn't seem to know what part of this scenario to start with.

Alfredo broke the silence. "You're going to do that? Make them stop?"

Nan spoke to Manny, though. "May I ask if either of you have ever really called the shots in this outfit? Even for short periods of time?"

"No," he told her candidly. "It was always Gaspar."

"Is there anybody in this organization who can step in and run it? Who could be trusted to run it right?"

"Well, there were a couple of guys..." Alfredo started diffidently.

"But you had to let them go." She gestured with one hand, a sharp final chop. "Look, in the future keep guys like that around awhile. I might think of a few questions for them. Understood?"

Manny was circumspect. There was no way to really gauge what was going on here, or where it was headed. "I understand that part, yeah."

"But not why I'm suddenly giving you orders? Because somebody has to. You see that, right?"

Manny and Alfredo consulted each other silently, nodded provisionally.

"We've been hit and weakened. We might be fighting for our lives here, right? And there's nobody to tell us what to do. So we have to run things ourselves for now."

Manny didn't look at the other man this time, just said, "We?"

"Meaning me." She said it with a snapdown finality, let it lay for a moment, then went on in a softer tone. "With your very welcome help. Any better suggestions?"

"But you don't know..." Except that Alfredo wasn't all that sure what she did and didn't know, anymore.

"No, but you do, right? And what we don't know, we can get somebody who does. What's the alternative?"

They thought it over, but came up short.

"So unless you have any objections..." she waited politely for comments that never came. "We're the executive council right here. I act as director until my husband tells me different. How about it?"

The room seemed to hang static, for a long moment, even the air ducts holding their breath. Then Alfredo shrugged. "Like you said, what's the alternative?"

Manny stood and motioned Nan to come sit in his chair. "Here. More comfortable."

Nan rose, crossed the room in a smooth glide, and took a seat. And, she could feel, the lead. "Thank you, Manny," she said, and nodded at Alfredo to signify that she wasn't just talking about having a place to sit. She waited until Manny sat on the couch, then looked at them both with her hands folded on the table, exuding executive will.

"First order of business," she said. "We find out who these fuckers are."

Chapter Thirty

A tall, skinny inmate with the sandy hair and freckly complexion that other blacks for some reason call "red" paused in his endless circulation between the rows of bunks and steel lockers, leaning on his pushbroom to see the end of the checker game. The players perched at one of the six steel "picnic tables" bolted to the floor, concentrating on their game above the sounds of two televisions, one tuned to Discovery Channel and the other to a raucous booty-bouncin' MTV video.

Chavez, a serial loser in his late thirties, arms covered with faded, inept barrio art and still wearing dungarees dusty from the dairy, seemed pleased with his move and leaned back to admire the effect. His opponent, a young black slacker called Freeway, looked up at him with an expression of empathy, even universal melancholy. He explained, "Now, understand me here. I am *not* a homosexual."

That took Chavez, a Shelltown junkie who was hard to get a rise out of anymore, aback. "So what, man?" he expostulated. "Make your damn move."

"Well, I wanted you to know that," Freeway continued in the same gently forgiving tone, "So that when I say that I'm about to fuck you..."

He made two jumps on the board. "I don't mean nothing that come to the biblical sense."

He jumped one more in the unfolding series of devastation. "I mean I'm going to pillage your village. The *chingazo*, like you folks fond of saying."

His last jump landed on Chavez' back row, awaiting a crown. Chavez gaped at the unexpected rip up the guts of his mindless defense and stared at Freeway with as much shock as distaste.

Freeway raised his eyebrows and showed a flash of gleaming teeth. "Was it good for you, too?"

The sweeper laughed and Freeway joined in, like a *mallate* magpie, but Chavez managed to keep his humiliation covered and chilled. "Asshole, you said you were a beginner."

"Compared to my master," Freeway said, bowing over steepled hands with a serenity copped from a hundred Kung Fu Flix, "I am

116

an egg on the bottom of the sea. Up for another one, double or nothing?"

Chavez didn't reply, just shoved three cigarettes across the table and shook his head at the perfidy of *negros*, smart-asses, and the overly young.

"Chavez!" It was a new guard, looking around to see if there was a Chavez in the dorm. "Visit."

"Right here. Who is it?"

"Do I look like your social secretary?"

No, *gabacho*, you look like a pimp in a stupid uniform, Chavez thought, getting up and walking towards the officer.

"Attorney visit," the guard added, remembering that he had to tell them that.

Chavez' wide, lazy shrug took in the entire dayroom, trustee barracks, and prison yard. "Do I look like somebody got an attorney?"

"So you're declining the visit?" Good. Save time and trouble.

"Hell, no," Chavez said quickly. "Anything gets me out of here for a minute. Away from these treacherous *negritos*."

Freeway accepted his accusing glower and nodded at his wise decision. "Sure, man. Maybe your lawyer turns out to have nice titties."

No such luck, though. There was nobody in the cramped attorney visit area but Manny Basto, sitting with his TekWar briefcase and a yellow pad in front of him. He motioned Chavez into the other chair with a distantly polite wave. As the con sat, Manny pushed a light aluminum ashtray towards him and handed him a pack of smokes.

"*Gracias, ese*," Chavez nodded, lighting one up and sticking one behind his ear. "All that good shit. But listen, I don't need no lawyer, Homes. I'm on the farm now, three months to make honor camp, I'll be for the Outs by Christmas."

Manny smiled cynically. "Out the gate by eight, in the spoon by noon, back in the pen by ten."

Chavez acknowledged the aptness of the refrain, took a deep drag.

"You think you're never gonna need a lawyer again?" Manny spoke without emphasis, but he had something that made Chavez pay attention. "In your life? Or maybe a friend?"

"I got friends."

Manny glanced around the room. "Didn't help much did they? *Oye, wey,* you can do yourself a big favor just by doing us a favor."

"So it's 'us', huh? Uh, oh."

"Just talk to me a little."

"Sure, I get it. *Como sí, como no.* What's 'us' wanna know?"

"Who did Señor Gaspar?"

"Oh, shit." Chavez sat a little straighter, dropped the hand holding the cigarette to his lap. "Well, *sí señor.* That kind of 'us' is worth doing a favor. You his lawyer?"

"*Claro que sí.*"

Con upsmanship wouldn't let Chavez resist. "Didn't help him much, did you?"

"Who, me? Oh, hell, no. Just got him down to a nickel when the DA was offering twenty and licking his chops."

"You got it, *compa.*" Chavez did his best to radiate reliability and cunning. "I'll ask around."

"Be really careful who you ask."

Deeply offended, Chavez swept an index finger to encompass not only the physical prison, but the "down" mindset. "Scuse me *cabrón*, but I live here, okay?"

Nan occupied Manny's desk chair as if she'd had it delivered herself. Alfredo and Manny had pulled curved-leg, upholstered chairs up to the desk for this war council. Nan was a concerto of earth colors, a severe buff dress topped with a short chocolate jacket, burnt orange earrings, and auburn wig. Outside it was in the seventies with bright blue skies, but in the den-like office it was all about Autumn.

"I don't see any question," Manny argued. "They were all three around. Getting visits. These guys are like, The Chiapas Hillbillies, you know? Who's going to visit them?"

"Not exactly conclusive," Nan said, but knew there would be more. Manny liked to move in one solid step at the time.

"Well how about, they're smoking now? Suddenly they're buying ice cream from commissary. Got a TV. Walk around like they're bigtime studs."

"Well, then..." Alfredo said with an air of conclusion.

"Good enough for me," Nan seconded.

Manny looked at both of them then nodded twice, crisply. "*Dicho, hecho.* Who do we know can take this?"

"Maybe it's better, somebody we don't know, see what I mean?"

"That's a good point." Nan was learning quite a bit from working with these guys. So were they. "Who then?"

Alfredo had thought about it. "We could go to the *changos*."

"Beg pardon?"

"*Negros*," Manny explained. "Maybe Crips?"

"They say if you go black, you never go back," Nan said with a slight smile.

Manny didn't return the smile. "Let's hope once does the trick."

Alfredo was fairly impressed with the condition of the crack house. Cluttered up but not filthy, well-fortified with everything from diamondplate to expensive steel doorframes. And packed with armed, belligerent black teen-agers wearing various blue clothing items and head rags. This might be the crackhead's Hilton, he thought as he walked through the room behind his host. He noticed his nephew Stebi, who he'd brought to watch his back and serve as token entourage, checking the place out approvingly. Probably wondering if they need a roommate, Alfredo thought.

Their host, X-Rock, was the old-timer in the place, around twenty-two. He was also wearing blue, but with more style and bling, including a gold Mercedes emblem on a heavy neck chain. Alfredo realized the thing had to have been made. He'd paid a jeweler to make a gold replica of a ripped-off car accessory. Amazing. He caught Stebi openly coveting the Benz necklace. I'll tell Tina to put it on his Christmas list, he thought.

X-Rock led them into a bedroom, obviously a private office. And judging from the bottles of Clorox visible by the toilet in the attached bath, where they kept merchandise they might have to dispose of in a hurry. The "office" was mostly locked cabinets, but

119

also had a couch, probably intended more for quickies than sleeping or sipping cappuccino, and a low boomerang-shaped table in retro orange Formica. Okay, where's the lava-lamp, Alfredo thought. Ah, there it is, over on top of the flash safe.

"What this could do, understand," X-Rock was lecturing, "could start a color riot in there. If all the facts were known, see what I'm saying."

Alfredo nodded his understanding of the delicate fabric of gangbanger racial checks and balances.

"The problem with the, uh, 'diversity' bullshit. Got its, you know, ramifications."

Alfredo nodded, said, "So can you hang with it? Or not?"

X-Rock made a deprecating grimace. "Hey, nothin' but net, Julio. Might be able to get permission, even."

"Good. It's fine with us, of course. Ask your main man inside there how's his sister doing? Tynicia?"

X-Rock laughed gleefully. "Oh, my, man done took names."

"He's gonna say she's pretty sprung," Alfredo went on. "Then ask him, what if somebody grabs her off the street, takes her in to kick? This nice facility up in Orange. Then some real pro rehab. Plus we pay for three, four guys."

"You should be working for me, pops. You got a flair for sales. Could you throw in some coupons? Christmas turkey? No interest until 2012?"

"This is major for us. You do it right, we do you right." Alfredo slipped into ironic "ghetto" diction, "Word."

X-Rock cackled again. "Damn, you taco-benders picking up on some *real* English 'round here."

Chapter Thirty-One

Nan didn't pay any attention to the bell from the outer gate: there were plenty of guys down there to get it. She was doing a light workout in her bedroom, barefoot in a GymWare support top and an athletic thong she thought of as a "jockita". She had a light coat of sweat and a sunny attitude as she ducked and bounced to a Spirogyra CD. But when her little silver "in-house" cellular chimed she stopped and answered it, controlling her hard but measured breath while dabbing at her temples and forehead with a hand towel. She frowned and stepped to the balcony to take a look.

It was worse than just any old cop at the door, it was that DEA slimeball. She tapped her fingernail on the phone a couple of times, looking down at the arrogant manner Gaithers displayed to a growing semi-circle of henchmen and retainers. "I'll be right down."

She set the phone on a dresser, quickly stepped into the khaki skirt she'd hung on the doorknob, fluffed her moist hair, and went down the stairs with her bubbly mood deflated.

The clot of bodyguards hulking around the gate parted as she approached, creating a gauntlet of armed, hostile men she walked through to confront Gaithers. He watched her come without expression, ignoring the troops. Nan stopped three feet from him and didn't bother with any pretense of social polish. "We've got plenty of brushes and cookies. If you're selling anything else, contact my husband's attorney."

Gaithers eyed her for a moment, then glanced around the façade of the house. Casing the place, Nan thought: don't let this guy near the silverware. Finally he looked right into her eyes, a gaze so opaque and featureless she thought of the glass eyes on stuffed snakes tourists buy in Tijuana. He said, "Actually, I think talking to me for a few minutes might save everybody a lot of time and trouble."

"You don't strike me as a trouble-saver, actually. And every time I see you, you waste my time. I'm in a bit of a hurry. Why don't you give me your message of cheer so I can close the gate and hose the driveway down?"

Gaithers didn't react to her scorn, just eyed the glowering goons around him and said, "Might be a good idea to tell these gorillas to take a hike."

"They're not really the outdoorsy, trekker types. And I kind of like their company."

Gaithers pulled a compact radio from his pocket and held it up. "Want me to call up some of my gorillas? With like crowbars and sledgehammers?"

She looked past him to the car he'd parked across the driveway, a bland gray Crown Victoria that practically had "Property, U.S. Govt." stenciled on the doors. Two men inside, looking straight ahead. "I can buy radios myself. And sledgehammers. What's harder to come by are search warrants."

He dropped the radio back in the pocket of his squarish looking suit with the air of a bridge player whose deuce had drawn out a trump. Where does he get those clothes, Nan thought, Eastern European Surplus?

"Not so hard for me." He pulled a DVD in unmarked plastic box from his other coat pocket. "Take about five minutes after I show the judge this little flick."

"So what are you here for? Popcorn?"

"You'd be interested in it, as well. So would Lt. Mobley. And especially Agent Reach."

Uh-oh. She knew the best bet was to slam the gate in his factory-second face, but there was something about the way he'd said it and her own guilty knowledge that made her say, "Okay. Five minutes."

She turned to the alpha male bodyguard and said, "So what do you think? Would I be safe for five minutes with a Federal agent?"

The guard spit about an inch from Gaithers' foot and eloquently replied, "Fuck that shit."

"Oh, I don't think so," she said brightly. "Thanks boys, I guess I'll be okay. Why don't you all go around back and play in the sprinkler for awhile?"

The pack moved reluctantly away, glowering and menacing towards Gaithers. Nan caught the attention of the spitter and said, "Oh, and don't forget to make that call to the caterer, will you, Raul?"

She turned to Gaithers, crossed her arms on her chest and waited.

"You want to do this out here in the hot sun?" he asked with what he probably thought was a disarming smile.

"I don't want to do it at all. But spit it out."

Gaithers raised his hand slowly and pointed up where the roof tiles overhung. She followed where he pointed and saw the tiny security camera. When she looked back at him again, he pointed out another one at the corner of the house. "You sure you want all this on the record?"

I can't believe he knows more about my own surveillance than I did, she thought, chagrined. But he's got a point. She turned and headed for the house, sensing him moving silent behind her in his ugly suede clodhoppers from Volume Shoe Source.

By the time she opened the front door, she knew the best place to talk. Right here in the entry. Nobody would bother bugging a place that people just walk through and the smooth marble walls of the minimalist, Southbeach Chic foyer couldn't conceal much, anyway. She took three strides inside, then turned, stopping him right inside the doorway. "So what's on your mind, Agent Whoever?"

He flashed his badge again. "Gaithers. I'll make this brief. So far those clowns have been working on you for implication. My interest is completely assets. I've got the goods on you, and you know what I'm talking about. You'd be better off opening up. It could work out good for you, that way, matter of fact. Piss me off, and you're not going to like it."

She laughed in his face, a good loud laugh that touched every element of derision and despising. "For *that*, I interrupted Buns of Steel? If you turn around you can see the gate, so probably even you can find it okay. If not, I'll get you some help."

He stepped into the house in a ponderous, studied method that called the phrase "breaking and entry" to her mind. He's inside now, she thought. I might not have played this so well.

"You think you're a pretty hot property don't you, you bimbo? Think you can make fun of me just because you've got Mobley ready to bend over and kiss your ass and are fucking that idiot Reach into being your little lapdog."

Well, there we have it, Nan thought: the fat's officially in the fire. But there was one thing more she wanted to get crystal clear. "We're not really very official here, are we, Agent Gators? Should I assume you're taking a kind of personal interest in this assets thing?"

The minimal mask over his larcenous, blunt-instrument persona was gone now. He took another step towards her, moving with emphasis on his bulk, looking down at her, barefoot on the marble floor. "You bet you ass, bitch. And your ass cuts no ice with me. I've been in this too long. I've got you by your perfumed little pubies. You're my meat and I'm going to have it. All of it. Including my retirement package."

"Okay," she beamed with hostess brightness. "I think it's time to say *Ciao*."

She brushed by him, moving quickly, and held the door open, motioning him out like a maitre'd.

He turned with her and followed her to the door. But instead of leaving, he stepped close to her, trapping her against the wall, towering over her, surrounding her with mass and intent. "You sit here with your tits and clothes and gangster hubby and figure you know your rights, that about the size of it? Think your puss is solid gold and the fix is in. You think I can't touch you, don't you?"

She looked up at him, made a distasteful face. "Well, I'd certainly hope not."

"Hope again, bitch." He reached past her head to pull the door from her hand and push it shut. "I can touch you all I want. Anything you got I can fucking take and you'd better bygod believe it."

He lifted his hands to the level of her chest, gave her a grin so artificial and inappropriate it reminded her of a Halloween mask badly imitating some real-life creep, then pushed his hands forward to grab her breasts, pushing her up against the wall as he squeezed and ground them. Not the squeezes of a man seeking pleasure: a brutal, mechanical attempt to hurt, intimidate, and objectify.

Nan had long since realized that, quite apart from the money, there are certain advantages to being a whore. And sexual aplomb was one of them. Violations of person that would send what she thought of as "amateur women" into shock were business as usual for her and left her mind clear of all the panic and revulsion that clouded the process of coming to grips with what steps to take. She had experience with situations like this and her approach was: Keep your shirt on, wait for a break.

She started to say something, but the rogue agent suddenly slid his left hand up and across her chest to land his forearm against her throat, snapping her head back against the cool stone wall of the foyer. Anything she'd wanted to say or scream would have to wait until the pressure against her windpipe relaxed. The crush of his wide arm, which wouldn't leave a bruise: he wasn't exactly a virgin, either. He'd learned how to cover his tracks and his position protected him from anything she might do about him manhandling her.

Grinning right into her eyes with a flat raptor gaze that granted her all the tender human concern he'd give to the balky padlock on a cashbox, he reached down and insinuated his hand into the waist of her khaki skirt. There was something insidious about the way he hooked his fingers between her stomach and the fabric that made it seem like perverse grudge sex, a slow, hostile penetration. Then he jerked once and the skirt tore down from the rear zipper. He hooked it downward to clear her buttocks and fall at her feet. And I was worried about keeping my *shirt* on, Nan thought.

He relaxed the arm on her throat slightly, cat-and-mousing her, she realized. Might as well play with the nice kitty. "You must be out of your mind," she said calmly. "You know what my husband is going to do to you for this?"

"Is he?" His blank, plastered-on grin didn't alter a millimeter. "When he finds about you and pretty boy humping in the joint while he's waiting for you to show up and spread the hams for him?"

Nan laughed in his face. "So you think I'm crazy as you are? Screwing a Federal agent right there in Inmateville?"

Gaithers' face didn't change, but she could hear the triumphant laughter in his voice. "Vidotape doesn't lie. You don't think they tape all that stuff?"

That hit home, all right. Everybody seemed intent on turning her into archives lately. But she had an edge on him. She'd been there. "Well, then they'll have some nice tapes of my *not* screwing anybody in that office."

Shit. He'd hoped he had her and she would break down behind the bluff. But he glossed right past it, playing it by ear. "You mean on the rest of the tape that got lost somewhere?"

Ouch. Maybe he had something there. And it wouldn't be the sort of film a husband would give two thumbs up. She turned a look of biting, distilled scorn on Gaithers, who leaned against her implacably. "I'm not used to having guys go to such expensive team efforts to get in my pants. You must not get much."

"Get in your *pants*?" he asked in an arch tone you'd use on retardates. "How easy is that?"

He punched his right hand into her bare stomach just hard enough to make her expel a puff of air, then slid his fingers downward again in that same slow, suggestive glide until he had a fistful of the front of her panties. He waited a moment, holding the taut Lycra bunched in his hand, staring at her face. Then he jerked backwards, snatching them off.

She felt a burn across her right buttock where the thong cut before it broke, but it was nothing compared to what was boiling inside her head or the blue-hot blaze in her eyes. She was running a fever of plans to cope with this, trees of plays teeming in her brain, but he protected himself well, used his bulk and greater strength to bull her up against a wall. His forearm pushed her head against the stone of the foyer, could choke her or even kill her with more pressure. He gave her a taste of that, leaning in on her windpipe until she choked and gasped. That ghastly, sick smile.

He jammed his other hand between her legs, prodding up, trying to enter her and rummage around. She clamped her legs together with all her force, but felt the rough, invasive fumbling getting more intimate. She wasn't going to scream for help, let them find her like this. He knew that, didn't he? If things got much worse he'd have to release her throat and she'd squall for help, no doubt about it. But for the moment, she stared into his eyes from a foot away, felt his thick fingers grubbing for a hold.

He had a cold detachment about his actions, but that didn't stop him from wanting to just tear her open and plunge in. Not quite the time for that, though, was it? And shaking her down was more important than hosing her down. He withdrew his hand and leaned away from her a little, brought his finger up to pass under his nose, inhaling her bouquet like a cigar aficionado. Grinning

126

his tight, meaningless grin, pushing on her neck just enough, showing her that whatever she might fear, he had no problem making it a reality.

She turned her head sideways, enough to rasp out a whisper. "Can you get on with it? A couple of seconds out of my life is no big deal, but all this foreplay is boring."

He almost let her have for that one. Smash her in the face, her head backed up against the wall with no place to go. But where would that get him? He looked down at her, taking in the firm belly and sparse, trimmed pubis. He yearned to bend this gang whore over that expensive table and fuck her to pieces, but then he couldn't really control her and a disturbance would bring all those beaners in and who knows who'd end up shot? But still...

She seemed to guess where his thoughts were heading. "Excuse me, but that call I asked Martín to make? Who do you think he called?"

He looked at her closely, not a lovely experience, and gave a short laugh like a sea lion, "Bullshit, you lying slut."

"I set that up when I first came here," she told him, letting the gloating in her voice sell him on the truth of it. "I say that and use the name Raul and they call up cars full of guys with guns. Stick around and enjoy yourself, dickhead."

He slid his left hand back along her throat, digging his sleeve buttons into her skin as they moved past. He cupped her jaw, ground his hand upwards past her ear, and sunk his fingers into her short, damp hair. He pulled a hard handful of it, lifting her onto her toes. He put the finger he'd run up her cleft into his mouth and sucked it noisily.

"Just a little appetizer, whore. I'll be back for more after Gaspar cuts your ass loose. You people are filthy with money you don't deserve and you'd best figure out you'll be better off if I get enough of it to make me happy."

He jerked her top down around her waist and slapped her left breast forehand, backhanded the right one. Then snapped his arm to the side, throwing her to the floor, and turned to swagger out the front door. He pulled it shut violently, but before the slam came Nan was on her feet. Kicking the skirt off her ankles as she ran into the office/parlor off the main entry, she vaulted the wide walnut desk and snatched open the drawer. She grabbed the big

Smith and Wesson revolver, checking to make sure it was loaded as she ran back to the front door, jerked it open and sprinted out into the carport. The car outside was pulling away as she got to the gate and tore it open.

As she burst into the street she saw Gaithers' car disappear behind the walls and palm trees of her neighbor, so she continued running until she was in the street with a clear shot. Standing barefoot in the street in a two-handed shooter's pose, she aimed at the very tail end of the dark unmarked Ford Vic, but it was two blocks up by then, and starting to make a right at the corner. She had no shot worth the risk. There were kids playing on the yards up there, some boys jumping skateboards. She bent her elbows, bringing the gun up against her face as if to comfort her disappointment.

Just as what she could still see of Gaithers' car braked to a sudden stop. She jerked the gun forward again, squinting down the barrel and hoping he'd come back this way. She had a pretty good idea why he'd stopped. And sure enough, she could see him backing into the intersection. Trying to get around the Lincoln that Alfredo had blocked him with and was determinedly poking forward as he backed and filled, keeping him from getting away.

Way to go, Big Al, she thought. Shove him all the way back here in range. But she was already starting to see blowing the DEA asshole away in the street as a less than stellar idea, so she didn't run up the street after her target. She could see the front of the Lincoln now, and watched Gaithers give up on trying to get around it. He opened the door and stepped out, holding a badge up towards the dark eyes of the Lincoln. She couldn't hear his words, but he was obviously getting worked up. The Lincoln sat long, black and sinister in the sunlight without any motion at all.

She had the sights right on Gaithers, but didn't take the shot. He was screaming at the Lincoln, had his gun in his hand. What a moron.

And there it was, the sound she'd been waiting for. Sirens up the street, coming in fast. One cruiser pulled up beside Alfredo, two cops jumped out of it to cover Gaithers, ignoring the Lincoln in view of this big ugly guy brandishing a firearm. Who matched the description they'd gotten of the guy trying to force his way into a house. Gaithers was yelling, but she couldn't hear him over the sirens of two more cars that converged from the other two blocks and slid to stops, indicating wariness of the gunman beside the Crown Vic. I told you, she thought; cars full of guys with guns.

Nan watched, richly enjoying the sight of four cops cautiously approaching Gaithers with drawn guns, forcing him to get on his knees and put his hands behind his neck. He seemed to be getting really apoplectic, and she wished she could hear. She slowly lowered the gun but then spun and brought it up on point again when she caught movement from the corner of her eye. She stopped with the gun at waist level, recognizing the neighbor she'd always thought of as "that adorable young matron with the rotten kids". Who was standing frozen behind an expensive double-wide Valco stroller with both the spoiled little bastards staring at Nan.

She looked down and took due note of her top wadded around her waist, the torn panties caught on one ankle, the hefty gun in her hand. She waved the gun at the neighbor lady in a cheerful fashion, rolling her eyes in mock exasperation.

"How many times have I told that little scamp what would happen next time he landed my newspaper in the pool?"

She walked into the house without looking back, though she wished somebody was getting Miss Junior League on tape instead of her for once. Passing through the foyer, she almost bumped into a maid, who dropped an armful of clean linens while almost jumping out of her skin. She leaned over to snatch up a tablecloth and spin it around herself sari style just as one of Gaspar's goons walked in with an unholstered pistol. She calmed his shocked expression with a smile and handed him the Smith. "Could you put this back in the desk, Roberto?" She took a towel from the maid and rubbed her hair with her free hand. "I'm fine, thanks. Just needed a little exercise."

She started up the stairs and turned, "That guy doesn't get in here again, though, not even if has a handful of warrants and busload of judges. Let them batter down the door like those hotshots on Most Wanted."

She held out the towel and the maid came close to take it from her, staring at her like you'd regard a zoo predator that for some reason was outside the cages. She shot the girl a look that invited commiseration and said, in English she knew wouldn't be understood, "Now see, a real woman would have gotten really upset having some scumbag put his hands on her like that."

She started back up the stairs, tossing more English back over her shoulder. "My take? Drop in the bucket."

Chapter Thirty-Two

RayRay Mobley was reading the morning's Union-Tribune as Reach knocked on his office door and walked in. He took off his reading glasses and held up a second section page for the agent's inspection. "You read this here? Three wetbacks gettin' shanked up on the Donovan farm?"

"Gee, I must have missed that vital item. So what about it?"

"It's about me thinking I might've brilliantly identified the perps in the Gaspar assault case."

Reach stepped back in sheer awe. "My God, Sherlock, you've done it again."

Mobley tossed the paper in the trash. "What's this Sherlock shit? I look like anybody named Sherlock?"

"Well, he answered to 'Holmes'."

"Your mama answered to so many 'Homes' she could start her own subdivision."

"See, you should have said, 'integrated subdivision'. Get it?"

"Now I got cutie-face white boys teaching me how to do the dozens."

"Maybe I should ask Señora Gaspar." He said the name and title archly. "About your theories."

"Shit," Mobley snorted, "You think you should go ask her what time it is."

"It's time to get a few things figured out."

"If you're hinting that I somehow infiltrated prison dormitories and slashed three inmates to bloody shreds, I think I can safely say I don't recall having done so." Nan looked cool and relaxed in her sherbet green pantsuit with light copper-colored silk blouse and jade earrings. But she sat erect in her chair, barely touching the back, hands in her lap, looking at Sean Reach with detached courtesy. "Other than that, I've got nothing to say on the subject. As I believe I've mentioned."

Reach slumped behind the desk and looked at her like she was the last word he couldn't get in a crossword. He started to speak, but she crisply cut him off. "And I don't think it's a good idea to talk about anything else, if you take my point."

She was really infuriating like this, that finishing school diction and corporate kiss-off manner. He ran his fingers through his hair in frustration, eyeing her wearily from under his eyebrows.

Her facade was stiff and buttoned-down, though she was dying to run her fingers through that same hair, tease him out of his sulk just to see the flash of his teeth and spark of eyes.

The subtle play of emotions he didn't want to reveal was fairly intriguing. She could spend some time studying the nuances of his face, no doubt about it. He was fighting some inner battle, and she saw the exact moment when he gave it up. He leaned forward with his elbows on the desk, pointed his hands at her with his palms pressed together. "Hell with it. Just tell me one thing and I promise not to go there any more. Okay?"

"Fine with me. You know how hard it is for a woman not to chatter about her husband's business?"

He snorted but maintained his eyes on hers. "Yes or no. Please. Have I got any sort of shot at all?"

"You flatter me, Sean. I truly mean that. But I'd like for you to read something."

She pulled a sheaf of folded legal-sized copies out of her purse, pressed them flat on the desk, and pushed them to him. He noticed the stapled papers were folded to an interior page, prepared and waiting to be served on him.

"Just the highlighted clauses," she said softly.

He picked up the papers knowing he wasn't going to like them, but unsure what form that dislike would take. He read the sections highlighted in baby blue, noted the date on top of the page. He looked up at her and said, "So what does this mean?"

"Signed." She pointed to her precise, elegant signature. "Sealed. Delivered."

"Amended this week. He made you sign a fidelity clause? How gross is that?"

"I made him write it so I could sign it, actually."

He just stared. Here it was again. A passionate, beautiful woman. A prostitute, for Christ sakes. And she was more interested in legality than her own feelings. "Binding contract," he said, shaking his head in disgusted confusion.

"I told you. I'm a by-the-books type woman." She reached and tweaked the papers out of his hand, refolded them, then met his eyes in utter seriousness. "And I'm already booked."

He sat still, roiling with frustration, heated replies, and the urge to definitive motion across the desk and all over her, lips first. Finally he muttered in sad resignation. "Okay. I give up. You've got some really weird ethics."

"Well I've got so few to show, I have to jealously guard the ones I have."

"They don't include your hubby and his jolly crew committing multiple murders, though, correct? That's not as immoral as..."

She got him off the hook by saying, "I don't really have a lot of indignation left in me after twenty years in the 'ho' trade. If you want righteous rants you've got the wrong girl."

He gave her a look that combined admiration and gallantry. "Twenty years. Yeah, right. So you got your start when you were twelve?"

She returned a flat look that froze the killer smile off his face as the silence built around her. He had a sudden vision of how she must have looked at twelve: hair almost colorless, flawless pink skin, hint of budding breasts below the long, graceful neck, no hint of gangle. An unbidden flash of anger hit him, aimed at men who would take advantage of need and pain in order to pillage a kid like that.

Then a second shot hit him, the crawling hunch that his anger might conceal some jealousy. He stared back at her, helpless.

"But I manage to work up a little for bullies," she went on. "People who pick on the weak, attack other people because they can't defend themselves."

There was no question about the frustrated possessiveness behind his next remark. "Maybe your husband could give you some tips on that. Take you to work with him some day. You could take notes."

"Oh, they have work release for vice monsters? I hadn't realized." She glowed with guileless pleasure at the concept. "That's just so open-minded."

He couldn't keep his disgusted expression from sliding off into a small smile. But she wasn't through.

"I don't think he's much of a bully, actually. Especially lying there in the hospital with machines doing what his kidneys should do if they weren't all smushed-up. I think for a gangster he generally takes on people in his own weight class. If you guys had been in his league, he might have taken you. But you're a bigger, stronger gang, aren't you?"

"But he wasn't exactly defenseless, was he? If he'd had a cheaper defense, he'd probably be sitting here for fifteen years. Which would suit me fine."

"Well, it is nice to always know where I can get hold of him."

He laughed and flashed her two "peace" fingers. "Look, I'm sorry. I didn't mean to poke into your past."

"Well we all have one. And they all have rotten spots to smooth over." She cocked her head and examined him critically, shook her head. "Not you, though. You're so squeaky clean it makes my teeth hurt."

"Actually, a lot of people have commented on how spotless your sheet is."

"I've always been a very clean girl," she replied lightly. "It's something men seem to like when they're out being dirty."

Again the clash between the two aspects of this woman knocked him for a loop. There had to be some central principle that tied it together, but he couldn't see it. And she wasn't exactly playing show and tell. He stared at her for a moment, then leaned back from the desk. "May I ask? What exactly do you want? I mean like, from life?"

Nan's enigmatic smile was somehow sad and amused at the same time. "You really want to know, Sean? It's pretty silly, actually. Just a good night's sleep. That's what I most want to do in life. Sleep. Doesn't seem like much to ask, does it?"

His eyebrows went up and he pursed his lips. He realized that she was actually serious about that and grasped for a conclusion. "So you can dream?"

"God no," she said, and there was no humor in her voice whatsoever. "That's what keeps me from sleeping."

There was only one more straw to grab for, and he overcame his humiliation at even thinking of it. "That contract only runs until he gets out, doesn't it? When he hits the street, he goes his way and you're not married anymore. Right?"

"You're a fast reader. But that's such a long way down the road." Something hit her, made her chuckle. "Especially with you guys so hot to hang more time on him."

He felt like he'd snuck up and underhandedly touched the cheese, only to have the trap snap down on him, crush him breathless. Was that what she... He couldn't believe that, but it made sense. Anybody else would buy it in a minute. Jesus Christ on a crutch! He felt big, vital parts of him pull back inside, like a threatened snail retreating into its shell. He knew he should shut up and get her the hell out of here, but he'd better play one more card. Official business only, Ma'am.

"I don't know what you think I do here," he said stiffly. "But I don't have anything to do with sentencing or parole or any of that. I work crimes, have no authority over sentences."

Nan saw him harden up and frost over, realizing how he'd interpreted her remark about time. It gave her a pang to think of his feelings about such a betrayal, a deeper one to know what he would think of her, believing she was playing him to soften Gaspar's sentence. But it might be for the best to let it lie just like that. For everybody concerned. She felt an odd sensation of losing something she never had, like that itching amputated limb you always hear about. She submerged her feelings with an abrupt change of the subject.

"Well, I was wondering how much influence you had in other matters." She saw a dangerous, hurt look come over him and hurried on. "That guy Gaithers you sicced on me. He's really crossing the line. He's harassing me, hinting at bribes. He even came to my house and made sexual advances."

Oops, second time today she hit home without meaning to fire a shot. Agents who come on to witnesses in their homes. Ouch. She could see that he was stunned by his own guilt, so she went very blunt. "Can you get that creep off my ass? Or know who can?"

He stood up and looked at her impersonally for the first time in the interview. "Not my department. Try complaining to his supervisors at DEA."

He walked to the door without looking at her, held it open to signal an end to the session. As she walked by she gave him a shy smile, but he was stony-faced. "Or work it out yourself," he told her curtly. "Cut a deal."

He closed the door firmly behind her, let her walk out to the visit area on her own.

As soon as she was gone, a wave of recrimination came over him. That Gaithers was an asshole and had spotted her as fresh meat. Whoever did her husband could get around to her. It's got to be scaring her at some level. She acts brave, but she's really a fawn surrounded by wolves. And she asked me for help and I gave her the cold shoulder.

It made him feel impotent and irritated that he couldn't help her. Then it hit him. She saw him as one of the wolves.

Chapter Thirty-Three

The embittered ex-wife stood in the living room of the tastelessly re-decorated ex-house, holding the receiver of an ornate reproduction of an early French telephone. Chela Gaspar was surrounded, framed, and replicated by a dozen beveled mirrors, chrome glistened from almost every piece of loud-colored furniture. Velvet paintings representing the Virgin, Julio Iglesias, and Pedro Infante in a police uniform hung by British countryside idylls done in bright primaries. She had asked who was calling and was less than pleased with the answer.

"*You!* You call me here at my home, you whore! *Pues, chinga tu madre, pinche piruja hija de la chingada...*"

She stopped in mid-screech and jiggled the button. "*Bueno?* Hello? *Se colgó.*"

On the other end of the phone, Nan took her finger off the hangup button and looked at the slip of paper where Manny had written three numbers. She glanced across his desk at him and dialed again.

Magi sat at a white desk adorned with gingerbread and gilt accents, amid furnishings that might have come from the Little Girl's Fantasy Catalog. She picked up a Sponge Bob phone on the first ring.

"Hello, Chela's residence." Surnames were uncomfortable around the former Gaspar household. "What? Oh my *god*! Who is this?"

The same answer drew the same shock. She held the phone away from her face and screamed for her brother. "Juancho, *ven!* It's that woman. It's about Papi!"

Juan Jesus Gaspar bounded into the room, took one glance at Magi's traumatized face and snatched the phone.

"We can't talk to you," he said firmly. Then hung up.

Magi shrieked, "Juancho! It's Papi! She said he's been hurt!"

Juancho thought it over, already regretting the decisive action he'd been proud of. "Let's go tell, Mom," he told her. "She'll know what to do." But he didn't sound particularly convinced.

Nan glared at Manny's phone, carefully hung it up, and told him, "I guess I'm going to need the address."

"I don't know..." Manny said dubiously.

"You *do* know," Nan snapped. "Same house, right? I want..."

She stopped, shook her head at herself. "What am I thinking? Alfredo, drive me over there. Right now, could you, please?"

Chela was pitching a hissy fit in the front room. Nan waited her out, a shapely cordovan pump tapping on the floor. Alfredo continued to wish he wasn't there at all.

Chela's rant had colorfully covered the characters of her ex, his new bride, and his idiot driver, but now she brought it around to action. She stepped towards Nan threateningly, leaning forward from the waist, both fists clenched at her side. If she could see what all that raging is doing to her throat lines, she'd seek help, Nan thought.

"Get your ass out of my house right now, slut! Two-bit bimbo!"

Nan raised her hands to shoulder height and clapped them. The sharp report caused both kids, sitting in front of their dinners in the adjoining dining room, to jump, and shocked Chela to a momentary silence.

"Two bit?" Nan said low enough for the kids not to hear, but in a tone that set a startling contrast to the demure, silent pose she'd held since walking in. "They lined up to pay a thousand bucks, you sag-ass frump. I'm not a slut and I'm not a bimbo."

She took two steps toward Chela, who in spite of being larger, heavier and the home team, gave back. "That's 'escort', to you. I give your ex good service and he gives me good money. I heard what you gave him was pitiful and you came out of it with a pitiful payoff. After taking him off while he was down."

She pointed a red-tipped finger right between Chela's eyes, backing her further off. "The only difference between you and I is I'm better at it."

Having shut up the incumbent, Nan stalked into the dining parlor. The kids leaned back, trapped, eyes wide. Chela launched into action at this, chasing her into the room, gobbling in fury. "Get away from my children, bitch!"

Nan slid onto a chair sidesaddle and examined the distraught children. "What is it with you?" she asked in a stern but not unkindly voice. "I've only known your father six months and I care enough to visit him. You're his *family* for crissakes. His loved ones. Did you know there's a chance he might not make it?"

"Shut up! Shut *up!*" Chela screamed. She seemed on the point of pitching into Nan, but some instinct kept her from following through. "You don't know shit! You got no right to talk to my kids, you tramp."

Without looking at her Nan called sharply, "Alfredo!"

He entered the room diffidently, abashed by the setting and his boss's fiery ex. Chela looked at him and snorted, almost spit. *"Pinche indio cabrón!* What do *you* want?"

"How do you shut her up?" Nan asked in a tone of scientific inquiry.

"Nobody ever found out," the big bodyguard answered.

"I believe it," Nan replied, then pointed at something she spotted where the carpeting gave way to the kitchen's tiled floor. "Whose is that?"

Magi saw that she was pointing at a dog dish and exclaimed, "It's Cesar's. You leave it alone!"

"The poodle," Alfredo told her. "Really stupid one."

"Where is he?"

"In the garage at meals because he's a pain in the ass."

"Works for me. Put her in there, too."

Alfredo looked at Chela. "I... uh..."

"Please, Alfredo. Thank you."

He scooped Chela up, kicking, and cursing, and managed to get her out of the room. A door slammed somewhere, muffling her squawks and a frantic yapping. Nan turned to the two scared kids.

She spoke in a soft, soothing voice, leaning forward earnestly and putting every inch of her serene, gracious face behind it. "Don't be afraid. I'll just be a minute."

She looked at them, saw very little calming, went on, "I don't know how much you know about your dad, but he's in intensive care. On machines."

Juancho stared at her pugnaciously. "We're not allowed to talk about him."

Nan's voice was like a ruler slapping into a teacher's hand. "That's just sick."

She turned to the little girl, a nice-looking kid at the point of tears. She spoke soothingly and gently. "Your father is unconscious right now. Because he was brutally beaten. He might be all right, or he might not. He might not be alive tomorrow."

Magi dissolved into sobs and the boy was obviously shaken. Nan went on in the same gentle tone, like talking to skittish horses. "Your father loves you very much. Look around at everything he's given you. Would you really let him die alone, never see him again? Is that how you want it?"

"My mother says..." Juancho's voice faltered at her glance.

"Forget it!" she said sternly. "Listen, you're old enough to start being a man. Your father's in prison: you need to step up and take care of your family."

She leaned closer across the table, speaking very quietly, and they leaned closer to hear. "You can't let anybody tell you what to feel about people. You love your father?"

Magi's cheeks were streaked and her whole face flushed. "Yes! Of course I do. But he..."

Nan pulled a fleecy white kerchief with intricate blue monogram from her purse and handed it to the child. She paused while the kid wiped her face and went on in a tone as gentle as any Madonna. "Honey, let me tell you something it can take a whole lifetime to learn. You too, kid. It's so hard to find anybody to love in this world. And if they love you back? It's a miracle."

Even Juancho was wet-eyed by then. Magi stared at Nan like she was a visitation from outer realms.

"So if you love somebody, you don't drop it just because they mess up. It's too precious. If you don't love people you end up with nobody. You end up being nobody."

Shakily, Magi asked her, "You've seen him?"

"Three times. They make it hard to get in, takes all day. Then maybe he can't even wake up."

Juancho, teetering between emotion and defiance, asked, "Why do you care?"

Nan shrugged and gave him a half-smile that he'd remember for years. "Because I like the guy, okay? Also, I'm his wife and he needs me to stand by him right now."

She swept the table with her gaze, soft but booking no excuses. "But he needs you a lot more."

Magi burst out again. "Oh, *Papi*! Juancho, we have to do something! What can we do?"

Juancho had made his call. Nan saw character in the boy, thought he'd stick with what he said. Which was the very staunch declaration, "We're going to go see him."

Nan hit him with a hundred watt smile that he felt all the way down. "Attaboy. Good for you."

She stood and pulled a card out of her purse. "Here's my personal number. I have yours, so..."

"I'd better give you my cell number," Juancho said quickly.

"Got you," Nan nodded. "I'm going to set this up and call you. Don't worry about getting out there. If nothing else I'll send a taxi."

She set the card on the table and stepped back, looking at them huddling together with scrambled feelings. "It's the right thing, kiddos. I promise. Stick to it and you'll always be glad you showed up when it counted."

She spun away without another glance or goodbye and called towards the garage. "Alfredo! Put a leash on her without getting bit. We're out of here."

Two armed state cops made a process out of examining Nan's paperwork before admitting her to a room with no picture window and much less in the way of electronic gear and exotic plumbing. Gaspar lay shrunken, but conscious. His head still had a turban of white plaster and gauze.

"Yo, Humpty Dumpy," Nan greeted him. "Somebody to see you. Let's spruce up a little."

She moved over to him, touched her fingers to his lips. "This is another no-talk deal, sport. Save it for your visitors. We've got plenty of time for you to bore me about your operation."

She pulled a brush from her purse and tidied his hair. She wiped his chin with the sheet, arranged his pajama shirt. She eyed her work then bent for a quick kiss on his forehead. He stared at her, trying to figure it out.

Done, she nodded to the guard standing in the doorway, who admitted the children. Nan had been watching for it, so she caught the lift that ran through him, the quickened breath and tingle. "They looked so pitiful hitch-hiking we just had to pick them up and bring them along."

She tried to slip away as the kids tentatively approached the bed, but he grabbed her wrist and held her. Getting the old grip back, she thought happily.

"Juan Jesus," he said in a rusty, weak voice. "Magdalena. This is Nan. My wife."

Nan slipped from his grip and headed for the door.

"They already met their wicked stepmother. Didn't you? I'll be outside when you're ready to go."

The kids continued their gingerly approach to the bed. Gaspar, greatly moved, spread his arms and Magi ran into them, sobbing into his chest. Juancho moved up behind, reached to clasp his father's hand.

Nan looked from the hallway, allowing herself to experience her feelings at what she'd accomplished. She kept her eyes on the reunion as the door slowly closed.

Nan sat in one of the awful plastic/steel chairs, reading a small hardback by Witold Gombrowitz. Alfredo sprawled over two chairs across the aisle, watching a particularly overwrought soap opera on a wall-mounted television. She saw a nurse open a door to the ward and show the kids into the waiting area. She marked the book and slipped it into her purse as the pair approached. Alfredo gave Juancho an inquisitive glance and the boy returned a thumbs-up, smiling.

Magi stepped up to Nan before she could stand, looking straight in her face. "I want to ask you," she said.

"Please do," Nan told her.

"Do you love my father?"

Oh, no, not the mouths of babes, Nan thought. She said, "It's not that simple a thing, honey."

"But you're his friend, right?" Juancho stepped behind the girl and spoke with a bit of attitude. "Is *that* simple enough for us children to understand?"

Nan smiled at him. "That's kind of complex, too, actually. But yes. Whatever else, I'm a friend."

"But none of that matters." She stood up and looked down at them. "What matters is that you came. It's wonderful. You could make the difference between how well he does in there. I mean it. Write to him, visit him. Okay?"

She started to follow Alfredo towards the door, but Juancho stepped in front of her. "Nan? Thank you."

She hit him with another sunshine smile and tousled Magi's hair. "Hey, no charge."

Nan waved out the window as Alfredo backed out of the driveway. Juancho and Magi waved back just as the door to their house opened and a furious Chela emerged to scowl at kids and adults alike, then turn and stomp off as the car ghosted down into the street and pulled away.

Nan sat, savoring the day for a few blocks-- and not without some personal sadness--before Alfredo broke the silence. "I can't believe you sometimes," he said wonderingly. "Most of the time. You know how much it hurt him, being split from his kids? How hard he fought it?"

"Who wouldn't?"

"When he hooked up with you..."

"Now don't say 'hook'," she chided playfully. "I'm living all that down these days."

Alfredo chuckled. "What I thought he was doing was closing the door, you know. Shut it all off, start something new."

"Maybe he was. Perfectly understandable."

The big henchman shook his head in wonder. "You're something else, lady. *Otra onda.* And you look like such a fragile little creampuff."

"It's a look that sells," Nan shrugged.

"Then you just march in and pull it off when Manny couldn't. And the way you came in on that thing at the farm. Man... boom, boom, boom, and it's all over."

"But it's not," she said flatly. "And you know it. All over."

Alfredo didn't like the sound of that, but it was probably true. "Well, we got rid of the rats in our shop. And up in the slam they'll think twice next time."

"But there'll be a next time," she went on relentlessly. "And we'll be up against people who thought twice. They got our message. Wasn't that massacre at the high school last year one of their messages?"

"Yeah, but..."

"I already told you. We have to make them stop."

"But there's so many of them. It'd take an army."

"That's what it's going to take," she said in a voice so level and pitiless that it made him look around over the seat at her.

"We're gonna have an army?"

"You can't have a war without one."

"If any other *morra* said that," Alfredo said after a somber pause. "I'd think she was a *loca*. But you..."

"What?"

"I'm just glad we're on the same side."

"Thanks, Alfredo. So am I. When we get home, would you have a drink with me?"

"Thanks. Maybe a small tequila."

Chapter Thirty-Four

Gaspar had dozed off, recovering pretty well but still weak. Nan stood over him as he lay limp, examining the leg that stuck out from under the blanket. A deep gouge there, sort of spackled over. The closer she looked at him these days, the more damage she turned up. It was like a disaster movie on the installment plan. He was a tough guy, with a lot of drive. But a thorough beating like this can pound the manhood out of a guy his age. She wondered how fully he'd ever really recover. Lost in that kind of thought, she didn't hear the light steps behind her. Didn't know there was somebody standing at her shoulder until she heard the little sour sound he made with his lips.

She swung around to see the Gaithers standing a foot from her, looking at her like a lizard watching a fly. He said, "Tell him not to get too used to the comforts here. At taxpayer expense. He's going back up to the joint next week."

"I've got this great idea," she said levelly. "Why don't you get out of this room right now and don't ever come near me again unless there's a witness present?"

"I've got an even better idea. Why don't you drop by my office where I have a tape recorder, then we can visit a few safe deposit boxes nobody else knows about, then you can drop down on those nice soft knees and start making me happy?"

"Let me put it to you a little stronger. If I ever see your face again you're going to end up in court and this will just be one of several incidents mentioned. The maid heard you at my house and Mobley asked me why I was so upset after the first time I saw you. I was just too frightened from your threats to come forward until now. How's that sound as a career move?"

"You're in no position to get snotty, Mrs. Drugdrop. This whole thing's coming down and there's nothing you can do about it but try to buy your way out of the wreck. He's going right back up where this shit can happen to him again. In fact, when the word starts getting around how he got some of his privileges and why he got stomped, I can guarantee he'll get more rough treatment and more guys rolling over on him. And I haven't even started with you. You have no idea what DEA can do to your house and privacy, do you?"

"Oh, I've gotten a few hints lately," she snapped.

"Not all you've been getting," he insinuated with an oily tone. "But I'm not an old lady like Mobley and you can't fuck me stupid like Reach. And don't forget I've still got tapes of you and him."

She looked at him sideways for a second, then stroked her husband's chest protectively. "You're going to just keep at this until you get what you want, aren't you?"

"Wouldn't you? You don't seem like the type of bitch that stops short of getting it all."

"He's badly hurt. I don't want him attacked again. I don't want my life being in an uproar."

"Then come across. Duuuh."

"This has got to stop. Look, what if I give you the name and location of somebody who's probably more central to this stuff than my husband is anymore? A guy who's been running the coke business and might have put this hit on Gaspar to take control? All you'd have to do is pick him up and shake him because he's got a lot to hide."

"Drug dealers kind of do."

"Especially drug dealers who like little boys."

He thought that one over. He'd known she'd cave in. And nothing she could do would stop him from taking her down anyway. She'd figured that out. "So what's his name?"

"They call him Psycho, but I can find out his real name. And I can tell you where to find him. I doubt you know anything about this guy. He's the connection from the south and now he's moving in on California. I'll give him to you. And we can talk about some sort of payoff. I just want myself and my husband to be left in peace."

"We can do that. When are you coming up with the information?"

"As soon as they move him back up the prison. I think he's safer in the sick bay up there than down here in town."

"Sure. That'll buy you off. But I still think we should belly up some. Seal the deal, you know. And not next week, either."

"Okay, that's enough of that. I want you out of here right now. And don't come back to talk to him until he's back up at Donovan."

"That's what you want, is it?"

"Yes." Her voice sounded like a pencil breaking. "That's what I want."

She reached behind her and grabbed the nurse's alarm, started a staccato finger dance on the button.

Gaithers started to move towards her, something dangerous moving in the depths of his opaque eyes. But there was already a nurse at the door, the heavy-set black woman in her forties, Nan was glad to see. Gaithers waved a dismissive hand at her when she asked what was wrong, but Nan immediately blurted, "Can you do something about this guy? He's making lewd remarks and advances, right here over my husband, threatening me. It's making me ill."

The nurse took in Nan's pitiful vulnerability and Gaither's aggressive pose and immediately turned hard and directive. "Sir, could you come out of the patient's room immediately?"

Gaithers smirked, showed her his badge, turned back to Nan. The nurse barked out, "Officers!" and the two cops from the prison were on their feet and in the doorway immediately.

"Please help me," Nan said, tossing in a little emoting. "Get this guy away from me."

The cops moved forward and the nurse faded from the door. Nan heard her call to the nursing station, demanding security. Gaithers, predictably, didn't submit to the cops graciously. In fact, whatever he said caused one of them to slap the badge out of his hand. They scissored in on him, grabbed his elbows and frog-marched him out of the room. He struggled in silent fury, not bothering to call out his office since they'd ignored the badge, but Nan heard him start cursing as they moved him down the hall towards the elevator.

The doors whooshed open and she heard more voices join the scuffle. She heard Gaithers loudly say, "Okay, okay. I'm leaving. Can you get me my damn badge?" Then they were gone. For now, she thought. I need a little longer-term plan.

She was looking at Gaspar's wan face as she thought. When his eyes opened, she was looking right into them. She was startled, but smiled warmly.

"You're too much," he said in a hoarse rasp.

"I'd better be. Things are heating up."

Gaspar nodded, but the admiring gleam stayed in his eyes. He cleared his throat and managed to speak fairly clearly. "Who's Reach?"

"He's that Fed. Did I mention he's adorable? One look at this guy and any woman in her right mind would get moist in the eyes. And what not."

"Is he why you got the contract rewritten?"

"Yeah. Sorry, but he got to me big time. I go weak in the knees every time I'm around him. How do you like me now?"

"Better every single day, *nena*."

She sniffed sardonically and reached two fingers to close his eyes, shutting off the fond approval shining out of them. "Sleep," she said.

Chapter Thirty-Five

Maru's head lolled back on the folded washcloth on the rim of the tub. From her double chin to the tips of the toes on her right foot she was submerged under sparkling, fragrant peaks of foam. An empty pint of Añejo floated somewhere in the suds. A CD player above the bidet poured out sappy Marisela and Lucia Mendez hits. She snored softly, a cute little snorkling gurgle.

She still felt a little guilty about this being the only vice she really practiced anymore, but she lived for her afternoon soak in hot water spiked with her collection of scented bubblebaths and costly emollients. Sometimes a little pot, as well, but nothing stronger. After a lifetime of tricking, muling and smalltime dealing, she was well aware not only of which way lay madness but fairly precisely how far.

The special pink phone she allowed in the bathroom during her soaks chirruped out a few notes of Julio Yglesias. Her head snapped forward and she spluttered as she kissed the cloudscape surface of the suds. Wiping bubbles from her eye with one hand, she flipped the phone open, squinted at the displayed number and grinned merrily. About time you got back in touch, *chica*.

"If you've gotten tired of that marriage craziness," she said without preamble, "you can always come crawling back to mama."

As she listened, her hand snaked out to the dish of See's chocolates on top of a stack of fluffy pink towels. Okay, two vices. But she thought of them as a sort of package. "I heard!" she exclaimed in delighted horror. "It was on the *tele* and everything. You need to fire your bodyguards. Get Kevin Costner."

She listened again, the tip of her tongue eviscerating a coconut cream with surgical precision. "Oh, so you want something. Never just call up to shoot it with old pals. Just kidding. Whatever you need, *güerita*. You know that."

She stretched languorously, bringing her feet up to the gleaming chrome controls of her retreat. With impressive dexterity she eased the tap over and cracked the drain. Fresh hot water flowed in, replenishing her bliss. She squirmed in the flow of warmth, but looked askance at the phone.

"Sorry, but messed-up tattoos aren't really much of an ID anymore. It's like saying a guy had on a sideways Raider's cap."

She gaped at what Nan was saying, then broke out laughing. "Well, that's different enough somebody might remember. Gross. All over? Full sleeves, the works?"

She reached for another candy then choked with laughter. "*A poco*? And you didn't *look*? Let me guess; maybe stripy, like a candy cane?"

She leaned back on the padded tub edge and fiddled around with the drain handle. "Well, next time take a look, will you? Professional interest. Yeah I'll put out the word."

She glared at the phone, injured. "Of course. Everybody. Both sides of the border, whoever we know. We can't have people running around killing kids eating ice-cream. It's un-American. And bragging about tats on their *pinga* but not even giving a peek."

She tugged a corner of a towel, but not carefully enough to avoid spilling the chocolates on the carpeting. Rolling her eyes in annoyance, she dabbed at the sweat on her forehead, but spoke seriously to Nan. "Listen to me, girl. I know you're tough and take care of yourself. But you're in some deep *caquita* now, right up to your expensive ass. Watch your back, hear?"

She smiled affectionately at the phone and made a kissing sound. "Who loves you, 'ho? Don't be such a stranger."

Chapter Thirty-Six

Nan stood to leave, smoothed the lap of her soft fawn skirt, and looked down at her husband. She'd learned that a muted, businesslike look worked best with the Sharp staff and the guard detail. She was all earth colors today, with a dark cinnamon merino blazer and a parchment blouse buttoned right up to her throat. The autumnal effect emphasized the reddish highlights in her brown wig. Beautiful natural hair that she'd bought while envisioning some third world girl running around sporting a russet stubble while growing the next crop.

She motioned to the wall, now bare of life support gadgets and displays. "I sort of liked you as Cyber-Gameboy."

Gaspar smiled up at her. He was still gaunt and his head looked like hell, but the vigor was returning to his look and presence. "Yeah, I'm all better."

"I looked all over for a 'Get well quick so you can go back to prison' card, but they just didn't have anything."

"I'll be glad to get back to the joint," he grumbled playfully. "Better set of people up there. And trustees can sneak me a smoke or decent food now and then."

"Ah, yes, your trusty sidekicks." She picked up her Giachio purse in nutmeg suede, continentally slim but big enough to conceal the Sig Sauer pistol she'd left outside with Alfredo but was generally never without these days. "So, the prison hospital in three weeks?"

She leaned over and kissed him quickly on an unravaged portion of his forehead. "We've got to quit meeting like this."

"I'll be there a couple more weeks," he said patting her awkwardly on the flank. "Then maybe we can get back to having conjugals."

"Well, I really have missed that luxuriant Boneyard ambience. So be a good boy, get well and you might just get lucky."

"I think I've burned up all my luck for this year." He nabbed her eye just enough to make it clear what he thought was his luckiest break yet. And she smiled to acknowledge the compliment.

"Okay, then. *Hasta la vista,* baby."

"Oh, yeah, I forgot," he said quickly. She'd noticed he always thought of last minute things when she started to leave. Poor guy, sitting here with no company but bored nurses, unsympathetic cops and network channels.

"The kids will be coming up to see me as soon as I'm cleared for visits up there."

"Ah, that's wonderful. They're great kids, Gas."

"Yeah, they are. But listen, they were kind of hoping you might give 'em a ride up."

"Of course. Or Alfredo can just..."

"No. I mean, you know..." he turned his hands palm-up and raised them to her. "They want to ride up with you. I mean, if that's okay."

Nan stood unmoving, one hand on the doorknob for so long he wondered if she was all right. Then she spoke so softly he barely heard her. "That's so much more than just okay."

He shrugged it all off, "They think you're cool. Want to be around you more."

She seemed to lock up again, just for a moment. Then said. "Whoa. I won't even try to respond to that."

Suddenly she laughed, an open, girlish laugh he'd never heard before. Her eyes were shining. "Oh yeah, any time," she blurted. "They want to come over for a swim, go shopping, hang out and let me watch them be kids, I'm there for it. As much as they can get away with."

She turned and pushed through the door. He heard her heels tap away down the hall.

She was pretty surprised at herself as she crossed the lobby of Scripps. She'd had a sudden vision in the elevator; sitting poolside as frolicking youngsters laughed, ate birthday cake, flopped bellybusters and squirted waterguns. Gaspar somehow there, too, smiling from a floating lounge chair.

You missed the Budget Rent-a-Spaniel, she smirked inwardly. But there was no denying that some alien feeling had welled up in her, something she didn't recognize or identify. Maybe I should check myself in, have that looked at, she thought. Probably one of those toxic normal feelings.

Chapter Thirty-Seven

It had been a deep, rich rush for her, chatting with little Magi on the phone. Children had never been a part of her life, something rather trenchantly enforced at times, and she'd never felt the urge to be around them, much less have them on her hands. So the tug exerted by Gaspar's kids--her stepkids, technically, right?--was a sort of sneak attack, though she'd enjoyed it so far. She was starting to see why most women were nuts enough to want to have children. They got to you on a different wavelength from the rest of humanity, didn't they just?

Kids, she reminded herself acerbically, who belonged to a hostile bitch who hated her guts and a man who'd paid her to marry him. Not exactly The Brady Bunch. But there was no denying that Gaspar's children, who she had originally approached as something of his that he needed and she was in a position to fetch for him, had sneaked into her affections. It hadn't been hard for Magi to convince her to pick them up in the cadmium yellow Mitsubishi Eclipse that Gaspar had stored in one of the three garages at her new house.

The first time she'd seen the car, carefully up on blocks with the tires and battery removed, she'd been surprised, first that a guy like Gaspar would buzz around in a little sports car, then that a mob guy with big bucks would choose a Japanese car instead of some exotic that would draw stares at nightclubs and Evil Drug Asshole conventions. By now she'd started to see it as an expression of the man. He liked a little fun, had an eye for beautiful lines, and wasn't ostentatious or insecure.

Magi, and to a greater degree Juancho, missed the little car, which their mother couldn't drive since it was equipped with futuristic impediments like a gearshift and clutch pedal. She'd begged her to bring it when she picked them up after the party and drove them up to Donovan. She was actually interested in driving it herself, but had presented objections to Magi just for the fun of the girl's banter and wheedling, zigzagging from adult-like behavior to giggle fits on a dime. So she'd had the guys charge the battery and put it in, replace and fill the tires, give it a tank of gas and run it enough to be sure it was ready to romp.

153

The kids wouldn't know, but giving them the ride they wanted had required her to sacrifice something she highly valued. She'd been militantly non-enrolled all her life and saw having a driver's license as a major concession to the world that wanted to fingerprint everybody alive, give them an ID number, and keep tabs on their pursuits. Three times she'd started to make an appointment with Motor Vehicles and backed out, but had finally taken the plunge. The prints, the picture (she was so dolled up for the shot that it amounted to a disguise), the registry with Them.

As she'd stepped away from the little line where you stood under the eye of the Big Bro Polaroid, she'd broken into laughter. The clerk looked up, but she waved him off, smiling. She didn't think irony was allowed in government buildings and this was a good one: after thirty years of outlaw anonymity she finally had marriage and driving licenses to make her a proper citizen because of her association with organized crime.

So she pulled into the parking lot of the Chuck E. Cheese in Chula Vista behind the wheel of a sleek, low-slung road toy, flaunting bright yellow driving glasses to match the newly-waxed gleam of the Eclipse. And a pale yellow knit dress with a red leather jacket from Tijuana she planned to ditch before presenting herself at the prison hospital visiting area. Her wig was sleek and black as the leather upholstery. She pulled across the packed lot in front of the pizza/pizzaz parlor, rolled down her window and stuck her hand out as a signal to Alfredo, trailing her in the Lincoln full of gunsels. The kids' cousin's birthday party would be breaking up any minute, giving them plenty of time to get up to Donovan for visitation hours.

His window whisked down, but he had to lean out to see her in the low yellow car. She also had to sort of scrunch down and peer upward.

"Look, you've got air-conditioning; why don't you park over there by the door where they can see you? I'm going to pull into the shade. It'll be an oven in this little thing in five minutes."

Alfredo peered out the window, squinted around the lot glaring with noon sun and glinting with reflections from chrome and glass. "If you can find any shade."

She'd already spotted her shelter. "That little alley thing there, where the dumpsters are. Honk when they come out and I'll pull out where they can see me. Think they'll spot this paint job?"

She pulled over to the recessed loading/dumping dock between Chuck E's and the Dollar Store and backed into the shade. She pushed the glasses up into her hair, turned off the motor, and turned the radio up. KSDS didn't come in that well this far south of downtown, but she wanted to catch the rest of Marian McPartland's piano jazz show. That old babe sitting there chatting, doing duets with Chick Corea: amazing. She kept her eye on the Lincoln as she listened to that pair skylarking around on the keyboards but didn't think anything when the Suburban with opaqued windows stopped behind it. One more "ChulaJuana" clown looking for a place to put his oversized gas-guzzler. But when the second one pulled in front of the car and stopped, blocking her view of Alfredo, she didn't like it one bit. Then two guys stepped into the mouth of her shaded alley and she liked it even less.

The long black coats and mirror shades were bad enough, but worse was the way they were just rolling right up on her. They came in here for her, no doubt about it. The shades and coat delayed her recognition for a second. The younger skinny one was just one more homeboy, black *cholo* chic all over him. But then she recognized the bigger, older one with black wool shirt buttoned at the top but open the rest of the way down, Scarface T underneath, black sag-n-bag trousers. It was the guy from that mess at the mini-mall, called himself Psycho. Not good.

She smiled nicely at these two fine young men and slipped her hand into her purse, reaching for the grips of her Sig Sauer 232. Immediately the younger kid--the driver from the mall, she realized--opened his coat by raising the AK he'd worn it to conceal. The gun had no stock and the end of the barrel had been sawed off to further shorten it. Full thirty shot magazine, though. Pointed right at her face by somebody who would have absolutely no compunction against turning it on and leaving it on until she was hamburger from her chest up. She laid the purse down and put both hands on the steering wheel. She looked past Syco and TeenGunner to the Lincoln as her only source of help: it was still cut off and she had a feeling what Alfredo was seeing through his windshield wasn't that much different from what she was looking at. Syco motioned for her to get out of the car.

Which was the last thing she wanted to do, especially not without her purse. But she knew better than to reach for anything. There was nowhere to run, nobody to call to, no jump on the drop. She carefully stepped out of the car and faced them from behind the open door. Syco walked up to the car with the measured threat of a big cat. The kid was keeping her right in his line of fire. Syco stepped forward, raised one foot and kicked her door shut. She jumped back to avoid being hit by the door and was suddenly face to face with the guy again. Caught unarmed in an alley with a damaging man and no guards, no sirens, no cavalry. On the other hand, it wasn't her first time in such a position, was it?

In spite of the nastiness of her previous conversation with Syco, her main thought was that it was a kidnapping. Perfect way to snatch the kids, and they'd be the perfect leverage over Gaspar, wouldn't they? But his first words cleared all that up for her, "It's now time we know us better."

Nan gave him a long, cool look while her mind shifted into overdrive, running odds, spotting outs, looking for an angle or edge. She stayed a hair shy of haughty as she told him, "I think I know enough already."

She caught the flicker in his dead eyes as he stepped within arm's reach of her and said, "What you know about me?"

She saw a small opening and shifted towards it. A major chink in a lot of tough guys' armor: identity. "Well, nothing you'd want to hear. What do you want?"

"Nothing." He had that almost poutish layoff so many gangbangers did these days. He motioned towards the suburban, and she quickly pictured the guns inside, the stained mattress on the floor. "Just a little ride. It'll be fun."

"Are you talking about fucking me?" A whore's kind of advantage she'd learned long ago. They start coming on, you name a price and they generally shut up. They're getting cute, you slam the nasty right in their face and watch *them* get inadequate..

Syco's lips barely twitched, a razor-thin smile. "That is surprise you?"

"Well, a little." Here's where the identity judo will either work or it won't, she thought. "I heard you don't go that way."

156

"What you're talking about?" He didn't quite grasp the phrase, but had his suspicions.

"Well, they're saying you mostly like guys. Little boys, actually. Lots of priors, and they've got a warrant on you for it."

There was a part of Syco--a deep-seated part where the beast that had clawed him up to leadership among tough, sociopathic killers lived--that stirred at that, roared for bloody thrusts. But there was also the chilled control that kept the reins on until the time came. He did pretty well at making one word slide out dripping icy menace. "They?"

"You know." She made a helpless motion that referenced their mutual victimization by the forces of law. "The cops. The Feds."

"They lie." He ran a stony, searching regard over her face. "I'm not *joto*. Not a faggot. You will see."

"If you say so, tiger. But they have this file full of evidence on you, show it around to everybody. They're looking for you all over town, talking to the Mexican cops about you. So maybe they're lying. But all those statements from victims. Photos of poor little boys..."

"There's not little boys!"

She detected the slightest cracking in his voice. A pressure point that could blow this whole thing up, one way or the other. Maybe he'd pull a gun and she could make a try for it. Maybe he'd lose it enough to give her a shot at his balls. Opening on deuces, but it beat getting into that car. She glanced at his teenaged gun-bearer, a question in her eyes.

She didn't expect anything back from JoJo and didn't get anything: he thought Syco was the bomb and knew for a fact the guy went for women. A lot. But Syco read the glance the way she wanted him to. This wasn't just between two people, it was gossip abroad already. And maybe the Feds really were doing this thing to him. Those bastards. He said, "Who is 'they'?"

"That special agent out of Washington. He's after your ass and telling everybody about you humping little kids."

"I don't fuck boys!" he snapped. First heat of any kind in his voice, Nan was glad to note. Then, out of the corner of her eye, she saw the bad situation about to go totally and completely to hell.

Magi and Juancho had slipped out of their dippy cousin's pizza party, eager to go visit their father. They spotted the Lincoln immediately, and assumed that the two Suburbans were some sort of escort their *Papi* had sent along. Juancho smiled fondly; he missed Gaspar's muscle pack, rides to school in the bulletproof Suburban listening to Martín and Lico clown around up front. He headed for the limo immediately.

But Magi had her hopes set on a spin in the Mazda, especially if she could take a turn around where her cousins and their stuck-up *fresita* friends could see her. She looked around for the sportster as she followed Juancho towards the cluster of gang cars. And saw it! No missing the loud yellow paint job over in that driveway. She skipped towards the Mazda happily and Juancho turned to fall in behind her. And there was Nan, waiting for them, talking to some guys who looked like minor-league soldiers in their Dad's mysterious firm.

Nan's brain, already revving so fast she was in danger of slipping the clutch, went over the redline at the sight of the kids approaching. What she came up with was that there was no way to stop them from blundering into this psychotic picnic, but she might be able to save them with a sacrifice bunt. She leaned into Syco's face and laughed with a scorn bitter enough to remove enamel, "You're going to need more guns than this to get me into that van with you, you baby-raper I wouldn't let your tiny, AIDS-covered dick anywhere near me."

Syco was obviously fighting the impulse to blow her away, and she figured her last option would be to kick him and run towards the end of the alley. If he shot her, great. It would warn the kids and draw cops. But he snaked his hand out with shocking speed, grabbed her by the throat, and spat into her face. "I will show you how much queer am I, fucking cunt."

Suddenly JoJo heard Magi and Juancho coming across the pavement and spun to confront them. Syco caught his move and looked away from Nan. Who immediately sneered, "Oh, I can see. Top dollar piece on your hands and you get interested in a couple of little kids. You animal."

Syco finally lost his control of the situation. His free hand came up and across, the knife edge of his fingers taking her across the temple and knocking her off her feet. "I will show to you an animal!" he screamed. JoJo was surprised at the way his hero lost his cool, but kept his eye on the two kids, who had frozen, aghast at the attack on Nan. Syco turned to face them and actually smiled. A smile which sent Magi into a screaming fit. She jumped from foot to foot for a second, yowling in horror and fear.

Juancho hesitated only a second, then plunged past his sister, straight at the two assailants. JoJo was impressed. For a rich boy, this one's got some *cojones*.

As he ran, he yelled at Magi to go get help, call the police. Magi stopped bouncing around and took off at top speed for the door of Chuck E's, yowling bloody murder. She saw her Uncle Dagoberto step out the door and headed for him. JoJo looked after her and saw her run into a cluster of well-dressed Hispanic adults with kids. Women swept Magi inside along with the other kids, two of the men had cell phones out and were yelling into them. Two more started approaching the dumpster bay, walking carefully, but with their arms in positions that suggested they might have handguns somewhere about their persons.

Lying on the ground, Nan heard Magi screaming for help and grinned through the pain that clenched the side of her head. Smart girl. If you can't make a play, make a scene.

Juancho tried to rush past JoJo, who was so intent on what was happening at the pizza joint entrance that he just snapped out a hand, palm first, to his chest, pitching him off his feet. Juancho hit the pavement with a jolt, his head snapping down on the pavement to fill his vision with sparkles. But he was immediately up, charging towards Syco. Oh, no, Nan screamed silently, Don't!

The kid launched himself at Syco, his face contorted with hatred and fear. Syco didn't even pay much attention, just batted his grasping hands away and punched him right in the eye. Juancho went down hard, his vision again exploding with jitter and flare.

JoJo called some gang slang to Syco, who took a few steps out onto the lot to see for himself. Nan rolled over twice and started crawling under the car, head first. It was too low for her to get under, but she found something that wasn't hot and wrapped her arms around it. She looked back over her shoulder at Juancho, who hadn't moved. She had to do something about that, but was at a bit of a loss.

What Syco saw in the parking lot wasn't good at all. People all over the lot were staring, several tough-looking guys were moving in, probably packing heat. He could hear a siren, still distant. Then another one. He figured they had about two minutes before things turned into a shootout. He looked back at Nan, curdling inside at the thought of delaying his extraction of revenge, but she was under the car. JoJo looked at him meaningfully. Time to go?

Yeah, *chinga su madre*, it was time to fucking go.

Alfredo and Magi's uncle Dagoberto were talking to the cops. A policewoman told her she and Juancho looked all right but an aid car was on the way, then went back to simultaneously soothing and questioning the still-hysterical Magi. Latinas in ridiculously showy dresses and baroque make-up hovered around, children in suits and darling dresses stared with delighted awe.

Nan walked over to Juancho, who sat on the hood of the Lincoln, everything inside him roiling with a complex brew of emotion, aftershock, and souring hormones. He looked up at her sheepishly, pointed to the red-purple puffball encrusting his eye. Nan thought the cheekbone was probably broken. You'll have the trophy shiner of the whole school, kiddo.

She leaned over to him, eye to eye, and smiled through the scrapes and bruises on her own face. She didn't really think there was anything she could say that wouldn't cheapen the moment, so she just put her hands on his knees, leaned closer yet, and planted a long, soft kiss on the non-impacted cheek.

She drew back and looked at him, giving him the full wattage of her approval. She didn't have to read the signs to know her effect on the boy: even more than on a grown man. He had just gotten a real kiss from a real woman. More than that, a favor bestowed by the Playmate of the Month, a smile and touch from the Fantasy Fairy. She reached out to cup his jaw on the uninjured side, gave him a pat that turned into a slideaway caress. She spoke with no lightness or exaggeration. "My hero."

Driving towards the La Neta hangout with Syco, JoJo was troubled to find that he wasn't all that sorry that his idol had failed. Had, in fact, been humiliated by women and children. He admired the rich boy's idiot charge, saw a lot of himself in the stupid gesture. He thought the cute little girl had come through amazingly well, also. But how about that blonde? Twice she'd escaped Syco, something very few had managed even once. He thought of her lying on the ground, then of what it would be like gang-raping her on the pad in the back of the Suburban. And was glad she'd gotten away clean. There was something about her, a tigress spirit that reminded him of somebody he knew way back, the first time he'd come to America.

He looked at Syco, who was seething silently over his defeat and trying to decide if there was really a Federal agent going around the region telling people he was a homopedophile, and for the first time it hit him. Someday he could end up running this gang himself. Nobody was perfect. He thought about that awhile, mostly in terms of how he would handle the job.

Meanwhile, Nan might have been calm and practical in dealing with the barrage of cops, medical personnel, and television stringers who descended on the Chuck E. lot, but inside she was fuming, and reaching for something she could use to scratch a major itch. Another visit shot to hell while things got sorted out. Gaspar's kids frightened and menaced. She'd had it with this. With a start she realized that she actually missed her visits with Gaspar. Even in the hospital, lying there... Maybe especially then, she realized. It was good to have somebody who needed her to be heroic, instead of wanting her to be weak, nasty and under control.

She was building quite a lot of affection for the guy. She liked making it with him well enough, liked the dry joking around. He was in her league, in a lot of ways. Who knew how old he was when he got bent? What his needs had been? She made a note to find out. The Fellowship of the Warped, she thought. Lifetime membership the only option.

But she had been hit hard, or more like infected, by the entry of Reach into her life and inner emotional structures. What would it be like to be really, truly, in love with her husband that way? To feel that desperate, gasping slide out of life that she experienced with Sean? To feel him in her like he belonged there, was born there, was filling her up and exploding her like a balloon?

Whoo. She clamped down on that whole sort of feeling/thinking, but realized that it probably wasn't a good idea to trample these awakening drives. Or she'd be as bad as the ones who'd beaten and greedied them out of her in the first place, cheating her of her very womanhood before it even arrived.

Now I've got the brand new untried libido of a thirteen year old virgin and the mind of an old Chinese madam, she told herself. What am I supposed to do with *that*? Decide between the fresh flame of a second chance at youth, and acting her age? Didn't it all end up that way if you played your cards right? The old man, the kids all grown up, the house, the hobbies?

Weekend husband, she reminded herself brutally. *Time share* kids. Then suddenly she thought of the barren sleekness of her flat in Mission Valley and cracked a knowing grin. She spoke out loud in the privacy of the Lincoln's back seat. "Better than nothing, sweetie. Better than you deserve. And no requirement to have babies."

But that was sidetracking her from the main point, and her anger. These damned contretemps with various men were fouling up her married life and she needed to put a stop to it. Starting immediately. Just as soon as she could get out of this parking lot and get to work on the problem. This shit, she swore grimly, must cease.

Chapter Thirty-Eight

The new executive council of Gaspar Enterprises was arranged about a long, gleaming hardwood table in Manny's conference room. The weather outside was typically relentless San Diego splendor, the sun tamed and toned yellow-green by palm fronds and calla leaves in the small court outside the sliding doors.

Nan sat at the head of the table, hunched over a sheaf of photocopies from the stacks, files and boxes strewn along its surface. Manny leaned back in his modernistic faux rosewood chair, poking at a slim laptop. Alfredo stood at a wetbar cleverly concealed by pullouts in the linen-paneled wall, dumping Trader Joe coffee grind into a paper filter.

The lawyer looked up from his screen, not enjoying what he'd been reading. "Everything I find checks with what I've heard about these SalvaTrucha maniacs. The press calls them MS 13 now, but it's the same outfit."

Nan looked up from her reading. "And it says they're not the Welcome Wagon?"

"Says they're a combination of the worst elements of street gangs, guerillas, and drug mafias."

Pouring Britta water in the top of the stainless Braun, Alfredo added, "Little tattooed *locos*, swarming like roaches."

"This article in the *Week* says they're mostly Central Americans." She read off passages she'd highlighted in pale blue. "Ethnic gangs in Los Angeles. Deported to countries that didn't want them back. Police manhunting them in Salvador and Nicaragua. Sprawling confederation of hardened criminals challenge local police forces. Spreading to Mexico, Canada, U.S."

Flicking on the Braun and rinsing a mug in the little sink, Alfredo spoke over this shoulder. "Combination of third world toughness and all-American know-how."

"And now they're up here? Tijuana? San Diego?"

Alfredo shrugged as he waited on the perk. "They do things the hard way."

"Not a good sign."

163

Manny read from his screen. "Recruiting from the poor, corrupting the Army, allied with gangs in California, Texas, and Florida."

He looked out the window, grim. "Al said it--swarming. Like killer bees or those ants that eat everything in their way."

"I hope you're not just saying that to make me feel better," Nan said with a light touch that didn't quite work. Then she had a thought, "Don't they have anything like a headquarters or home area?"

"They're pretty loose-knit. But I read something in "*Zeta*" about how maybe they're concentrating up in Solares and Vientos. *Infonavits*. Before the word went out down there not to mention them anymore."

"Info somethings?"

"*Infonavit.* Federal workers' housing projects. Instant slums, mostly. Vientos is like twelve years old and Solares has been around even longer, right?"

Alfredo nodded, trying to figure out how he could get some of the coffee already brewed without spilling the stuff still dripping into the pitcher. "At least. Means they're falling apart and full of *super-pobres*. Like some kind of laboratory vat for cooking up street crime."

"I think they took over a whole block of Solares," Manny put in, remembering more as they talked it over. "Moved everybody out and moved their people in. Crazy crack gangsters with tats on their faces and dicks, their murderous little girlfriends. A barracks for teenaged assassins. But who knows for sure?"

"So at least they aren't a completely invisible network like Al' Qaeda or something. But bad enough." Nan shuffled her newspapers restlessly. "So who is going to know the most about them? Here in this area."

Alfredo dumped the sponge he'd used to clean up the coffee he'd splashed around by being impatient and carried his steaming mug triumphantly back to the table. Sinking into a chair he said, "Does it say who wrote that article?"

Nan looked at the papers in her hands, laughed and smacked herself on the forehead like Homer Simpson. "Doh! Good one, Al."

The heavy Cantera table with a carved horsehead base positioned under a green umbrella in a nook near the jungle of palms, trumpet vine, and papyrus by the pool had become Nan's preferred home office. Wearing modest blue-white-green resort wear with a vaguely nautical motif, she leaned back against the canvas webbing of her rubberized steel chair and regarded James "Jimbo" Chapman, a charming/repulsive weasel who wrote for the tabloid *SouthCoast Week*. She knew he was thirty-six but like many dissolutes gone to seed, it would have been hard to guess precisely.

What she saw squared with what she'd learned: a greedy, amoral, womanizing glutton redeemed from the seeds of his own corruption by a degree of writing talent, a deep well of contraband contacts, and a sly, roguish humor. He licked his fingers clean of the residue of the baklava she'd offered him and refreshed his wine glass from a crystal decanter.

Chapman was very much in favor of living this way, and as usual his inner radar was pricked up for any hint of how he could get some of it for himself. He had put Nan in the "get some for myself" category the second he saw her, but was well aware of his limitations. Still, you bide your time and you never know where fruit will fall, had been his experience. She sure was a cool, piquant, platinum slice of honeybun, though, wasn't she? Sitting there in a couple hundred bucks of boutique sailor suit, that big blue tote bag hanging from the chair beside her like she was ready to ship out any minute. Well, he'd just try his best to seem like the next dreamboat leaving port.

Nan had silently watched his joyous genocide of the baklava population and decimation of two bottles of Chardonnay while weighing her appraisal of him. She decided he wasn't a guy heavily into foreplay. "I need to learn more about the drug gang scene in Tijuana."

He paused with his glass at his lips, eyed her for a beat, and sipped. When he set the glass down he wore the wry smile of a connoisseur of paradox. "Señora Border Snake asking for *my* info on the drug biz?"

I also do my homework, honeypants, he thought. Like I hear you've been doing on me. "Are you some sort of black belt in post-modern irony?"

"It seems to come with the territory. It's obvious from your articles you have solid sources. Like that piece on those Mara Truchas."

"I was lucky to get some good dish on that one. And could get a lot more. That's your main area of interest, then?"

"One of two. I want the best information you can get on these MS characters and I want it exclusive and private."

"Meaning I couldn't publish it? They want a follow-up on that other piece anyway. Why would I agree to restrict it to you?"

She reached into her bag and withdrew a thick stack of bills wrapped in two rubber bands. She tossed them on the table in front of him.

"Ah, so," he said sagely, picking up the stack and riffing through it. "I see you've studied the language and folkways of my people."

He set down the money and gave her a bland, neutral look. "But you've got to know that journalists are hard to, you know..." he made little quotation marks with his fingers, "...'swear to secrecy'."

Nan reached into the bag again and pulled out a massive Ruger Security Six pistol in .357, blackened for night ops and exuding explosive menace. She placed in on the table beside her, pointing vaguely in Chapman's direction.

"Succinct," he said, admiringly. "I think we can do business."

"Glad to hear it. The other 411. You did a piece four years ago about a mercenary bar in Rosarito. Ex-S.E.A.L. types, gunrunners, all that?"

"Ex-marines, bounty hunters, cashiered ass-kickers for hire."

"Well, we're hiring."

Chapman never needed an excuse to take a drink, but he raised his glass just to cover his surprise, give it a quick run through his brain. All he came up with was astonishment.

"I've got this straight? *You* are short on soldiers?"

"But we don't really have soldiers, do we?" she asked rhetorically. "We have street toughs. We've got pitbulls: we need timber wolves. Tigers. Kung Fu gorillas."

Chapman nodded comprehension. "Invisible flying sharks."

"That's the idea. Communication experts."

166

She'd lost him again. He was beginning to think this babe was more than just a wow-zow cleavage. "Communications?"

"I need to send a message."

"Ah." This was looking like one of those rare projects that kindled his long-abused curiosity. "I can talk to those guys. Gotta say though, just being around them scares the shit out of me."

Nan nodded happily. "They sound perfect."

"But then again," he said with the same wry smile. "So do you."

"Good." Nan's smile didn't change, but he saw something shift inside it.

"In way that kinda gives me wood."

"Well, how nice for you."

If she wasn't so screamingly fuckable, Chapman thought, this would be a fun chick to just hang out with. He drained his glass and stood up. "Let's talk next week."

"I'll call you Monday," Nan agreed.

He looked around at the blue shimmer of pool, then back at the deep end of her eyes. "Maybe you could pick up some tiramisù?"

Chapman was decidedly not a man to spurn the company of naked young women, but at the moment he was more intent on holding the wobbly attention of his drunken colleague. Blas Espinosa was his counterpart in the dissipated lowlife slot at Tijuana's scrappy weekly "Zeta" and frequent partner in the somewhat allied endeavors of disinformation and misbehavior. While leggy, depilated young chippies strutted by on the front bar of the Hong Kong, delicately placing six inch heels between glasses and ashtrays, he continued trying to make sure Blas understood what he was saying to him. And might therefore even remember it. Thus the uncharacteristic wave of dismissal at the lissome teenager who squatted in front of him, her knees framing his face. He did give her a little pat on the thigh as he nudged it aside to keep Blas in view.

"Everything," he said again. "Anything you've got."

"Yeah, sure," Blas muttered, trying to reclaim the attention of the squatter, who had lost her attachment to these two *pendejos* and was slinking down the bar towards some avidly interested conventioneers from Nebraska. "Yeah, if you're sure it won't get published, I can give you a lot."

"Publication is the last thing they want," Chapman reassured him. "And what these people want, they get."

"They show you money?"

"Good, big money, *amigo*. Also showed me a gun, know what I mean?"

Blas nodded with owl-eyed sagacity. "The *plata o plomo* show. Bring me money and I'll make you an instant expert."

"Great, you got it."

"Now get that girl back over here. You going queer on me or something?"

Since Rosarito Beach is just a half hour from the border crossing on a main highway, and has the first decent beach south of San Diego, it's inevitable that it would have a bumper crop of fun, sporty, tourist bars. La Malquerida is emphatically not one of them. Located within a pistol shot of the beach--a fact occasionally demonstrated--and just south of the main springbreak ghetto, "La Mala" is dark and squalid with that special air of no-nonsense drinking and resident iniquity. The customers Chapman could pick out through the dimness, smoke haze, and rattle of southern biker ballads were like a clinical illustration of the term "border scum" and looked well-practiced in the mortal arts. Not much change in four years.

Like so much of border culture, including the existence of Tijuana itself, the Mala's clientele was a factor of being just past the far reach of the leashes on the dogs of American law. San Diego hosts the Top Gun school, the world's largest naval base, the training center for Navy S.E.A.L.'s and a massive Marine presence just up the road at Camp Pendleton. Stir in the nearby presence of major drug cartels, sprinkle on a few black and Philipino gangsters hiding out from various warrants and recapture efforts, and there was definitely a local pool of men experienced in combat, accessible to forbidding weaponry, and rather blasé about matters of jurisdiction or moral consequence. "La Mala" was still their quarters and Chapman was chatting with one of the leading citizens.

He had a first name stamped on dogtags somewhere with his blood type and ID number, but nobody knew him as anything other than Lux. He was moderately tall and very lean, wore steel-gray hair cropped to "regulation length" and moved with the deceptively soft slide many athletes fall into. Sitting at a corner table, with both their backs to walls covered by a rummage-sale assortment of unit pendants, hats with the names of warships and Asian disaster zones, badly-composed candid pornologs, helmets, gasmasks, and athletic team posters, he and Chapman conferred over a bottle of cheap Mescal. From across the room Lux could have been an aging waiter/actor, a faded rock guitarist, a field archeologist. Within view of his pale eyes there was no doubt he was a professional in very sinister professions.

In his "Week" piece on the Mala, highly fictionalized to avoid reprisals from the understandably publicity-shy members of its flock, Chapman had scoffed at the Hollywood portrait of mercenaries and hitmen as big, bulgy Schwarzenegger types. Lux was the showfloor model of the prototype he'd noted: compactly built and normally muscled like Steve McQueen or James Coburn. And, as he'd been the last time, short on giggles and all about business.

"I don't really care how hot she looks, actually. Just how well she pays."

"She's rich, generous and the way I hear it, she's reliable. Talk to her and I'm sure you'll reach your own conclusions."

"Conclusions are what you might call my stock in trade. She looking to rock somebody's world, or keep her own relatively rock-free?"

"I think maybe both. She talks like she plans to hostess a world war. And very interested in those MS-13 types."

Lux looked off into the dusk of the Mal's interior, considering. "Mara Salvatruchas. Interesting. I've dealt with them before. Mostly in Nicaraqua."

"I'm guessing 'deal with' is the main idea here."

"So where do I talk to her?"

"You'll love it. Take your Speedos."

Chapter Thirty-Nine

But Nan invited Lux to Manny's office for his first consultation. He didn't sit around the conference table with them, choosing to stand with his back to the sliding garden door, light from behind him obscuring his expression and giving him a bright aura. His manner was modest and businesslike, and he talked like any other specialty consultant.

"No," he said calmly but with finality. "See, you don't want to include a gift card with this. What you want is maximum destruction, disorder and demoralization from out of an empty sky without warning or reason."

"That makes a lot of sense," Nan nodded. She'd selected a very conservative skirted business suit for this meeting, dark gray tropical wool with a faint claret chalkstripe. Lux looked like a tennis bum in boat shoes, chinos and black polo shirt. She had the impression he wasn't given to saying things that didn't make sense.

His weathered, ultra-relaxed poise and quietly radiant confidence looked good to her. She could see that he was a stud: deliberate moves, prior strategy, stamina and resolution to get it done. A guy who could reach out and kill without missing a beat, but wouldn't bother doing it for ego or honor or any of those stupid destructive distractions.

Studly in more than just the business sense, she thought. There was a banked virility about him, more powerful and contained than she was used to picking up on from a man. Whatever message he might inflict on other men, his communiqué to women read something like, stand by to get hammered into addictive oblivion. But she'd been immunized: one more advantage to being a whore in a man's world.

They sized each other up, members of the same tribe. Both sleek and healthy because they could deal with human meat unhampered by moral reservations about the rules of the veldt. She knew he saw her too, but was too professional to give her even a hint of the eye. She felt good about him working for her.

Lux glanced at her, then around the other two men. "The only message you want to send is, 'You're fucked'."

"I like it," Alfredo said quietly. He was regarding Lux from his own perspective; that of a man not used to feeling outclassed in the physical jeopardy department.

"If they don't know who hit them, it's one more thing they have to figure out before they can do anything about it."

Manny nodded judiciously, but was getting to like this guy. The *jefe's* wife had hit on a winner, was his impression.

"The best thing, I think," Lux went on, "Would be to do the tenement and that compound simultaneously."

"Good. Give them no warning or chance to regroup." Nan was already seeing the outline of how this would work.

Alfredo was on board with that. "Nail 'em all at once."

"But wouldn't that split our resources?" Manny objected. "Divide up and weaken and all that shit?"

"Definitely. It would cost twice as much. A little more than twice as much, actually. There'd be some co-ordination and logistical problems. But not as much as trying to do a rerun once the Maras are alerted and the cops are freaking out."

Nan gave a quick, brisk nod that both of the Chicano men knew meant the decision was done. "What would you need?"

"Well," Lux said with a wry smile that might have contained the only hint of flirtation since she'd met him. "We *are* mercenaries."

"You'll talk directly to Manny about money. Anything else?"

"Yeah. The sequel."

Nan arched a perfect eyebrow. "We'll need an encore after Destruction From The Skies?"

Lux nodded, all business again. "They'll figure out who it was, or else lash out at random. And their message will be 'Hey, fuck you, too.' But we'll factor that in."

Chapter Forty

Maru was breakfasting at the crack of noon, as usual, pretending to be dieting because of the Sweet'n'Low instead of sugar in her coffee and noshing breads and fresh fruit instead of a big greasy plate of *chilaquiles*. She slathered low trans-fat cream cheese on an onion bagel, licked off the knife and waved it like a conductor's baton to punctuate her phone conversation with Nan.

"Like the Trophy Lounge up in National City. Cruising Filipina fleet widows. But what really trips his trigger is *Negritas*. You remember Treshanna?"

Nan's reply made her smile. You could never tell for sure what that girl was really thinking. "Sure, I'll let her know. Anyway, she's got this friend named Calistoga or something, kind of a light hooker. Does stunts on weekends for dinner, gifts, maybe a take-home prize here and there. Any time she wants to get heavier, I've got calls for her. And that girl is *black*. I mean they call people "black and beautiful" who aren't any darker than I am, but that Califa or whatever is black as a hearse."

She stopped, routed back to the matter at hand, and went on in the tone she always dropped into for the juicy stuff. "Anyway she cruises meat markets like Gauchos and Capistrano, and she's seen the guy a couple of times...and I mean "seen" like you know, the full El Monte... at the Black Angus in Chula Vista."

Paddling some apricot jam onto the cheese-packed bagel and mixing it like an impressionist blending a palette, she laughed as she started to take her first nibble. "Yeah, they still call it the Black Anus. Little Calista might be a main reason for that. Anyway, he comes in there a lot the last few weeks. Real cockhound. Not a big spender, but throws good dope around."

Her second attempt to scarf the expressionist bagel got derailed by the novelty of Nan's request. "Yeah, yeah, I could arrange that." She hated to broach bottom line, but there it was. "It'd cost, you know. I mean, they..."

She gobbled a big chunk of the bagel while Nan responded to the idea of her having to pay whores for their time. Well, she was always saying things were ironic. "Sure, honey. Of course you get a professional discount."

She reached to refill her cup from her cool new French press but forgot about it as she dissolved into merry laughter at the next question. "Oh, she way more than *saw* it, 'mana. It's a snake. Like a rattlesnake head with big fangs. The rattles are on his belly and the snake's sort of wrapped around his *pinga* so it sticks out of its mouth."

"Impressed?" She laughed even harder. "I guess you could call it that. She told him she'd doggie all night if he kept the *coca* coming, but there was no way she'd go down on that thing."

Syco was single-mindedly unaware of the culture clash he trailed behind him as he glided into the American clubs where he'd been grazing and glutting during his junket north of the Border. He'd found his happy hunting grounds and was running amok. San Diego offered a wider range of tastes than he was used to in the barrios of Latin America. He'd dabbled around with Asian girls but they were skittish, and Filipinas, who were almost too easy but also sort of too skinny and chatty. Where he really got hot was with white, and better yet, black, women. They represented exotic tableaux not generally found in the slums of Tegucigalpa. And while he was still making up his mind, the black *vainas* were more fun to talk to and had bigger butts.

The clash was in the way he perceived his personal dress code, versus what everybody else saw. He thought wearing all black and red was cool and *machote*, a standing ad for his vigor and sexual animosity. Wearing a long-sleeved black shirt buttoned to the neck with the rest of the buttons left undone seemed like the height of cool for him, the sort of thing the hard bangers had always worn. And covered his tattoos until it was time to pounce them out there and start the juices flowing.

Whereas anybody in "ChulaJuana" saw him as a *cholo* punk who still thought the old-school barrio *bandilla* chic was with it. And those who got to review his tats generally thought they were horrendously creepy and completely gauche. But he had good dope and didn't mind doing some very liberal dusting. He was getting his way.

He'd done his usual predator stalk into Toritos, his tireless self-absorption backed up by the packets of top-grade toot in his shirt pocket and the hefty Glock 10mm in the small of his back.

And had spotted his prey before he even got past the passé ferns and into the waterhole.

He'd seen Treshanna before, but always hanging out with some limp-dicked Anglo in a business suit, or local "*chinaco*" with too much pomade. But there she was right there, standing alone just inside the bar, looking like some kind of African love idol among the dark wood décor and tacky silk leaves. She'd given him a sly smile, then looked away. He moved toward her confidently. Tonight's the night, had been the main idea.

But things weren't breaking that way, and he couldn't figure it out. It's like you put everything in the pot and turn up the gas and nothing happens. Put two roosters in a pit and they just stand around avoiding eye contact. He couldn't figure it out.

She'd been somewhat flirtatious, but he was wondering how real it was. She was showing him the goods, and he was impressed, but he couldn't seem to move in for the kill. She already had a drink, didn't want to slip out to powder her nose, wasn't giving off the scent. Finally he got tired of it and just popped the question straight out. A guy like him could do that anytime, it was just fun to screw around first. Up to a point.

He was totally unprepared for her reaction. Her big, dancing eyes widened and her lavishly red lips parted in surprise. "You saying you want to take me home? You *hitting* on me?"

No, you stupid *changuita*, I've been talking to you for ten minutes because I'm so interested in listening to all this crap about where you got your hair done. "Yes, I am hit you. I have great *coca*, you have great ass. What do you thinking?"

She tossed her head back as she laughed, heaving her tantalizing cleavage. "Oh, I'm sorry honey, I thought you just wanted to... I didn't know you swung that way."

It pissed him off not to understand English expressions, especially when somebody just might be laughing at him. "What is 'swung' mean?"

She leaned forward and touched his upper arm lightly, "You know, sweetheart. I heard you're like this." She made a vaguely floaty gesture with her hand, the golden nails flashing in the indirect lighting.

He was rigid with frustration, ready to blow up all over the place. His "controlled" speech sounded like it was being crunched out of a pepper grinder. "I don't knowing what 'this' means." He imitated the gesture in a savagely derisive manner.

She moved closer yet, giving him quite a lookdown and a deeper waft of her no-prisoners perfume. She spoke as quietly as the music and hormone jabber made it possible to hear, "I know you're into guys. Everybody does. You don't have to act like this. You want to get high, talk some shit, it's okay."

He froze, solidifying into some sort of volcanic stone right in front of her. He'd heard her, all right. But he had to make sure. "*Into guys?*"

"Yeah. It's okay. This America, girlfriend. You can go where you want. No shame, no blame." Her eyes sparkled with inner humor as she held up a hand to stage-whisper behind. "Just make sure they're old enough, okay?"

Of the dozen questions that blasted into his livid mind, the one that popped out was, "Who was told you that?"

"Common knowledge, sweetie. That cop was pretty serious about it, though. Pictures of little boys and shit. But hey, I don't listen to cops much. Still want to do a line or two, talk about it?"

He wasn't frozen anymore. A red heat pulsed through his frame, screaming at him to hit the bitch, to pull his gun and air out the room, to scream and tear off his clothes, show her who he got hot for. But even as he thought that, he felt himself wilting and shrinking away. He screamed, "I am NOT liking *guys* or *boys*! I am *into* women, stupid nigger whore!"

The bar froze and turned eyes on him. Treshanna drew away, sneering in scorn. "Well, you ain't into *this* woman, asshole. Why don't you get your narrow racist butt over to Third Avenue, cruise the Boy's Club?"

She'd said it loud and with the perfect flair to send the bar into whoops of laughter, mingled with boos. Her own take was Hollywood-grade scorn and disgust that radiated off her and diminished his very presence. If Treshanna had gotten the slightest hint of how close she came to getting repeatedly shot to death right then and there, she would have hit Nan up for a whole lot more money.

Chapter Forty-One

"You don't have this place wired or anything, do you?" She peered around the interview room suspiciously, obviously trying to avoid the main issue. "This is just between you and me."

"Could you tell if it is or not?" Gaithers shot back at her, enjoying pushing her towards corners. He was already anticipating watching her squirm in so many ways.

She hadn't been at all surprised to arrive for her visit and get whisked straight into see Gaithers, instead. In a different office, further back in the bowels of the prison. As soon as she walked in the door she'd pulled a hand-held alarm klaxon out of her purse and showed it to this creep. Her finger didn't leave the button the entire time she was alone with him. She gave him a look reserved for scumbags. "Why not try just being straightforward for once? You want me to answer your questions but don't even have the stones to give me a simple yes or no?"

He waved his hand to encompass the room. "No bugs." He held up his other hand with three fingers erect. "Scout's honor."

I'd love to see which merit badges you got, dickhead, she thought. Then scooted her chair closer to the desk, looked him right in his rapine eyes, and got to the point. "He calls himself Psycho. His real name is Pablo Bocanada. Originally from the state of Tabasco."

She saw no flicker in the blank eyes to indicate whether he bought the contrived fiction she'd worked up with Alfredo. She assumed the fact he wasn't taking notes meant the room actually was bugged. One more Boy Scout gone bad.

"Yada, yada. Who is he? Where? What does he know?"

"He knows way too much, is the consensus. And he's been looking pretty shaky. If I were you, I'd move fast because little Pablo might not be around much longer. I think if you tell him Alfredo isn't very happy with what he knows about the deal he cut with those Mexikanemi guys, he might decide he's safer talking to you than walking."

"I know a little about my own business, thanks," he said sourly. "All I want from you is information. Where can I find him? Is he hiding out?"

176

"Hardly," she chuckled humorously. "He's out strutting what he's got every weekend. Almost sure to turn up at the Angus in Chula Vista. The one on 'H'."

"The Black Anus," he smirked. "Pussy posse."

"Oh, you boys and your cute nicknames," she deadpanned. "He gets a few drinks down and he talks easier, I understand. He should give you everything you need on anybody below him in the food chain. But he's got nothing on anybody higher up."

"You wish," he snorted unpleasantly. "You want to send me off chasing the nickels while the fat cats, including your hubby, skate."

"My *hubby* is already in prison, you dork. This guy is basically Accounts Receivable. He knows where it comes in and how. They're careful not to let him know about the main players, though. Where do you think I heard all his?"

He didn't move for a long time, watching and weighing her. It sounded right and she wasn't trying to light it up any bigger for his benefit. And she'd be out of her mind to be making it up. All he had to do was tell this Psycho she'd set him up and she'd be dead. He couldn't read anything off her but a desire to get him off her back and resentment about having to spill. He decided, nodded to her slightly. "He's got to talk, and what he says has to put people away. You understand that, don't you? You're not getting any slack for throwing us some homeboy who pissed you off."

Like that would get rid of you, anyway, Nan thought. She pursed her lips, became extremely concerned. "I can see that. Look... if you don't mind me telling you your business or anything?"

Gaithers imperiously waved her on.

"One thing I'd caution you about, the guy's a diddler."

Gaithers showed no reaction. "Likes 'em with no fuzz on their pussies, huh?"

"Likes them with no pussies at all. On the side, you understand? He hangs around women, but his real action is chicken hawking. Nobody cares as long as he keeps it out of town."

"What do I care?" he demanded.

"Nothing, but I'm just saying it's a sore point. If you start using loaded words like "faggot" or something around him, the way you guys do, he's going to lock up on you. I'm giving him to you with a big blue bow. Don't screw it up, okay?"

"Do I seem like somebody who screws up getting people to spill their guts?"

Nan didn't answer, just glared at him, stood suddenly and left the room without closing the door.

Chapter Forty-Two

Nan stepped out of the Lincoln as the power doors shuddered down behind it, looking with interest at Lux directing a half dozen men at work in the garage. Always curious about mechanical contraptions, she walked over to watch. Most of the men seemed to be cut from the same bolt of cloth; the same relaxed attention as Lux, like a knife in a scabbard. One was much older, a scrawny old-timer who looked like a psychedelic casualty from the sixties. His drawn face, receded gums, and papery bald scalp gave him the look of a skull, but he moved with precision and controlled vigor as he worked at a bench, assembling a collection of shiny steel and black composite. Occasionally one of the other men, working on three other benches, would pause and he would glance over and point a finger or step up to interlock two machined widgets into oiled harmony.

Alfredo followed her reluctantly and Lico, standing against the inside door on the opposite wall, was the only one of his men in the garage. Nan was aware that Alfredo and the troops felt abashed in the presence of Lux and his men. They were Wise Guy Muscle, used to swaggering like leopards through herds of ruminants. Next to this crew they felt like barrio boys with zipguns.

It wasn't just the DeathCheck ordinance, either. The gangsters were fighters, even killers if it came to that. They'd take somebody off in the course of a day's work, not think a thought about it. But these new guys were natural-born killers, the industrial strength, big league version. Trailing bodycounts like forgotten *futbol* goals, walking weaponry.

On the other hand, she mused, the hardware was certainly part of this little road show. She admired the symmetry and click-in finality of the weapons being put together, and was impressed by the assembled products being wiped down and leaned against the wall. Mostly recognizable as military grade long arms. But some of it was decidedly alien. Two benches had bundles of steel tubes laid on them, multi-barreled furies that were taking quite a bit of time to assemble. And those things over there looked like cannons. She watched, fascinated, for ten minutes before saying, "Why don't I think you guys picked this stuff up at Big Five?"

Lux gave her one of his almost smiles and said, "Well, we're kind of Bad Heat R Us. You wanted the whole nine yards, this ought to get it done."

"But come on," she persisted. "This stuff isn't just illegal: it's like, unavailable."

"Well, not to guys who've used it and know where they keep it," Lux said companionably, toggling the shell extractor assembly of one of the miniguns. "Lots of guys we work with actually sell this stuff down in the jungles. There's even a little factory outside of Ensenada that knocks these beauties off."

The older man, who Nan realized was of an age to have served in VietNam, smiled at her, enhancing the skull impression. "Each piece copied one by one. This German guy set it up originally. A hand-machined minigun is an expensive way to build, but they get a hell of a good price for them."

"As well you know," Lux said dryly, drawing a Halloween grin. He told Nan, "There's not a hotshit cartel gangster in Miami or Bogota not dying to have one. Makes Tony Montana look like a wienie. They like to put them in back of Suburbans, pull in front of people and open the rear doors, scare the crap out of them"

"That would do it."

"Then a lot of it's just rebuilding. There's this gunsmith in El Cajon who does some refit parts. You realize the only difference between a lot of legal rifles and full-fledged machine guns is just a little part called a 'selector switch', right?"

"Stands to reason," she said, continuing to stare at the minigun's ring of barrels. Amazing what guys will soup up in their back yards, she was thinking. She could see the purpose of this stainless Gatling gun very clearly: you push a button and it spins around spitting out death too fast to even think about. Fine with her. She didn't really want to think about it, anyway. "Well, you're doing a great job on the assembly line, guys. If you want refreshments, just ask."

"Thanks, I could use a lemonade or something myself," Lux said while fastening the stripper assembly onto the receiver group. "It is pretty neat looking stuff, huh? I mean, you know, just seen as an art object or something?"

"The Contemporary Art Museum in La Jolla would fall all over an exhibit," she agreed. He'd picked up exactly on her absorption with the ordinance.

Lux jerked his head dismissively toward a pile of greasy green tubes against the wall. "That ugly stuff over there you can pick up anywhere in Latin America. You see mortars and grenades sold in public markets some places."

"Yet we consider them backward and underprivileged."

Chapter Forty-Three

Some of the things Syco appreciated most about the United States were the hardest for him to understand. So much of it seemed on fast-forward, but then a lot was just jumbled up and ass-backward. And the place he was walking into was one of the things that seemed most confused.

There was a certain element of anti-Americanism among many illegal entrants, but the Mara field marshal definitely didn't share the sentiment. He was thrilled and intrigued by the country: infatuated like a man in the presence of an exciting woman that he has plans to make his very own. For that matter, the U.S. hadn't treated him badly. Unlike every other country he'd lived in, where they'd locked him up, beaten him, tortured him, exterminated his family, and tried to kill him. Of course, this place probably just hadn't gotten around to it yet. In the meantime he was slurping it up and loving it. But much of it made no sense at all. You take this "Black Angus" place.

He had scoped out the parking lot carefully before JoJo dropped him off. Good kid, shame he couldn't come in, but here you couldn't go in a bar unless you were twenty-one. No women in their teens allowed! Ridiculous. Not that he was complaining about that part of it. But as he walked across the lot he took a closer look at the Angus and just couldn't figure out what they were thinking.

The interior was his idea of lavish luxury: thick carpet, posh furnishings, free snacks, top-quality liquor, huge screens for sports events, cute waitresses in formal costumes. Any such place in Central America would be an architectural extravagance located in some ritzy enclave, probably with a wall around it and guards. But here the exterior was an ugly box situated on a common street between a 7-ll and a cheap taco drive-up. The entire block was crappy strip malls, gas stations, and fast foods. Well, whatever. The important thing was he was here and the place was full of available *chicas*.

He moved straight to the bar with no more than a quick scan of the dining room. That was another thing: who would come to a puss palace like this, then go in there and *eat dinner*? He made his usual gladiator entrance to the bar, going largely unnoticed. Things looked good tonight. A nice racial blend, some exotic stuff he hadn't seen before. He decided to circulate, got a drink from the bar and moved to the darker area in the back where he'd noticed some of the nicer pieces often hung out. He spotted the winner immediately.

He'd almost been put off black women by the *pucha* the other night. But this babe was just too fine for words. Better than that Chalistra he'd picked up here before, the one who got all virginal about his viper figurehead. This one didn't look like she'd shy away from anything: built, gorgeous, eyes full of hell... and giving him the once-over. He moved towards her like a matador, completely unaware that he was being reeled in by an expert.

Dorothea Tompkins, doing business of late as "Amaryllis", had a hard time keeping a straight face as Syco rolled in on her. Jiveass little strutter with that *cholo* drag and attempted mustache. And hung like a mouse, or she missed her guess. Anybody who'd tattoo a snake around their unit. Well, thank Jesus she was getting paid for this one without having to experience that little delight first hand, so to speak. She looked him over from his waxy flat-top to his stupid spaceman sports shoes and hosed him down with the look she thought of as Max Meltdown.

He stood there breathing at her, so she glanced sideways at a chair, cagey cool on top of all the subtly advertised volcanic fires within. He sat down and said, "Whut up?"

Another original conversationalist, "Amaryllis" mused. "Isn't that my line?"

He had no idea what to do with that so he said, "What is your name?"

She gave him a little more smolder and murmured, "We really need names here, honey?"

He nodded. This was going really well right out of the box. "I am Syco."

And it shows, hotstuff. Well, time to turn that old trick. "Nice to meet you. Hey, wait a minute, though... aren't you the guy supposed to be all gay and shit?"

A leaden bolt fell through Syco's chest and guts. Again! *What?* He stared at this second bitch to come up with that vile *calumnia*.

He felt like grabbing her hair, banging her smirking face to the table top and finding out where she was getting this *pedazo de mierda.* Instead he said, "I am not homosexual. I like women, not men. Find out."

"Not so much 'men', way I hear it," she replied in a voice dripping righteous scorn. "More like Little League."

"That is one *lie!*" he exploded, again drawing the attention of an entire bar. He dropped his voice and said, "Who says that things about me?"

"The cops, that's who," she told him in a voice audible to anybody interested. "Got pictures of little kids you been queering off. Listen to me, Short Eyes, I got a little boy of my own."

She stood abruptly to leave it like that. But her inner drama queen couldn't resist playing for the cheap seats: she attempted to hurl her drink on Syco. His hand twitched up with startling speed to block her toss, shatter the glass, and splatter most of the ice and soda water all over her already sheer and clingy dress. She drew full attention as she stalked out of the bar trailed by her provocatively swishing rump.

If Syco had any inclination to reply to her physical insult with violence, as he would have in the drinking spots in his own world, it was drowned by a crushing descent of mortification and rage. He just had to understand was happening here. Thirty minutes and two drinks later he'd decided he looked like some other guy who was a faggot baby-raper, so people were confused about it. Forty minutes later he was talking to a Federal agent.

Aside from their mutual desire to sexually subjugate Nan Gaspar, Ronald Gaithers had only one thing in common with Syco. He was also completely deluded regarding the way people evaluated his appearance. He saw his working attire as a clever disguise, a dress-down that allowed him to pass under the social radar while maintaining instant readiness to slap on the cuffs. Everybody else tended to read his pleated highbelt slacks, suede loafers, synthetic white shirt with single-Windsor tie and K-Mart knockoff London Fog windbreaker as being an almost defiant statement of geekhood.

Not that he gave a damn what anybody thought. He didn't even pay any attention to the decorative and blatantly available women in the place. He had pretty definite tastes in women, liking them cowed and reluctant; hating to do it but having to anyway. Fear and distaste were aphrodisiacs that would drive him into a fury of thrusting, slapping and punching. One of these days.... Well, anyway, he was working on a couple of those right now. One in particular.

He spotted Syco immediately and sized up his proudly assembled look as "*Cholo* pimp piece a shit, Type C". The guy in his chippy gladrags sitting there surrounded by poon practically drooling for it and he's all by himself and not even looking. Easy to believe that stuff about him being a bootie bandit.

Syco looked up from his ruminations on character assassination and spotted this guy casing him, wearing blend-in subterfuge so frumpy and oblivious he just had to be a cop. This was one Saturday night that just wasn't working out for him at all. He eyed this *pantalón,* itching for a reason to hate him. And the guy must have decided to make it easy, because he walked over and sat down facing him without a *porf*a or *permiso* or *chinga tu madre.* Well, he was in the perfect mood to deal with assholes and cops.

Gaithers was known even among his brusque colleagues as lacking "bedside manner". He took his chair, looked Syco right in the face and asked, "Is your name Pablo Bocanada?"

Syco almost regretted seeing the thing blow over. This guy comes in here staring at me with a hard-on, doesn't even have the right guy. Same way they screwed up and hung this *joto* baby-banger rep on the wrong guy. Incredible. He sneered, "No, I am not. Go look some else place."

Gaithers didn't change gear or non-expression. "Do you call yourself Psycho?"

Syco almost heard the click of his whole organism jumping back to alert. Nothing that showed in his face. "Do I look like Syco to you?"

Don't flatter yourself, puke, Gaithers thought as he said. "You work for a man named Humberto Gaspar?"

Carajo! This was triangulating in a way Syco didn't like one bit. Who *was* this *tarugo*? "I don't knowing him. And I don't knowing you. Get out from my table."

Gaithers loved the part when he pulled out his wallet and flashed the buzzer on them, stamped things all crystal clear. He dangled the badge and ID insultingly close to Syco's eyes and grinned at him with derisive spite. "Gaithers. DEA. Want me to spell that for you?"

Syco was completely unfazed by the badge and dramatic revelation of "secret identity" even though he had several thousands dollars worth of coke on his person. He wasn't connected to any dealing or trafficking north of the *linea*. It had to be some sort of witch hunt. He looked at the wallet as if to read the fine print, then spat on the badge with surgical precision. The only one in the bar who saw him do it was a leggy Campechana with an adorable smile and infectious laugh, sometimes known as Mariposa. She rather admired the spitting act. Decisive, accurate, and a real statement.

She was at the "Black Anus" hoping to get some of the money Maru had promised, but that Salvatrucha clown hadn't given her a tumble. On the other hand, there might be other action in this place later, so she'd stuck around.

Gaithers folded the wallet without cleaning it off, stuck it in his windbreaker pocket and left his hand there. Syco didn't much care for that, but wasn't all that worried since he'd eased his monster Glock out when he first caught sight of this *zanahoria*, and was holding in under the table pointing right at his dick.

"Cute," Gaithers remarked acidly. "If you'd like to smear some shit on the wall, feel free. But I think you're better off talking to me. I might just be the one guy who can keep your ass alive and out of prison. And pay you a little something, too."

So he was obviously out of his mind. But it might be worth hearing out. Syco put on a sneer and waited.

"I know about your whole thing with the Gaspar bunch."

Okay, that might have something sensible behind it. But why would drug cops care about that?

"I know you're in deep shit with them."

Well, yeah. I guess that would be the case, wouldn't it? Do I look scared? "You talk very much shit."

"You want shit?" Gaithers figured he might as well play a big card now, see what it might shake out. "You think Alfredo doesn't know what you're into with those Mexikanemi types? You think he's going to let you get away with that?"

Great, he was back to *chiflado* talk. "What you want from me?"

"It's more what you want, sonny. You want to live--don't wanna go down when we bust the whole works--you talk to me; We cut a deal, you walk out alive, free, and a little stash to boot."

"Talk to you? Deal?" Syco finally figured out what the guy was doing, but none of the rest of it made any sense. "You mean you want me to be rat? To put somebody finger?"

"No need to think of it like that. Think of it as life insurance and good citizenship."

Sound counsel for somebody who might be best described as an anti-citizen of at least four countries. Syco looked him over a minute, possibly to decide if this was some sort of complex gringo-style joke. Then he said, "I don't put things in the ear of police, *pendejo*. If I have one thing for you, I put it in your ass."

"Yeah, I hear that's your style," Gaithers drawled. "But if you want to..."

He broke off because Syco's face was finally moving. In his head it was like the reels of a slot machine were suddenly coming to a stop, all showing the same thing. "You hear what?"

"I hear your ass is dead if you don't deal, kid."

"No!" Syco snapped out. "What you said. You're Federal police?"

"Yeah, duh. You might want to keep your voice down."

"You are say lies about me?" Syco's stifled anger had finally found a blow-hole in the sheet of ice up top and was surging towards it. This guy knew who had smeared him. Maybe even he was the one. He raised an aggrieved voice against this cowardly injustice, "You have little pictures, *puto*?"

Gaithers looked around at lots of people checking this out. Not good. Easy to see why they called this fairy "Psycho", no doubt about it. He looked the guy in the eye and said, "You calling *me* a *puto*, you little faggot? Am I the one who swings both ways?"

Two tables away Mariposa saw a chance to put in a lick. Might be worth something. All she did was laugh.

The clear timbre of her engaging laugh cut through the sudden quiet of the bar and, as often happened when Mariposa really cut

187

loose a belly-laugh, the guys at her table joined in and the whole place had a good one, not really knowing why, but somebody had said "faggot" and then there was all this nice-sounding chortling. A good laugh had by all. Until the pounding report of big 10mm rounds going off in the small, crowded club slammed a big steel door on everybody's ears and changed the laughter into screams. Mariposa's scream was also distinctive and contagious.

The impact of the first shot to Gaither's crotch gave him no time for regret or second-guessing. He never even felt the pain of his left testicle being mushed or the pelvis behind it shattering into fragments that sprayed out into his intestines. The hydrostatic shock from the overloaded dum-dum round took care of all that in milliseconds. As he was blown backward over his collapsing chair, the second shot tore through the underside of his right leg, exploding his femoral artery in a fountain of bright, hot blood. He hit the floor like a holiday pudding.

Syco felt better immediately. He stood up calmly, displaying the Glock and the thin spray of blood on his pants and shoes. Nowhere near as bad as the way the people behind Gaithers got drenched. He circled the room with the pistol, everybody there getting a peek down the little black tunnel to oblivion. People stopped moving, stopped screaming. He moved smooth and serene to leave the club. He only wished those two black bitches were still here. See what they thought about his *macho* at that point.

He took two steps, passing within a foot of the cringing Mariposa, then stepped back on an afterthought and pumped two more rounds into Gaithers' face. He toed the dead agent's demolished head over to one side and put another round into the ear. You want something in your ears, *pinche placa*? My compliments.

He stepped to the next table, the merry-makers there frozen and shrunken in fright. He reached to pick up a ring of keys from the table and leaned over to ask the guy, "What car?"

The guy stared at him, gaping and incapable of speech. Syco brought the gun closer to bear and everybody smelled somebody pissing his pants. The girl beside him blurted out, "Blue Toyota Camry, Arizona plates. Around back by the taco place." She looked at the Camry owner as Syco pocketed the keys and left. No

188

longer her boyfriend, she realized. She waited until Syco was gone, then got up to call a cab.

At her table, ignoring the gabbling and post-showdown bravado among the Anglo idiots she'd been sitting with, Mariposa sat silent and motionless under the impact of what she was starting to put together. She had no schooling and could barely read, but she was far from a stupid girl and what she was adding up was that she'd just seen an execution by proxy. The whole thing of putting a wasp in that guy's ear had come through Maru, but she knew from Treshanna who'd paid for the little viral campaign. Tresh had thought it was funny to get paid by a former stable-mate and she'd agreed. But now she saw a plan behind it and got the distinct feeling that it hadn't mattered who got shot back there. Probably would have been a bonus if both of them wound up dead. She got up and left the table without a word of farewell.

She shouldered through the panic in the kitchen and slipped out the back door. Cutting across the corner of Analberto's Tacos, she moved quickly through to the Motel Six, a layout with which she had a working acquaintance, and emerged at the bus stop on Broadway as the first police cars screamed into the Angus lot. She realized something else, sorting things out as she sat demurely in hopes the 932 would come by pretty quick. Her laugh had been part of it. She'd seen guys like that react to being laughed at in her time. She might have been the one who delivered the *coup de grace* back there. Maybe she could collect something on that.

She was glad the bus came by in only six minutes. As she sat in the back row, ignoring the comments of a bunch of teenage gangbanger wannabes, she decided not to mention her role in that Fed getting shot to anybody. Whatever Nan might pay her, it wasn't worth it to make any contact with her. She liked Nan okay, working with her. Classy, good-natured, fun sense of humor. But she was starting to see her as somebody who wouldn't think a thought about getting folks shot dead.

Chapter Forty-Four

The southwest block of Solares was a bachelor barracks. There were women in there, but they were hardened, gun-packing *jainas* who fought and killed with the men, wore the tattoos proclaiming bombings and mutilations. The Mara control of the building was absolute: they'd moved all the families out two years before, generously and with goodwill. The big project up in the Vientos hills was occupied territory, but Solares was an outpost, a fort overlooking the city and garrisoned with the youngest and baddest. There were guards on the roof, sentinels in old cars on surrounding corners, watchers at the doorways. At four in the morning the Mara slept, but with one eye open and a gun in each hand. The rooftop snipers died first.

They had heard the pipey clatter of a two-stroke engine, but assumed it was a *moto*, some early morning delivery scooter. Before they fully realized that a black-painted ultralight was sweeping down on them, the engine of the open "GoKart with wings" went silent and twin M-16's mounted on the frame opened up, triggers tightened by release cables from the pilot's stick. The little flyer banked, yawed, fell back into an unpowered glide while the guns raked sixty rounds across the roof. All five teen-agers at that post were killed without firing a shot. One boy, mortally wounded, managed to point his gun at the sky, but the pilot leaned out to put a .357 pistol round through his head from a mere nine meters away. The motor cut back in and the ultralight banked into a turn towards the soccer field below, where a car waited to evacuate the pilot to the safe house out past El Florido.

Six street corner *vigilances* heard the shots, but had no time to react. Six men in black flak jackets appeared from around corners or doorways, all pointing stubby M-39 grenade launchers at the lookouts' cars. The result was so well co-coordinated it almost sounded like one blast, but the Maras who'd awakened and looked out the windows saw several columns of fire in the streets around them.

Fifty young warriors were bailing out of bed, looking for somebody to shoot. Several focused on the vehicle that was pulling up in front of the lobby doors. It was a glass delivery truck originally, but the sloping side rack was currently all steel plate. A small window amidships revealed the multiple barrels of a minigun, a hand-machined copy of the General Electric/DeGroat original. Five Maras ran through the foyer, pouring fire on the truck with their Chinese-made Kalashnikovs. Their shots were deflected high into the air by the angled plating. Then the minigun replied: in two seconds over a thousand copper-jacked 7.62mm rounds vaporized the lobby glass, eroded the walls like a hurricane of lead and almost literarily obliterated the Maras.

Other armed, crazed hotshots ran from side doors and jumped out windows, trying to outflank the truck. They found that the passenger window of the cab was also steel plate. And that aimed fire from the rooftops at the ends of the block was picking them off with a deadly precision.

Their plan quickly shifted to crouching inside the front windows, popping up to reconnoiter or fire blindly. Almost all of the gunmen in the project were at the front windows when streaks of fire whooshed in from the night, blowing big holes in the façade and turning young killers into chopped meat.

All four mortars were in the beds of two beer trucks on the public basketball court three blocks away. All trajectories had been computed in advance and there was no fumbling for range or target, just a swarm of sonic bees appearing out of the night to blitz the Maras straight to perdition. Within two minutes, before the ultralight had landed and the beer trucks fired up to lumber off to warehouse hideaways, there was no returning fire from the riddled project.

An armored car with signage from the Baja's largest bank pulled into the street and waited for any other signs of resistance. When nothing happened, two men climbed from the glass truck and carried the minigun to the back door of the armored courier, which opened for them. The glass truck started up and lurched into reverse on shredded tires. It backed up thirty feet before the driver hit a hydraulic lever and the big steel plates slid off the rack and crashed to the street.

The truck pulled forward, letting the plates clang down to the street with a sound like a two-ton skillet falling on a tile floor, then crunched over the curb on bare rims and drove into the lobby. The driver jumped out, covering himself with a compact Bullpup semi-auto tucked into his elbow, ran out to the street, leaped into the open door of the armored car, and slammed it behind him as it quickly rolled up to speed and around the corner. Thirty seconds later the big tanks of heating oil and nitrate fertilizer left in the glass truck detonated and the building shook itself to death then collapsed into its own corpse.

At about the moment that the vigilance cars around the Solares fortress exploded, another vehicle nine miles across town blew up much more spectacularly. The rusty old Dina panel truck had been sitting across from the front doors of Infonavit Vientos, a festering four story building of inferior construction even for a government housing project. Perched on the lip of a precipitous *barranca* in the uncontrolled western ooze of the Tijuana urban amoeba, Vientos was a more recent, but more thorough, infestation of the Mara Salvatrucha into the TJ ecosystem. They had appropriated the entire sprawling tenement and turned it into a community. It even had its own clinic. The fact that it was not just an armed camp, but also family territory, had made setting up the second blow against the Mara much more difficult to plan and implement. But Nan had insisted.

When the huge bale of high explosives in the Dina blew up, it didn't just cause a deafening thunderclap and disorienting fireball, it also peppered the front of the building with thousands of rubber erasers. The hail of high-velocity rubber blew out almost all of the windows in the front façade and shattered mirrors and pictures throughout the front apartments. But they didn't kill anybody. Several people were hit, but only a young woman who'd been on the toilet when the carbomb blew was injured even slightly, a badly bruised cheek just under her left eye. But there was nothing to suggest anything to the Maras other than that they had been sprayed by a fusillade from ambush.

Within seconds after the detonation, two vans slid around the corners of the front street, parking diagonally just in from the intersections. Their side doors flew open, and in each one a roof-mounted rack swung down in a manner made familiar by Vietnam helicopter door guns, revealing twin miniguns. As Maras ran out to fight, a bearded Viet-Vet with a fringe of gray around his balding head swung his gun in an arc, etching a jagged seam of death through the street. In the other van a young black ex-gangster wearing earphones and dark glasses grinned as he tipped his gun upward, tearing chunks out of anything at the other end of the three-quarter solid line of hot metal he was waving around.

At the mouth of the stinking muddy alley that ran behind the tenement, a black mid-sized pickup truck sat silent and dark. In the middle of the block, across from the rear doors, three men lay on the roof of a grimy shed left there by workers who'd built this junk housing. Two had light Ingram sub-machine guns on shoulder lanyards and Italian automatic shotguns in their hands. The third rested his head on the composite shoulder stock of an M-60 machine gun, fed by a belt of rounds from a green metal ammunition box. They moved to ready positions as a group of women and children erupted from the rear door.

The stream of kids and young women from the beleaguered building swelled, then started milling in small groups in the alley. The kids cried and ran amok, the women stared back at the building where their men were fighting for their lives. As soon as the flood of half-dressed refugees stopped, the headlights of the pickup snapped on to light up the scene like a chiaroscuro Guernica snapshot. Rotating red and blue lights strobed from on top of the cab and a loud, hateful siren started its techno-Euro warble. Panicked once again, the flock of families and camp followers ran away from the truck, to the other end of the alley where a narrow stairway led down to the streets below.

When they had all fled, the truck snapped back to darkness and silence. Two men stepped out and hopped up into the bed, leaning over the cab roof to steady their weapons, an old Browning automatic rifle and a modified assault rifle from Fabrique Nationale with a gaping M-39 grenade launcher attached below the barrel. One of them carefully placed a black box on the roof, with wires leading to the front bumper of the truck, where three slightly curved olive-green packets were mounted. An embossed legend was visible on each Claymore mine, "This Side Towards Enemy".

As their women ran back to cover, the Mara mounted the same undisciplined frontal wave that had served them so poorly down at

193

Solares. Twenty or so had been abolished anonymously by the whirring whoop of the cloned miniguns from the dark doors of the vans. They were dying like roaches and most hadn't seen the face of a single attacker. Their street was a death-belching firepit, their home was being chipped away and looked more and more like a death trap. They fired into the night, furious with hopeless fear.

Warbling sirens brought two police cars into the street, skidding around the corner almost sideways. For the first time in their young, violent lives the Mara were glad to hear the cops arrive. One *patrulla* skidded to a stop, the driver staring awestruck at the hellish pageant of demolition he'd barged in on. Two young cops jumped out of the following car, pistols in hand.

The nearest black van reversed with wheels cocked over, shunting around to reveal the open side door. Inside, behind the smoking black tubes, a graying death's head smiled at them cheerfully, reached to ratchet the receiver clear and leaned back on the grips to take aim. Both cars left streaks of hot rubber in reverse gear as they dived back around the corner.

A little under a mile to the east, on an overlook whose view of the endless sprawl of Tijuana's night made it somewhat of a "lovers' lane" at times, a shiny diesel pickup had been parked since late afternoon, hitched to a fifth-wheel trailer called a ToyHauler because the rear door could be swung down to create a ramp for wheeling in dirt bikes, ATV's and other gas-guzzling motion toys favored in the Baja badlands. But that night it fell open to reveal the slotted muzzle of a 75mm recoilless rifle on a bolt-down mount. The truck started up immediately and idled while three men slapped a projectile into the breech, locked it down, and fired.

They fired eight times, each shot coming after one of the gunners moved a lever a minute degree, which translated into the incendiary shells slamming into the entire third floor of the Maras' homestead, one streetfront apartment at a time. The floors above and below shared in the benefits of the explosions, which also deranged the rear units and left the entire building burning, falling, smoking, and sagging in abject defeat. The rear door of the trailer lifted and the truck was on its way to a campground on the beach at Km. 62 within a minute of the last shell rocketing off into the darkness.

There were few Maras alive inside the building at that point, and they were staggering out, running for their lives. But there was nowhere to go. The tattered survivors ran back through the building, all resistance gone. Without shame or pause they fled after their women. When they burst into the back alley they milled for a minute, regrouping, then the pickup's headlights flicked on again and a horizontal rain of metal blew through them like they'd never even been alive.

Chapter Forty-Five

As soon as the attack started, Syco was up, armed and heading for the front with JoJo right behind him. This wasn't a police raid or some other gang. Both of them had been through military attacks before and it's the sort of thing that once experienced tends not to be forgotten. They ran through the panicked corridors of the Vientos warren, Syco screaming for the women and children to withdraw like they'd been taught, for the males to follow him to the third floor front, where the heaviest armament was located.

He jumped into a front apartment on the second floor, looked out and fired, then ran for the stairwell. "I don't see anybody out there," he yelled at JoJo and Montero, a local warlord who had joined them, carrying an AK-47 and machete. He motioned them up the stairwell and was waving another group of men upwards when the firebombs slugged through the front windows and blasted the world into rubble and flame.

JoJo had been protected by the stairs, but Syco lay in a burned, bleeding heap in a back apartment, wedged under a fallen concrete *viga*. JoJo ran to him, seeing the rest of the guys collapsing into mindless panic. He fired three shots in the air, hammering sharply in the closed quarters. He pointed to the stairway and screamed at the top of his lungs, "Down! Out the back! Follow the women. Go, go!"

Without thought or question, they obeyed the youngest survivor in the building, heading for a retreat, another day. JoJo quickly bent over Syco. It didn't look good.

He felt like crying. The destruction around him meant little: it had never been his home. But this was his most trusted mission so far: guard Syco's life. He could already tell that he'd failed and it was bitter in his mouth.

This kid had made his own bargain with death when he was seven years old; stood right in front of the end of all life and stepped right up to take it. He'd sealed the relationship in blood a year later out in the jungles, swinging up the barrel of a rifle as tall as he was, ripping slugs through the sweaty fatigue shirts and shocked cries. That had been before he found his new family, had been back when he was Jose, Pepito, *hijo mio*, beloved son. One thing he'd known half his life was that he would never shirk away from laying down his life for his family.

He knelt by Syco, trying to pull him out from under the beam while the flames licked closer, breathing in the toxic stench of burning synthetic upholstery and carpet. He was crying as he clawed at the concrete, tugged at Syco's flaccid limbs. Not from the pain in his bloodied hands, or the burns on his legs, or even the loss of an admired companion he'd fought with and camped out with in rainy jungles and heavily patrolled border swamps. He cried out of frustration and failure.

Syco was still breathing; a shallow, shaky rhythm. But he was pinned down for good. JoJo pulled away his shirt, hoping for some extra space, and saw a piece of rebar stabbed deep into his leader's chest. The flames were all around them now. He wanted Syco to live, but he didn't want him to come around. They were both on fire. He jumped away as Syco's hair burst into flame. He stood looking down for a second, brought up the muzzle of his AK, and fired once, right between the eyes. And that was that.

He was about to pass out in the acrid smoke, losing his vision and balance as he inhaled the chemical poisons. His pants leg had been on fire, but he'd managed to beat it out. He stumbled through the rubble and flame like a blind man, fell into the stairwell and bounced painfully down to the first floor landing. He was hurt bad, he realized. Broken bones, seeping burns. He smoldered in shame and fury. He staggered for the back door. Two feet before he got to it, he saw the back alley light up like an apocalypse ballpark and explode into a roaring rattle of death. What comrades he could see through the door were carried helplessly to one side as if by a sudden, fell wind. He tripped, fell on his face, bloodying his nose and knee. He lay there a moment, shaking his head clear, then the bangfest outside stopped and everything was all over.

He used his rifle to get to his feet, limped to the door, and peeked through. He saw a pickup truck pull forward and three men with weapons jump from a roof to the bed. He willed himself to pull his gun up and burn the bastards down, but he just couldn't do it and the truck rumbled away in reverse. He felt like passing out. He leaned in the doorway, heaving sobbing breaths until the smoke cleared out of his lungs enough for him to move. He hobbled numbly across his comrades' shredded bodies, like so many logs or dead dogs in the alley.

He found the stairway and staggered down it, slumping against one damp concrete wall. At the bottom he fell forward, lurching out into the midst of a huddle of silent, terrified women and children. He was looking right into the face of Lina, Montero's woman. All he could see in her eyes was a question. He burst into hacking sobs and fell to his knees.

Three days later, bandaged, splinted and nursed back to health by Lina in a filthy shed behind a butcher shop in Lomas Portillo, JoJo had a clear mind and plenty of time to think and put things together. He lay in a hammock with two sleepy babies, the morning edition of *El Mexicano* open on his chest. It was still crammed full of news of the massacre, everybody from the Mayor to the Governor, to the President of the Republic, to the United States State Department squawking about it and nobody with the slightest idea who did it. *Narcos*, they said. The answer to everything. The first thing JoJo had figured out during his convalescence was that if he hadn't tried to save Syco, he'd have been in that alley, blasted into dogfood with the others.

Also that the surviving Mara women, who were disbanding and drifting off to other places, resented him for having lived through the attack when all their men died. If he hadn't been so obviously damaged and heroic, that resentment could have led to a blade slipped between his ribs. Lina, on the other hand, had just transferred her allegiance to him. She had slipped into the hammock with him last night, wanting comfort more than giving it. The survivors who remained looked to him for leadership, though he was younger than all but two of them. Though broken and defeated, he was the male of the pride.

Another thought that had come to him was the way the attack at Vientos had unfolded. Not a sudden, unavoidable smash of death like had happened in Solares, but an articulated pressure from the front. They had known everything about them, had known the women would leave and the men would stand and fight. Until it was their time to stumble out into the steel blizzard of the alley.

Now, sifting backwards, he remembered that a reporter had asked questions of some of the children, bought them sodas and cigarettes at the little store by the school. Even though no paper in Tijuana had run any story on the Mara since the new mayor took over.

And hadn't there been a social worker at the school two weeks ago? More questions. Safety and hygiene at home. The kids had reported these inquiries, and he knew their responses had been reported elsewhere. So whoever had struck down from the night and killed his family had more organization than just soldiers and big guns: they had *known*.

It also occurred to him that all that intelligence had been used to spare some lives when it would have been easier to just kill everybody. All that had been needed was one big bomb, like the one they did in Managua that time. The people behind the raid didn't want to kill women and babies. Which meant it wasn't *narcos*. Or anybody he'd ever fought against. It was almost like it was ordered by somebody with kids. A woman perhaps.

As soon as the thought crossed his mind, it dragged an image with it. He saw the face of the woman from the parking lots, who had eluded Syco's claws twice. She'd stood up like a man, summoned help very cleverly, had no fear whatsoever: he could see that clearly. Again she reminded him of somebody he'd known long ago, back when he was another person entirely.

And now, after they had struck at her, her husband, the children at that restaurant, they had gotten wiped out by white men with sophisticated foreign weapons. It could have been her. No doubt about it. And he had nobody left, couldn't go to her for revenge. But he knew who could. He'd see about that tomorrow.

Meanwhile, there was Lina. And these two babies. And the other ones outside.

It would take some major effort to bring them back. And it looked like it would be up to him. They would be back here, take power again. The Mara Salvatrucha wasn't like a tree you could chop down. It was like asparagus, an underground network that put up shoots here and there in order to feed and grow. But they would need a seed to grow around. And he was it.

He spoke softly and Lina was immediately in the room. "I have to go somewhere tomorrow, a couple of days. Then we're going to leave. Everybody."

She nodded without expression. She'd been brought up here from Guatemala without explanation, now she'd go somewhere else. The men spoke and she did what they said. Her only question was, "Where will we go?"

"South". He never even thought of the word "home" anymore.

She nodded again, satisfied, but he went on. "We'll be back here. This isn't over."

"No." Lina was no blushing bride. She'd killed on command, had hacked off a policeman's genitals with a banana knife when she was thirteen.

"Where are you going tomorrow?"

JoJo picked up a fretting baby and laid it on his chest, patted it gently. "To make sure they know it isn't over."

Chapter Forty-Six

Like the guy'd been sitting there waiting for him. As soon as he stepped in the office door, Mobley picked up a copy of the Union-Tribune, snapped it out, and held it up in front of him, flashing the headline: TOLL MOUNTS IN TJ DRUG WAR.

"I got a couple copies," he said from behind the paper. "Want one for that scrapbook of yours?"

Reach had read it already, but stepped across, took the section from him and looked it over. "They found some more bodies under the rubble," he said blandly. "Sure know how to keep milking a massacre."

"Next time you're jammed up jelly tight with the comely Miz Gaspar, might ask her what she's got lined up for an encore."

"For a guy your age, you don't mind jumping to conclusions, do you?"

"Don't take no 'Sherlock'," Mobley snorted derisively. "That crazy bitch is firing up the whole border on us."

He stopped, hand to mouth, "Oh, forgive me. I didn't mean to insult the object of your infatuations."

Reach, downcast with embarrassment, held out his palms. "I think I'm over all that."

Are you, now? Mobley thought as Reach suddenly burst out, "I wanted her more than any woman I've ever known. And now I'm thanking God I didn't get any closer in."

Aw, for pity sake, man. Little horseplay is one thing, but we got enough guts being spilled as it is. "Hey, now you're thinking with the big head, my man."

Reach nodded absently, but was obviously wrapped up in feeling sorry for himself. RayRay hesitated to go on with him moping like that, but decided it might be the best time for it. "So, in possibly related news, our buddy Gaithers got taken out, too. Are we thinking that in between mopping up international gangs she pops a Fed or two to keep her eye in?"

"I'll give you a freebie to jerk me with. She asked me to get him off her case and I said I couldn't and wouldn't. Looks like she opted for self-serve."

Mobley grunted and stood. He walked over to the coffeemaker and poured a cup, one cream, no sugar, and carried it over to Reach, who took it with an appreciative nod. "Thanks, Ray."

"Best be glad you're better-looking than that DEA asshole, huh?"

Reach laughed out loud, almost spilling the coffee. "Can we agree that she's gone totally out of control?"

"Sure as hell out of our control." He turned to get his own coffee, muttering, "A million beats in this world and she has to walk onto mine."

Reach sipped the coffee, looking into middle distance. Mobley almost didn't hear him murmur, "And the hell of it is, all everybody had to do was let sleeping beauties lie."

Chapter Forty-Seven

Reach had been in the border area almost four months, but was a Tijuana newbie. So he might have hoped for an enlightening exposure to Mexican color, or at least vignettes of the downtown tourist zoo parade, in this excursion to meet the TJ cops Mobley always referred to as his "counterparts". If so, he was bound to be disappointed by Taqueria Cinco Esquinas.

The bus they'd grabbed at the border crossing took them right to the door, except there was no door. Reach's crash Spanish course in Virginia had actually given him more of a command of the language than Mobley, which he found humorous. So he didn't have to count the five streets to figure out the name of the smoky, pungent open-air taco shop at the intersection where they converged. He realized the lack of doors and shutters meant it stayed open twenty-four hours. The sort of place cops would know.

No trouble spotting the "counterparts", either. Their tan *municipales* uniforms created a buffer area around them in what Reach took to be a fairly raffish clientele with high criminal content. But for all he knew everybody in Tijuana looked that way. They'd occupied one of the two sidewalk tables, the one beside it unoccupied even though other customers were eating standing up. Mobley was obviously used to this and plopped down at the other table. Reach joined him, sitting carefully on a grubby plastic chair bearing a faded ad for Negra Modelo beer.

The older cop, a big guy with lots of shoulder who looked every bit as banged-up, hard-bitten, and criminally-inclined as the customer base, pointed at Mobley and raised five fingers in the air. The guy chopping *carne asada* on a slice of tree stump obviously had one eye on the big cop at all times because he nodded instantly and whipped five corn tortillas onto the grill like a Vegas dealer. The younger cop, clean-cut and good looking, nodded at Reach and asked him in good English, "How many tacos do you want?"

Apparently food came before introductions down here; not a bad concept, actually. Reach had noticed the tacos were rolled-up tortillas, nothing like Taco Bell. "Four, I guess."

"You're *Federal*, right? I'm Benito Reyes." He held up four fingers and got the same quick nod from the *taquero*. He inclined his head towards the older cop. *"Y presento Sargento Alonso Bernal.* Ugly sucker, no?"

Reach gave his name to Reyes and Bernal and shook hands but got very little feeling off the older cop. Who was mostly thinking, *Jesucristo*, this one's even prettier than Reyes. And wondering if *Federales* from *el otro lado* were as big shitheads as the Mexican variety.

There was no waitress, but Reach saw the cook motion for a customer to take the two plates of tacos to their tables. The guy glanced over and shook his head but the cook, wreathed in fragrant smoke, waved his knife emphatically and the guy carried the plates over, set them down and bolted away. Then had to approach them again to lay down four cold Coronas. The tacos tasted greasy and smoky, sensationally good. Mobley was tucking into them with his usual voracious gusto. Beats the hell out of a donut shop, Reach thought. He alternated bites of the savory beef and sips of beer, scanning the area while Mobley brought the Mexican cops up to speed on their reasons for coming down to chat.

The *taqueria* was a concrete cave full of smoke. Reach figured you could poke around and find mammoths painted on the walls back there somewhere. No frills at all, just a huge grill behind waist-high windows which served as counters and sideboards for bowls full of radishes, guacamole, cilantro/onion mix and scary-looking *chile* sauces. Buses thundered up, belching heavy smoke just feet away from their table, and unloaded working men and families. The other four corners were all essentially third world versions of convenience shops, except the dingy barbershop where a guy was getting a shave with a hand-held razor blade.

Behind the two cops he could see down the fifth street, which pitched steeply downhill and gave a panoramic view of the valley below. A valley sliced in two by a long iron fence with periodic standards holding arrays of floodlights that could have held their own illuminating Yankee Stadium. The southerly view of the United States Border. Maybe Reyes and Bernal were making a point.

In fact, that's exactly what they were saying at the moment. Mobley had referred to the Salvatrucha gang as "those little scum from down South" and Reyes quickly spoke up. "Also from the barrios up in *Los*, don't forget."

Bernal nodded ponderously, never missing the chance to remind Mobley of things like that, "*Pues*, thank you for train them."

"Don't mention it," Mobley replied, rolling up another taco and folding the end over to minimize the drip of hot grease. "Thing is, you seem to have an idea how they fit into all this. And we don't have much of a clue."

"They're enemies of the Altamira operation. You noticed he's Mayor now, by the way?"

"I don't understand how a drug kingpin gets elected Mayor of a big city," Reach said without thinking and drew blank looks from the Mexicans, writing him off as naïve.

"Drugs and kidnapping are the only way they know to make out," Reyes said to Mobley, obviously dealing Reach out of the conversation. "And the only place they can cut it out of is Altamira's operation. So they're enemies of the most powerful man in Baja. One of the most powerful families in the country."

"You mean 'were' enemies, don't you?" Mobley asked pointedly.

Bernal snorted like a buffalo. "No 'were'. You kill the ants on your table, are no more ants?"

"So it's not over with, huh?" He didn't expect an answer to that, just turned around and held up three fingers to the cook. He got the nod and smiled contentedly. "And you're thinking it was Altamira wiped those guys out? Then why are we talking?"

"No." Reyes was very definite. "We think it was done by Altamira's *gallo* from your side. Sr. Gaspar."

"Well now that's very interesting, matter of fact. Because we kind of get a hunch it was Gaspar's wife."

Reyes and Bernal both stared incredulously. Mobley swigged from his beer and shrugged. "Hey, he's been sick, okay?"

"You think a *woman* sent that attack?"

Mobley pulled a black leather fanny back around to front center and pulled out some small black and white close-ups of

Nan, laid them on the table in front of the two uniforms. Reyes picked one up and stared at it with an intensity that seemed to go beyond police work. "That's our babe," Mobley teased him. "You getting some 'hard' data there, *amigo*?"

Reyes laid the shot down and picked up another one, a profile from the same surveillance session. "She just reminds me of a girl I knew in school."

"Shit, kid, where'd you go to school? The Playboy Mansion?"

Bernal was also intent on her picture, tapping it thoughtfully with a blunt finger. "Remind you of school days, too, Lonso?" Mobley bantered.

"No," Bernal said thoughtfully. "Other pictures. We take. She came here, to Altamira."

Reyes took another look at the picture and his eyebrows shot up. "*Ujule!* He's right. We thought she was just, you know... he has a certain reputation. For quality."

"But she's not *puta*, she's Gaspar's *esposa*?" Bernal couldn't believe it.

Mobley glanced at Reach, enjoying himself. "Well, actually a little of both."

"You think she took charge while Gaspar's in prison? Or in the hospital?"

"That's exactly what we're thinking. She brought in mercs when Gaspar was in traction, a coma, a world of hurt."

Bernal couldn't look away from the shot of Nan, her face peeking out from under the wide brim of a white summer hat, as though flirting with the camera that was supposedly hidden in a phone company van across the street from her house. He spoke slowly, a sense of wonder in his broken English. "We have drug murder here all the days. *Matanzas, masacres. Bandas* of *narcos* fight for millions of dollars, *ya sabes.*"

"Yeah, seems I heard something about that," Mobley offered conversationally.

"Tijuana, *desgraciadamente*, has the fame for this. *Narco-masacres.* Twelve dead *narcos* today, ten tomorrow. I think record is twenty."

Reyes saw where he was going and put in, "Now we've got 246 people dead. So far."

"And this was made by a *woman*? By a *prosti*?" Bernal didn't try to mask his incredulity.

Mobley spread his hands, no explanation to offer. "Yep. Whore with a heart of full metal jackets."

Reach also signaled for more tacos. He said, "I am woman, hear me roar."

Chapter Forty-Eight

The lowrider that edged around the corner, lights off and oversquare engine barely turning over, was the flagship of the La Neta fleet, Poker's own car; lovingly hand-built, burnished and fortified. A different breed from the boxy early sixties look favored by the new school *cholos*, this was a *clasico* '54 Chevy with fenderskirts and awning, chopped, channeled, frenched, reversed, lowered and dechromed into a sleek abstraction that combined the look of spacecraft from old serials with cruising submarine creatures. None of that hydraulic bouncing and dancing jive: this was a lowrider and it bygod rode low. The multi-coated, hand-rubbed midnight color revealed ephemeral highlights of neon purple as it skulked along under the street lamps.

Nobody would want to face Poker Cabrales in a fight, and several who had were no longer around to brag about it. His pocked face and shaved head carried their scars, his flat Indian features had been pounded rounder and flatter, combative tats crawled from the rolled-back sleeves of his Pendleton and down to his calloused, battered hands. But he sensed that he was out of his element as leader and warlord of the gang, a position that had been thrust on him, essentially, by attrition. He liked working on his car, bare-chested with weightpile muscle rippling and hands greased black to the wrists, bending wrenches under the old eucalyptus behind his shanty at the edge of Barrio Lobo. Talking to girls and drinking cold Tecates in a blare of *rancho* music at Las Milpas.

Not scheming ways for his *gente* to fight clear of the pressures of sustaining income in an area increasingly dominated by big international outfits. He didn't let himself realize it, but his biggest dread was that he was presiding over the death of his way of life, and his homeboys. And making all the wrong moves.

But he'd agreed to this *rifa* and it made some sort of sense. Those Mara Salvatrucha *locos* were the only group strong enough to oppose the Hispanic *narco-mafia* and he couldn't throw in with the Gaspar *bola*, so he'd allied with the little psychos. Now somebody was pounding the Maras and they thought this might make that stop. So here they were, La Neta in full combat mode;

eight burbling, low slung rods loafing down the suburban street like a pod of killer whales. Full of *vatos* with shotguns and AK's. Pulling right up in front of the house.

Poker's window, *blindado* with a deep purple film, whispered down and he regarded the house solemnly. Beside him, Yato leaned over and gave it the eye. No lights inside the walls, no sign of motion, no traffic on the street. He looked at Yato, then turned to poll Shady and Pharow in the back seat. Neither made any movement, but he caught a hint of nod from Pharow, who was a lot smarter than he was. He turned back, took a breath, stuck the big old Browning .45 into his waistband and took his sawed-off Remington twelve gauge off the floor. "*Pues...*" he said softly.

He jerked his head around, bringing the cutoff up to the window, as a thin whining sound came from the garage in the Gaspar house. The three wide electric garage doors were rolling slowly upwards, showing them a widening slot of complete darkness inside. Vision and gun barrels fixed on the garage, they didn't notice that two dark vans had slipped into the street ends, blocking off any exit from the block, straddling the street with their side doors facing the La Neta battle group. The garage continued to open, still revealing nothing inside.

The lights in the garage came on like a punch in the face. At the same instant the doors of the gunvans at the corners banged open. Poker and his *carnales* stared into three helpings of heavy weapons squad crouching behind concrete street barriers, aiming at the lowriders with a wide selection of very butch-looking guns. The two gunships in the street made the same sound at once, the ratchet of miniguns being cleared for firing. Poker looked through his chopped-down tinted windshield, then back out his side window, staring into the face of inevitable, instant death. The gangbangers sat motionless in shock, a frozen tableau in the wee hours up on Lobo Mesa.

They didn't find out how long they would have sat there before doing something desperately crazy or too craven to think about, because a guy walked out of the garage in the aura of intense light from the halogen spots aimed outward from the rear walls. Wearing black fatigues, beret and shoulder holster, he strolled nonchalantly in front of the field of massed fire, looked over the immobilized shorts, and swaggered up to Poker's window.

He bent his knees to look through inside, lean and hungry guy with Siberian eyes, and nodded to Poker and Yato. He inspected the guns on display in the car, then glanced over his shoulder at the men behind him. He granted Poker a wolfish smile.

"Hi, I'm Lux," he said with the cool friendliness of somebody who respects his opponent but holds all the cards. "I'd like to invite you in for a drink. I mean, if you don't have other plans."

The blue glow from the lights in the pool, the warm flicker of tiki torches, the soft indirect lighting around the patio; all very beautiful and soothing. But Poker sat stiff and unsoothed, the tumbler of Don Julio untouched on the stone tabletop by his elbow. Pharow, beside him but slightly distant from the table, had already tossed his drink down and felt like he could use a couple more. Poker ignored Lux standing behind him, and Alfredo over to the side with his arms crossed on his chest. He was only interested in Gaspar's wife. Right up in the top five finest *jainas* he'd ever seen, sitting there in that silky robe the color of British Racing, treating him very politely and asking him to call her Nan. And obviously in charge of this whole *chingadera*. He just couldn't think of anything to say to her.

So he said, "*Oye*, Las Maras are our friends. Allies, you see what I'm saying. Against those *pinches* Gaspars."

"Excuse me?" Nan was still polite, but slightly offended. "I *am* a Gaspar. Did I hurt you? Or your people?"

She leaned forward, the sweet hostess falling away from a firm, determined look. "Did I get your little brother killed?"

As she'd intended, that reference to past scrapes dragged Poker out of his dither and stony *machote*. His fists and tattooed throat clenched as he barked out, "Your husband's bodyguard shot him! Alfredo was there, saw the whole fucking thing!"

Nan gave a sigh, shaking her head in disappointment. "After he pulled a gun on about twenty armed cops. Don't be such a homie. Who paid your brother to get involved in that thing? Getting a sixteen year old kid to do a hit for them?"

"And were going to kill him afterwards, anyway?" Alfredo put in stolidly. "Those friends and allies of yours."

"Hear you tell it," Poker sulked. He glared around him, looked at Pharow, who was showing nothing to nobody. He spotted his drink and took a deep swallow.

"Look, Poker." The steel edge clicked back into its sheath and she spoke to him in understanding, respectful tones. "You don't want us to bring you in--pay you--I respect that. Not a problem. Consider a truce. A cease-fire before more people die."

Truce. *Gabacho* word for "give it up". Poker glowered but was starting to lose sight of why he should be pissed off at her. He fell back on gangbanger basics. "We're not afraid of you."

Behind him Lux gently remarked, "Do you want to be?"

Poker didn't respond.

"Those Maras down in Baja weren't afraid of us either. Now they are."

"That's why they sent you instead of coming themselves," Alfredo chipped in.

"Do you see a kind of pattern there?" Nan asked bluntly.

"You should think about sitting this dance out, *compa*," Alfredo suggested mildly. "Or if you want, we could pay you to go shoot those little assholes for us."

"Either way, we don't end up shooting each other. Here where we both live." Nan appealed to reason without being condescending. "Smart guys think win/win. But if you mix it up with us we both lose. And for what?"

Poker looked from her to Alfredo and took another pull on his glass. He just couldn't figure this one out. He wished Pharow would jump in.

Behind him, to his right, Pharow had been scanning the setup from under the roll of his watch cap, sizing these people up. He could see that Poker was frozen on dead center. He loved the guy, but he wasn't who you wanted making big decisions on short notice. He suddenly said, "How about we think this over a little?"

Nan smiled at him and motioned towards his glass. One of Alfredo's guys, a *vato* he knew from grade school, stepped over and poured him another measure of Julio.

Nan swept her wide blue gaze across both of the Neta guys. In a soft tone with no hint of malice or wiggle room, she said, "That's exactly what I hope you'll do."

Chapter Forty-Nine

Several underlings stood around the mayoral office at various points, none taking a seat on the stiff chairs and sofas. They were in complete attendance under the antiquated banners and framed pictures of past Tijuana mayors, looking at all times at *Don* Altamira, faces blank of anything other than quiet respect. Several of these aides had been puzzled for several days as to why *Don* Altamira would not take pleasure in the public destruction of the Central American gangs that were the only challenge to his power. Aides that hadn't been around long enough to know that trying to second-guess or predict him was a waste of energy.

One of the battalion of attorneys he kept busy or poised for action was broaching the subject and everyone in the room was curious about what they would learn.

"The entire situation is totally out of control, *Don* Altamira."

"For now," he replied. He was an average-looking man without bluster or pose, especially among underlings. "Perhaps these people are unaware of my future plans."

Most of us are, the lawyer thought. "You don't seem pleased that this scum has been burned out for you."

"Would you be pleased, *licenciado*," the Man said with a faint accent on the title that everybody there knew was not a good sign. "To have to stand for governor of this state in three years if your administration was nationally noted as a war zone?"

The attorney stood silent, waiting.

"For that matter, how happy would I be about my campaign for the nomination, which I remind you is not yet decided," Altamira went on, "If I become widely associated with bloodbaths and the wanton annihilation of public housing?"

"There is no point in discussing things with those MaraSalva *vagos*," the attorney ventured.

"No, I'd think not," Altamira agreed. "Especially since they mostly seem to be converted to charcoal and cat fodder. But there will be more of them. Soon."

"If it's true that Gaspar's people did it, we can certainly pull them back into line by their ears."

"Let them know that I don't much care for having my city converted into a stage set for Armageddon? I would hope so."

"It's hard to tell exactly what is going on," the attorney said, not at all liking what he was telling his boss. "Gaspar is now in the prison hospital wing, as close to impossible to communicate with as anybody could be. You spoke with his wife yourself and detected no threat."

"A fascinating woman," Altamira said. "Of many depths and levels. I think we can assume she's the source of all this damaging publicity."

Another underling spoke up from where he'd been standing by the door. "Actually, Señor, it seems that she influenced a San Diego journalist to write an article saying that what happened was a cleansing, a crippling blow against the drug trade."

The first attorney nodded, chagrined to have been robbed of mentioning that. "Our investigation indicates that the weekly publication schedule means the article had to have been written before the attacks took place."

"And saying very much the same thing Blas Espinosa wrote in "Zeta"."

"Not a co-incidence," the lawyer answered quickly. "She is not only creating heavy damage and attention here, but she is manipulating our own press and we have no control over her."

"Then we have little choice, do we?"

The attorney paused only slightly before asking, "But to eliminate her?"

Altamira's left eyebrow moved only millimeters, but got across his dismissal of what had been said. "Of course not. We exploit her."

Chapter Fifty

It had been a heavy week, to say the least, but Nan felt some of the load come off her shoulders as she stepped into the waiting room in white jeans and golf jacket over a silk blouse in holiday red. Just entering the prison had a calming effect on her, which she found richly amusing. But why not? The cares of the world were outside strong walls now, she was in a circle of protection where she could lay around in her underwear joking with her husband, talk about the kids, get a little roll in the hay. She shook her head, stifled a laugh. Yeah, sure: Honey, I'm home. Practically a TV wife off *Family Ties* or something. I'll have to decide on a proper Christmas gratuity for the guard. Who looked up and saw her, then nodded towards the side wall. Where Sean Reach leaned in the doorway, waiting for her.

He read something in her face as she walked over to him, because he immediately blurted, "Listen, no funny business this time. I promise. I'm really sorry about all that's happened."

"Don't be down on yourself, Sean. I was there, too. And I let down my position as much as you did. But I'm not really sorry about it. You've opened my eyes quite a bit."

"I just wish..."

"Don't even go there, okay? I wish I'd met you years ago. But you wouldn't have been interested before I married The Antichrist, would you?"

He grimaced involuntarily. Brings out that dimple, she thought. Wish I had a camera. "I'm in no position to judge you," he said. "That's pretty obvious."

She glanced around the visitor area. Funny place to be having this talk, but nobody was in earshot. She looked back at his face and felt another twinge of her deep-seated unworthiness. Nothing like superficial physical perfection to haul out our deeper qualities for review, she thought sadly. "I know you don't think much of my morals. But I have always stood firm behind my business ethics."

He didn't have a response for that one. She always seemed to fade back into some complex mirror world whenever he expressed any feelings to her.

Nan thought his speechlessness was rather affecting, but let him off the hook with a sad smile and shrug. "Hey, if people ran their sex lives as honestly as their business there'd be less broken families."

"You know a lot about broken families?" He knew there was a hidden trigger or catch down inside her, the secret that would explain everything. And he'd give anything to be able to find those buried drives and understand them, soothe them away.

"I could write a book on it."

The stood silently a moment, staring at each other. Two kids with a sheet of glass between their noses and the Christmas display of toys and candy. She suddenly remembered something she should probably do.

"Oh, by the way, thanks for getting that Gaithers creep off my case. I haven't seen him since."

Once again he'd gotten lost in the serene beauty of her, only to have steely realities break the surface and snap in his face. He regarded her carefully, trying to evaluate. He said, "He was shot to death in a bar. By some Latino-looking gangster. Nobody you know?"

"Whoever did it, I'm sure they had their reasons." She left that hanging, hurrying on to the other thing she had to get done with this guy. "Look, this might be the last time we talk, at least without a lawyer present."

He sagged almost imperceptibly against the door jamb. "I came here to ask you something, but I think I just got the answer."

She'd already given her exit line, and should just pivot and walk off, but something in his dejection wouldn't let her. Why should he be hurt? He was the only one in this whole mess without hidden agendas and blood on his hands. She moved six inches closer and dropped her voice. "I want to tell you something, Sean. Just me to you. I'm quite attracted to you. You're everything I admired and couldn't have when I was young: straight, strong, dedicated, clean."

"I was until I met you."

"Ouch," she grimaced. "Okay, then, you deserve this one. Nothing ever worked out for me with men like that. Like you. I finally figured out I didn't feel like I deserved them, that I wasn't worth it."

He looked at her searchingly, spoke gingerly. "And now?"

"It seems to be changing for me. I'm learning I can have decent feelings for a man, stand by him and deserve whatever he gives me."

A flash of hope flashed across his face, then broke into a scowl. "You're talking about *Gaspar? He's* your morals coach? Jesus Christ!"

His hurt and anger made her want to pat him on the head and give him a cookie. An insight flashed through her head and changed the man she was looking at. She suddenly saw where her infatuation with Reach came from and it was silly and banal. Television. How's that for insipid?

Her only companion and confidant in those school years, laying there suffering, listening fearfully for the steps coming up the stairs. Her TV escape turning into books, uneasy sleep becoming the only luxury and solace of her life.

And all over TV, these strong-jawed, clean cut, incorruptible, crinkly-smiling heroes who couldn't be bought off, who wouldn't hurt people just because they had them in their clutches. Straight shooters. And here he was.

Maybe everybody's just running around trying to find their place in the phosphor glow of commercial fantasy. But there was a difference between the stationbreak idyll and the synthetic family ties her marriage had delivered her to. The Gaspar Show worked. And had documented support. She looked at Reach as if from a slight height.

"It doesn't matter who he is. What matters is who I am. It's ironic, because I look at you and see what could have been. And now I'm telling you there isn't ever going to be anything more between us."

"Why?" The word wrenched out him with enough force and emotion to make her glance toward the guards and waiting visitors. "Why? Because I'm crazy about you and got out of line?"

"It's even sadder than that." She spoke with a soft regret that registered in him as finality. "There's a war on. People are dying."

"*Talk* to me about it," he pleaded. "I can..."

"And you're one of the enemies." She stepped back, and gave him a smile that suckerpunched him right under his heart. "Goodbye, Sean."

Her expression snapped into an impersonal, businesslike mask and she turned away and walked towards the portal to the conjugal visit compound. He reflexively held up his hand as if to stop her and the guard stepped to bar her way.

She stopped, stood still, then turned and looked at him, waiting. His shoulders slumped and his arm fell to his side. He nodded at the guard, who checked Nan's ID and motioned her into the visiting area. Five minutes later the guard glanced at the doorway, and there was that Fed, still standing there with his thumb up his butt.

Chapter Fifty-One

It was cool in Boneyard 11, but not chilly: the blinds glowed a soft yellow in the calm, silent afternoon. Gaspar was barefoot, but otherwise fully clothed, lying across the bed with the thin, chintzy blanket over his hips and chest. Nan sat on a pillow in her red and white seasonal outfit, her back to the wall. She wasn't wearing a wig, and her silvery crop made her look like a Scandinavian athlete. If figures it would be a sweatbox in here when we were sexy newlyweds, she was thinking, but now that it's nice and cool we're all bundled up and decent.

She watched Gaspar closely, gauging his recovery process. He was doing much better, the pallor fading and the haggard look diminishing. But he still had a way to go.

He picked up on her examination and gave a reassuring gesture with his thumb. "The back's much better. I walk around the yard all the time. Not that I'm ready for any back-breaking sex yet."

"Good. Because I'm not putting out until you get way better."

He sighed. "Well, there's always that kid in the laundry, I guess."

She reached to gently brush hair back from the shiny pink scar over his left ear. "I can't believe I encouraged you to go work on the farm. You might have been killed."

"They could have nailed me anywhere," he said, touched by the concern in her voice. "If I hadn't been out on the farm a few months I might not have lived through it."

She nodded, continuing her scrutiny of the scar in his scalp. "What doesn't kill us make us stronger, they say."

He rolled his shoulders, hunching up on the other pillow to look at her more directly. "This made us all stronger, this whole thing."

Nan nodded agreement, but said, "Thing is though, staying this strong is getting really expensive."

"And receipts are down."

"When it rains it pours. I've had a few talks with this Altamira. But I don't think he's going to open you up any more territory or anything. That's what's been bothering me most: we can't expand or grow."

He was following her, then suddenly broke a smile. "Uh, oh." He eased up on an elbow and moved to a sitting position beside her. She turned sideways to face him, the couple leaning on the wall and looking at each other from two feet of distance. "So you came up with a solution, am I right? Rob banks. Kidnap the President. Stick up Iran."

Nan made a self-deprecating moue, but moved in on the topic she'd been waiting to open. "We're limited with cocaine. And the pharmaceuticals and weed and stuff. Altamira has a ring around our necks, like those fishing ducks in China."

Gaspar eyed her almost warily. He'd figured out there was really no limit how far or in what direction his delightful wife might move, given impetus. "It's never been a problem."

"You never had to field an army before. I'm running the numbers, looking around."

God help us, Gaspar thought affectionately. "Let me guess, go legit? Pork belly futures? Car parts? Mutual funds?"

"Not a bad route to keep in mind for less troubled times. Isn't that what all the robber barons and Godfathers do when they hit a certain point? Start endowing schools and buying up churches, collecting Good Guy badges? Even Scarface was going that route."

"But that's not what you have in mind?"

"Not at the moment. What I came up with is wholesale heroin distribution."

He stared at her a minute, then broke into happy laughter. "*Madre mia.* For a hooker, you really think out of the box."

Nan hadn't changed her position or expression. "It seems like the only place to go, given your position and resources. Sinaloa isn't the only place *chiva* comes from. The Far East isn't really all that far these days. Apart from not even being east. Some of Lux's merry men have worked for a few Asian import/export types and enjoy cordial relations with their reps."

He watched a shadow of puzzlement cross the focused smoothness of her brow. "Who also smuggle people, apparently. Wetback coolies? I can't figure that one out. How do you market an unlimited supply of something with no demand?"

"But they wouldn't mind more outlets for their *chiva*?"

She spread her hands, offering to the comprehension. "So we branch out. More biz, more bread, more whup-ass."

"Actually you figured out a major advantage of *coca*," he told her. "It only grows in one place. It's like a God-given monopoly."

"There's that. Now you take the commodity I'm most familiar with. If I had the only one in the world, what could I charge?"

"Probably nothing. Halliburton and Blackwater would snatch you up and stick you in a bunker in Guantanamo. You'd be a strategic stockpile that could only give it up for Presidents and Senators and shit."

"Ancient white crooks who can't get it up anyway. Sounds like a government solution, all right."

He rolled away from her, leaning back against the headboard and staring at the blank wall. "You impress me, no two ways. Thing is, I've thought all that out before. Well, the Asia thing is a new twist. What I came up with was, No."

"But we really need the cash. We're right on a sort of line between really whizzing on our fence lines or just bleeding to death until they roll us up."

"Here's part of my thinking. *Chiva* isn't the same business as *coca*. Different people, different *onda*, understand?"

"Sure, a different vibe. But..."

"Coke is pretty harmless. You've done it right?"

"A time or two. No residual damage."

"There. And who uses it most? Anglo assholes with money. It doesn't really impact the community. But smack is poison."

"So you sell it uptown. Look I put a lot of work into this. Planning, account research, contacting people..."

"You're amazing."

She heard the refusal behind his compliment. "But you're going to totter out of the hospital and just over-ride my decisions? Write off all my work?"

"Yeah."

"Okay."

"Okay?" He turned to give her a searching look. "That's your only comment on this?"

"No, I have one other comment. Would you like to hear it?"

Boy, is this a moment, Gaspar thought. Wonder if she'll call in an airstrike. "*Con permiso.*"

"God, it's good to have a man around the place again." She ducked over and kissed him on the temple.

He sat for a moment, entertaining understandably mixed thoughts and emotions. He noticed he was shaking his head like a clown and grinning like an idiot. "Did I already say, 'amazing'?"

"We've all missed you," she said, cuddling against his side. "And I'm glad you're back. I just want to get you back into shape: I'm actually getting a little horny."

"*Ay, ay ay.* Well, listen, there's one more thing about this I wanted to mention."

She pressed against his left arm and nipped his shoulder girlishly. "Oh, I'm all ears."

"What you were saying about moving into square business, getting good Joe medals? It's a lot tougher making that move if you have a jacket for opiates. People draw a line there and it sticks to you."

"So going legit is part of your plan?"

"I'm already in it. So are you, sort of. Know what's the closest thing I've found to narcotics?"

"Don't tell me, give me three guesses. Um, Cheerleaders? Video games? Tiramisú? Bureaucracy?"

"Southern California real estate."

"So I'm living in part of an investment portfolio?"

"I'm all over it. Greenfield subdivisions. Downtown highrise. If the Chargers really move to a new stadium in Chula, I'll cash in big time. If not, I cash in later."

"Now that sounds exciting. But in the meantime, if you don't mind me mentioning a few nagging *problemos*..."

"I've got another plan for getting more money. Maybe you can work on this a little until next visit. And maybe by then I'll be ready for you."

"In your wildest dreams, invalid. Let's hear your secret plan."

"Expanding the coke business."

"But wouldn't Altamira take a dim view of that?"

"Well, he wasn't exactly Mr. Support during our time of trouble, was he?"

"Not what you'd call. He seemed a lot more concerned about the Maras getting blown up. I got the impression it created headlines and furor for him."

221

"Yeah, well, see? He's a *politico* now." He almost spit the word. "Different set of values from business people. He's got the city by the sack and can steal more than we can earn."

"Okaaay." She drawled it out, thinking. "Well what about your fellow evil drug lords? They aren't going to be too nuts about you grabbing more territory."

"We're a different outfit now. Thanks to your mercenary psychos. We're stronger, bigger. And a hell of a lot scarier."

"I prefer the term 'assertive'."

"We'll see what we can assert." He rolled toward her and extended his hand to stroke up the side of her neck and gently cupped her jaw. He caressed her cheek with his thumb, looking deep into blue skies. "And what about you? Going back to the dishes and cookbooks?"

She cocked her head, listening for a faintly ringing bell. "I think I've heard of those somewhere." She took his hand and moved it to her lips, kissed it, and lowered it enough to say, "Look, I love this stuff. I just learned a new game and I'm good at it. I'm stoked. You should keep me on."

He laughed and leaned forward to brush his lips on hers. "I can't figure out if you love me for myself, or just my drug war."

Nan's eyes smiled into his, a midsummer glory. "You hear what you just said?"

She leaned in for a longer, more sensual kiss, then whispered along his cheek, "Does it matter why?"

"Doesn't seem to." He reached out and took her shoulders, pulled her across him, twisting her body to his and holding her close enough to feel her breathing and heartbeat. It was the longest kiss they'd ever shared: a lazy, lingering exploration right there on the tacky bed inside the flimsy walls of Boneyard 11.

Chapter Fifty-Two

She'd worn a firetruck red teddy and a cute thong with fuzzy red heart in front to celebrate Valentine's Day, but now they were both tossed on the floor. Nan was under the cheesy blanket, cuddling up to Gaspar in the slight chill of the trailer unit. She didn't want to get dressed. She liked it cool like this, as close to cold as San Diego ever got. The hustle, sweat and bother of hot days weren't her cup of tea. She liked it cool, calm, dry--the blue haze over the sea. A positive value on body warmth.

It had been a fairly heavy few months, she thought as she lay with her fingers in the thatch of her husband's chest. Her talks with Altamira, coached by Gaspar and rehearsed with Manny, had been an extremely delicate tightrope. Yet somehow she'd managed to get her point across without triggering the delicate cobwebs of macho, protocol and attitude in the powerful Mexican boss. Her point being that she wasn't afraid of him.

There was little he could do to them north of the border and she'd demonstrated pretty conclusively her capacity for reaching into the south with scorched-earth ferocity if she felt she had to. Lux's men said they thought they could fight the local Mexican army to at least a tie if need be, and were only half joking. Experience counts in such matters and any one of these guys had seen more combat than the entire infantry division stationed on the old Rosarito highway.

Similarly, without being disrespectful or arrogant, she'd let him know through excruciating euphemism and obscure name-dropping that they could make do without his supply lines, and would do so by introducing new sources that were beyond his control.

After three meetings, during which Nan's intelligent discussion and the weightless calm behind the high blue beams of her eyes had fanned into a hard white flame Altamira's zeal to collect her, it was agreed that he would increase supply to them on a need-to-ship basis. Understanding that any jurisdictional disputes on the U.S. side would have to be settled there without his help or influence. So far they'd handled that pretty well.

A Latino group in the eastern valleys and a tough biker coalition up around Riverside had taken umbrage at new players on their respective turfs, and ended up nursing bloody stumps. The bikers had probably been wounded beyond their ability to recover, leaving a rich area for cocaine and methamphetamine sales by default. Police in both areas expressed deep concern over the outbreaks of mass casualty ultra-violence, but were reluctant to connect them with that nasty business in Tijuana back in December. After those two campaigns they hadn't run into any undue trouble from anybody else.

Meanwhile, the Mara Salvatrucha had returned to the Tijuana area. They had learned an important lesson, however, and stayed in small cells scattered over the metropolitan area, not concentrations like the ones that had proven so easy for Lux's men to devastate. It was hard to estimate how many of the Central American gangsters had infiltrated back in, typical in a city whose very population figures are a matter of guesswork. They had also apparently not yet decided exactly how virulent their infestation would become.

Nan had invited Jim Chapman over for a discussion of that very matter, plying him with grilled prawns and Chivas. Chapman had a related chat with Blas Espinosa, who in turn took the conversation to a cop of his long and fruitful acquaintance, a tough, useful veteran Sergeant named Alonso Bernal.

Which led Bernal, his young partner Reyes, and three other very case-hardened cops to get the drop on JoJo, who had moved into an old rancho in San Antonio de los Buenos with a woman and two kids. He and Bernal ended up sitting in a patrol car on the beach at Rosarito for a few hours: eating hotdogs, watching pelicans dive into the waves and talking about the near future.

JoJo found Bernal a very interesting guy, for a cop. Not so much his initial message that they could harass Altamira all they wanted to, but if they made a move against the Gaspar machine in California their previous obliteration would seem like a summer clambake by comparison. He'd more or less come to that conclusion himself. Besides, they had their hands full in Tijuana.

What really blew JoJo's mind was a further idea that Bernal moved to after he got the impression that the teenaged Mara leader was a smart cookie, extremely resourceful and capable for his age. JoJo was shocked at the idea at first: an alliance with cops seemed like a refutation of every Mara instinct. But the more he thought about surreptitiously teaming up with elements of the police, apparently some sort of secret death squad within the force--hardly an alien concept to Maras--to oppose the Altamira regime, the more sense it made to him.

So basically it was a time of relative peace and prosperity. Nan's visits to Boneyard 11 weren't interfered with, Gaspar was getting to know his kids again and Nan was enjoying stolen moments with them as well. There was certain ongoing Federal activity against them but nothing like the pressure that had mounted in the fall. She was getting the impression that the overall official regard of the situation was relief that the newly brawny Gaspar outfit seemed capable of keeping that crazed-assed Salvatrucha outfit from seeping into the region.

Lying on her man's chest, Nan felt the cadence of his breath and the hardening of his arms and shoulders. He was definitely recovered, a tribute to his undeniable vigor. She'd put together a lot of his backstory by then. What he wouldn't tell her, she'd wheedled out of Alfredo, who was as proud of his *compadre's* past as Gaspar himself was eager to forget it.

Essentially it was the story of a teen-aged gangbanger not that different from Poker: rival gangs as a matter of fact. But Gaspar had been the one with the smarts and determination. He'd started out scrapping his way into the gang with just his fists, then fought his way up on sheer drive and guts, and ended up becoming the tough guy who was sharper, cagier, and more brutal than the other tough *vatos* in Barrio Lobo. So when the Altamira family made their move to the border, and looked north for support, firepower and distribution, he was the guy with the go-to.

She touched his biceps and ran her fingers over his scarred knuckles with a certain pride. The thing she was aware of above all else was that they were colleagues, a matched pair. For better or worse, they deserved each other. She stretched slightly to bring her lips near his ear. In a drowsy whisper she asked, "Okay if I take a little nap? It'll pay off for you, I promise."

But she didn't hear his response. She lay on his chest, under the thin blanket and drifted into a deep and dreamless sleep.

Linton Robinson

Author

Linton Robinson is a veteran, award-winning writer and journalist with credits in the top magazines in the United States. He has lived in Latin America and in the border areas for many years and written for papers on both sides of the line.

His work is informed by work in law enforcement, psychology, and smuggling.

To follow Lin and his increasing number of novels, see his website at LinRobinson.com and his Twitter page @LintonRobinson

To join Lin's newslist and get advance notice of new books on the way, sign up at LinRobinson.com/mail

The Borderlines Series

"Boneyard 11" is an offshoot of the Borderlines novels, the "fourth book in the trilogy" drawn from the TV series that remains in development and moves towards production. It says here. The series takes place in two fictional, isolated communities across the California/Mexico border from each other and is comprised of many intertwined lifelines of characters based on people known in the larger communities on which "Barrio Lobo" and "Grupo Bravo" are based. Fans of "Boneyard 11" will want to take a look at the books in the trilogy, starting with "Mary of Angels". Bonus chapters from that book are included here.

Bonus Chapter: Mary of Angels

The Camponeta family didn't realize it, but their crossing was uneventful, a stroll in the park, as the Jungle Woman said. She arranged them in an order of march, young ones near their parents, his older brothers bringing up the rear, herself in the lead. She told them how it would be, told them they needed to keep quiet and obey her instantly if she gave them orders. The old cop laughed and said they'd better listen to her. But she was serious now, on the job. She led them down from the cliff, walking in furrows eroded into the rock and dirt. It wasn't an easy walk, but they tumbled out in good shape at the bottom of a rock draw, stepped out onto a smooth sand *playa* where a tall link fence ran out of sight in both directions. Their angel walked to a certain place in the fence and looked exasperated. Pepito came up behind her and saw that the fence had recently been repaired with shiny new links. He looked at her, at the fence. He pulled out his scorpion knife and started cutting at the chain links.

Jungle Woman smiled at him, then touched his hand, motioned to put the knife away. She reached into a bag that hung down her back and pulled out a pair of bolt cutters with sawed-off handles. She quickly cut the links in an "L" shaped cut that allowed them to open it like a door and step through. When they passed, the hole fell shut, wasn't noticeable. The sandy patch led into scraggly brush. Pepito knew this kind of brush meant there was river ahead. He was an expert on rivers at the age of seven. Jungle Woman gave them plastic bags to tie on their feet so their shoes wouldn't get wet. She picked their way through the brush and marsh and shallow skims of water without meeting anybody or saying a word. It was here, moving on wet trails through black vegetation, that Pepito saw that she was The Jungle Woman: her silent panther moves, her twitching nose and ears, her big eyes staring right through the dark.

There was more business with fences, some crawling through places and under things, but the trip was nothing like the scary stories they'd heard. Pepito realized that not everybody was lucky as they were. There were probably only so many angels to go around. They were into some sort of town, seeing cars and people, and nothing had happened. They'd made it. Pepito exulted. Then disaster swooped down on them.

The family had entered a sort of tunnel, five feet wide, between a chain fence around a place where people lived in trucks and trailers, and a long wall of corrugated sheet metal marked, SWAP MEET SATURDAY, SUNDAY and, TIANGUIS, SABADO Y DOMINGO. Pepito, still ecstatic at crossing the last river, told his brother Mateo, "These people aren't so bad. Look, they made this path for us here."

Jungle Woman laughed and said, "No, they just got tired of people like us cutting their fences, so they gave up a little right of way to protect their property." And at that moment, halfway through the "tunnel", is when it happened.

There was the roar of a horror monster and a fierce round wind. A blinding light came out of the sky to pin them to the ground by their own hard-edged shadows. The family froze, too terrified to think. They stood staring up into the smiting light from the sky. Just like chickens.

Jungle Woman didn't even look up at the helicopter that jacklighted the family. She looked quickly at the ends of the passageway. Sure enough, Pepito could see that there were uniformed men at both ends, pulling up on little motorcycles with four wheels. He saw all at once that the hospitable highway he'd commented on was the perfect trap. His family was in a dither as the *migra* moved in from both ends of the tunnel, big men with helmets and batons. Some of his family squatted down, some ran or jumped in fear, crying. Juanes was at the point of fainting. Pepito looked for a way to crawl over the fence, but realized they'd never make it before the men with clubs caught them. He reached into his pocket, found his scorpion. He glanced at Jungle Woman. She was the angel here, could she possibly cope with this?

Even as the thought crossed his mind, she was in action. She pushed his father and older brothers, yelling at them to move, to run toward the closest group of *migra*. They balked: it was crazy to charged armed men. She yelled at them, swatted them to move. Pepito lurched forward, his knife in his hand. He ran screaming toward the *migra,* who stopped, startled. His family, spurred by his move, ran behind him. Jungle Woman pushed them on. She even slapped Juanes' face and pushed her into a stumbling run.

They ran right at those policemen soldiers, everybody screaming in fear.

Jungle Woman sprinted into the lead, running past Pepito, who charged on stubby legs, his scorpion sting held out in front of him like a cavalry saber. About thirty feet from the *migra*, who were standing still, staring at them, she snatched the back of Pepito's shirt and swung him up on her back in one smooth, powerful motion. He grabbed her shoulders and hung on. Her leather pack was like a saddle for him, he could feel hard objects inside it. He was definitely a mounted lancer then, pointing a thirsty blade towards the uniforms. Then Jungle Woman grabbed a section of corrugated metal and pulled it out from the wall as she ran forward. It peeled away until the end hit the other side of the "tunnel". She spun and snatched a handful of the chainlink fence that was behind the galvanized steel. It opened, another of her magical doors into new worlds. Behind the chain fence were hundreds of cars, parked close together in the darkness with their lights off. The cars were all watching a movie.

The family blundered through the hole into the drive-in cinema and stopped, stunned by the sheer weirdness of it. Row on row of motionless cars, all pointed at opposite ends of the walled lot, where two enormous screens showed soundless movies. One screen showed animated Disney figures, leaping around in the sky frenetically. The other was a five story woman, naked, kneeling over a man in bed, writhing in emotion. They stared at this spectacle. In the cars, people stared back at them.

The Jungle Woman yelled for their attention. She was leaning against the section of wall she'd jammed across the pathway: men were pounding on the other side of it. She pointed, "Go over there where the lights are and wait for me. Everybody go a different way. Run. RUN!" The Camponetas ran towards the refreshment stand, scattering among cars full of startled movie-goers. The men behind the wall section ran into it in unison and it slammed shut. She lifted her feet and the impact threw her through the chain fence into the drive-in. She steadied Pepito on her shoulders as she ran after the family. The two smallest children were in their parents' arms, the older kids were dashing and turning like wild goats. Pepito turned his head to see the *migra* pull the steel outward and come into the huge collection of cars, running behind

4

them. He looked up at the helicopter, which had veered inside the cinema and swooped overhead, shining the glare down on them like God's own flashlight. Even carrying Pepito, the Jungle Woman was faster than the others, and she headed straight towards the refreshment stand.

Pepito felt her hard back surging between his legs as she loped through the lot, rounding cars, sometimes pounding across a hood if there were chairs of viewers in the way. He was impressed beyond his ability to conceive of it. She had shocked him with a display of daring and superhuman strength, ripping the steel away like wallpaper. Then he saw the cutaway and was even more impressed. Better than strength: she had been ready for this unforeseeable attack. She'd planned in advance, had known the path was a potential trap, had come here at night to cut these wires and work the fasteners loose. Pepito was awed, felt like peeing his pants. Which he fortunately didn't because he was still clinging to her rippling back, riding her like a movie cowboy.

The Camponetas provided a bit of distraction and unbilled entertainment bonus for the drive-in customers: a ragged bunch of wetbacks fleeing through the gaps between cars. They blundered into folding beach chairs crammed full of children. They kicked over a barbecue where big, beer-swilling dads were grilling *chorizo* and chicken wings. They plowed into a little girl with three huge boxes of popcorn, flushing clouds of white *palomitas* into the air. The helicopter dodged around above them, spotlighting them for the pursuing officers. The movie audience didn't like the helicopter, whose light blotted out the screen images and wiped out their night vision, any better than the Camponetas did. Clusters of children atop cars cried out in fear, confusion and delight. Horns started sounding all over the lot. People leaned out to scream at the sky, shoved obscene gestures upward. A group of sailors in a convertible threw beer bottles at the swerving chopper. One of the bottles fell onto the windshield of a "low rider" car. Four *cholos* in head rags and wifebeater shirts erupted from the *ranfla*, cursing. One of them whipped out a pistol and fired at the helicopter, which jumped straight up like a flea, peeled off and juttered away towards the freeway.

Most viewers had no idea why their film pleasure was being disrupted until a ragged kid or angry patrolman tore by their windows. People applauded the gasping Camponetas as they plunged through the cars, wide-eyed as spooked horses. Horns beat out Mexican beats, including the "shave and a haircut" riff, which to Latinos says, "*Chinga tu madre...cabrón*". A guy handed a hotdog to an amazed Marco as he stampeded by, then a stick of cotton candy to the traumatized Juanes.

Doors opened in front of running *migra*, piling them up. One stocky father stepped from his car and shoved two stiff arms into a charging patrolman's chest, knocking him off his feet. Winded by the run and the blow, the officer reached gasping for his gun but the father, a tattooed barrio tough, stomped on his hand. Then his nose. Other officers gave up on the chase to rescue their fallen colleague, but the tattooed father was defiant and when a group tried to subdue him, people boiled out of surrounding cars and swarmed all over them, yelling in Spanish. The ensuing rhubarb drew in all of the *migra* officers and over fifty movie-goers. It was featured in newspapers and TV news. Four officers were injured badly enough to miss days at work, three were disciplined. The theater threatened to sue INS. Several Chicano gang-bangers started wearing T-shirts showing a pistol aimed up at a black helicopter quartered in red crosshairs. No charges were ever filed.

But the Camponetas didn't see the events that made them anonymously notorious: Angeles formed them up at the refreshment stand, counted them quickly, and led them out through an exit with hinged steel spikes in the ground to prevent unpaid cars from entering. She herded them down the short driveway to an access road. They could hear the two-stroke whine of the *migra* FourRunners. Unconcerned, she hustled them across and into a ditch where a grating barred access to a five foot culvert. Whipping the bolt cutters from her pack, she slammed the husky brass padlock. Pre-softened in preparation for such an event, the lock popped open and she pulled the grating out for the family to slip into the dark, moist shelter of the culvert. Pulling the grate shut behind her, she reached out and popped the lock back in place. Bent at the waist, she trotted down the echoing tunnel with the family strung out behind her.

At the other end she had her way with another lock and led them out into a brushy sinkhole. She let them rest and relax, told them to take the bags off their shoes. The family looked around this leafy bower, then back into the black pipe they'd emerged from. Their breathing slowed, their postures softened. Marco said, "Now we'll never know how the movie ended," and everybody laughed. Pepito watched the Jungle Woman size them up, then pull out another pocket phone and make a call. All she said was, "Now. *La Pipa.*"

Within ten minutes they heard a vehicle stop up above the brush, stand there with the motor running. Pepito snuck along behind Jungle Woman as she went up to check it out. She told him to bring the others up. When the Camponetas crawled up to street level, Pepito was already sitting in the open side door of a rusty old panel truck, motioning them to come to him. Jungle Women held them up, fed them out in groups of two. They huddled together in the dark of the windowless truck, smelling old fish and machine oil and traces of marijuana leaf. Pepito sat near the curtain at the front, listening while Jungle Woman and the driver chatted and played *Radio Frontera.*

They were only in the truck for thirty minutes. When the doors opened, they spilled out onto a cement patio. They stood looking around at a two story stucco structure with parking spaces and numbers on all the doors, like a hotel. On the roof was a very old sign with broken neon tubes and the name, MOTEL FRONTERA - VACANCY. The truck driver was a short, powerful man with shoulder-length hair called Gacho. He wore knee-length shorts and a dirty shirt that said PADRES. Jungle Woman handed him money and he gave her a salute.

A slim man got out of a big new car and approached her. She counted the money he gave her and nodded to him. She waved her arm at the family: take them, they're yours. His mother and father ran to him, calling him Teo and hugging him, but the kids stayed put. The small ones had never met Tio Teoforo before and the older ones knew he didn't much care for children or displays. He waved at them in welcome and they filed by to shake his hand and thank him for paying their passage to California. He showed them into their new home, a room on the upper floor with a number seven on it and a discolored place beside it in the shape of a number one.

Pepito hung back. He walked back to Jungle Woman, who was talking to Gacho about money. He stuck out his hand to her and she shook it solemnly. She asked to see his knife. He pulled it out and showed it to her. She examined the cheap little blade, gave the boy a long look. She smiled and shook her head, handed the knife back. She said he was a crazy brave boy, to be careful here in The North. She patted his hair, then suddenly squatted down and hugged him. Then she stepped up into the truck and Gacho started it and they drove out of the parking lot into the night and were gone. The Jungle Angel, the Pony Woman, had brought him here to thrive and left him to the task. He put his knife in his pocket and looked around his new world.

The only person outside was an interesting old *gringo* standing beside a large basin of murky green water, pissing into it. The man nodded to him and held up a bottle with a little gold liquid in the bottom. He said, "Bottle in one hand, dick in the other. Easy come, easy go, huh, kid?"

That was pretty deep, Pepito thought, a symmetry he'd never thought of before. The old *gringo* who could speak the language asked if his back was still wet. Pepito checked carefully then shook his head. The hairy *gringo* laughed and shook himself off.

Pepito explained that they had no home and had come to find money and a fine place to live and the man said, "Welcome to the club." He taught Pepito how to shake hands. People don't hold your hand here: you stick out your palm and they hit it. The hairy *loco* went to a room up the stairs. His family went to a room downstairs. It was a big room with a big bed and a place to cook and another place to wash. There was a small room to hang clothes in and that's where Pepito would sleep.

They had crossed the last water. This was the land of honey, of their legends and lullabies, their new home and life. Everything would be wonderful now. He told his father that he was welcome to the club, that he knew the handshake. So now he belonged in America.

Less than thirty-six hours after La Flaca and Pepito galloped through the drive-in up in San "Yskidrow", Ado was singing about it on the afternoon *Linea* runs. He'd heard the story three times from bus passengers by then, each time with more embellishments. His wife laughed at the story, then quickly cleared away the remains of their dinner so he could start writing about the *autocinema* baffling the *migra*. She added some comic flourishes to his account, resulting in something he rarely did, a comic *corrido*. This approach was not unheard of: even the Tigres del Norte had humorous hits like *"Las Gueras de Califas"* or *"Vivan Los Mojados"*. But both of those drew from long-standing sources of Mexican humor and myth: California Blondes and Long Live Wetbacks were almost more graffiti than nuggets of humor. But Ado's latest, *"El Show dela Migra"* drew it's humor from an actual event, with the Mexican pride and genetic hatred of the Border Patrol as a side dish, rather than main course. Instead of broad, *cantina* clown slapstick, Ado was sly, telling it straight-faced as an epic battle to let the absurdity of it pull its own weight.

> *They laid their ambush with a helicopter*
> *And a dozen men with guns on motorcycles*
> *They would trap these sneaking pollos*
> *Who tried to see the main feature without tickets.*

> *But ten minutes after midnight the critics were enraged*
> *There was enough popcorn and Pepsi and McPollo for all*
> *And in the spotlights of Hollywood*
> *People who watch movies in cars all want a happy ending.*

The song kicked the collective butts of *Linea* crossers and straphangers: the first time Ado sang it he made over twenty dollars in tips. He immediately produced fifty cassettes with the single song on them, and sold them out in two days. His wife wanted him to spring for two hundred tapes, get a price break, but Ado told her these quick passions had a way of blowing over as quickly as they started. She laughed and told him she much preferred the slow type of passion that a woman had to stoke for six months before she could get a man to quick fooling around with his guitar and pay attention to her. "You see," Ado told her, "That's the sort of thing that you can rely on in the long run."

Two days later they heard the gamecock crow on *Radio Ranchito*, the signal of a song of special interest, followed by a digitally enhanced cut of *"El Show dela Migra."*

"Okay, okay," Ado told his smiling wife and son, "I'll go make a few hundred more. We can always tape over the ones that don't sell." In the back of his mind he was already hearing a sequel to the song. Not a Part Two, his competitors would do that. No, something focusing in on that skinny *pollera* with the fine *trasero*. He'd start asking around, get more information. Radio! Think of that!

OTHER BOOKS SET IN MEXICO

Anybody interested in fine writing about the border--or an examination of the invisible lines that divide and unite us--should be aware of "Imaginary Lines", published essays on the region written by Lin and Ana Maria Corona, a Mexican writer. Girlhood tales of cooking, interviews with gigolos and matadors, backstory on maids...it's a magic mirror of two worlds from two different perspectives.

"Sweet Spot" is a unique kind of crime/politics/sports novel set in Mazatlán's famous Carnival. Informed by the years Lin lived and reported in this amazing city, it sprawls across travelogue, cultural guide, murder mystery, romance, and baseball. One of the best-reviewed works of fiction to come out of "the Sicily of Mexico".

Made in the USA
Lexington, KY
28 July 2012